A Matter of
Life and Depths

A Matter of
Life and Depths

Cruising Sisters Mystery

K.B. Jackson

TULE
PUBLISHING

Chapter One

"MY CHOPSTICKS ARE poking me in the rear."

"I told you not to put them in your back pocket. I also told you that you didn't need to bring your own. I'm certain they'll have plenty, both on the ship and in Yokohama," I said, my head down as I dragged my over-stuffed suitcase behind me like a pack mule.

My sister Jane grunted, lugging her own bag up the gangplank of the *Thalassophile of the Seas*, the private residence cruise ship on which we'd recently decided to live full-time, currently docked at the Port of Seattle in preparation for departure that evening for a two-week cruise to Japan. We had disembarked when the ship had stopped in Los Angeles for maintenance and flew back to the Emerald City where I kept a small place for those times the ship wasn't sailing.

When Jane and I began our new lives at sea, it only made sense to sell the big house I'd shared with Gabe. Every memory we'd made there had been tarnished by his betrayal, and I certainly didn't need the space. A condo in Seattle was the perfect solution.

"You know these are my lucky chopsticks, Char."

"I don't think seeing a Sir Anthony Hopkins lookalike at the counter of a sushi joint in Turlock makes those chopsticks lucky."

"It was him! I know it!"

"Welcome back, mesdames." There was no mistaking the suave French accent of Xavier Mesnier, head of security onboard the ship.

As we made eye contact a bead of perspiration dripped from my forehead to the tip of my nose. I shook my head in an attempt to dislodge it but only managed to make myself dizzy.

Xavier was the kind of man who possessed an air of both intimidation and safety at the same time. He was intense but kind, strong but also gentle under the surface of his gruff exterior. We didn't start our acquaintance on the best foot—something about him arresting my nephew for murder didn't exactly endear him to me and my insistence on involving myself in his investigation hadn't made him my biggest fan either—but we'd developed a modicum of congeniality toward each other (perhaps even a hint more than congeniality) in subsequent months since Jane and I had made the ship our home.

Although I'd never confirmed it, I assumed he was about my age—early to mid-fifties—based on the graying temples of his otherwise black hair and the fact that his olive-toned skin had just enough weathering to indicate he was past the half-century mark. The crinkles around his eyes were the type that came from smiling and laughing, but I'd yet to see that side of him. I'd only seen him serious…about his job, about his responsibilities.

While Xavier hadn't been thrilled about my involvement in the murder investigation, at least he'd listened to me and respected my input.

I wasn't used to that.

Gabe had often been dismissive of my thoughts, opinions, and feelings. He was condescending about my job as a librarian, annoyed by my anecdotes, and disinterested in my friends. The funny thing was, I hadn't even noticed. I had spent so much time hustling for my worth in the relationship I had acclimated to the way he'd treated me.

I cast off thoughts of Gabe like last week's trash.

"Did you miss us?" Jane let go of her suitcase handle to swat him on the arm.

"I have been awaiting your return with bated breath." The hint of sarcasm could not be disguised by his heavy accent, although I was rarely able to discern between what was mordant wit and what was just him being...French.

He'd shaved his goatee since the last time I'd seen him.

I waved my hand in front of my chin. "This is new."

"It is spring." He shrugged but didn't elaborate. "How was your time ashore?"

"Not quite long enough to get my body to stop swaying like a buoy."

"You officially have sea legs." His mouth hinted at a smile.

"I suppose so. How about you?" I asked him. "What did you do with your free time?"

"We have added a few staff members for this voyage who

specialize in the cuisine and culture of Japan, and I would like to be able to communicate with them, even if only in a rudimentary way, so I took a course in basic Japanese."

"Of course you did." Jane's suitcase began to roll away from her and down the gangplank. "Ack!" She managed to stop it before it vaulted itself into the water and dragged it back to where Xavier and I were standing. "Well," she huffed, "I'm ready to go take a nap now. *Sayonara*, Xavier-san!"

With that, she marched off, leaving us in awkward silence.

He opened his mouth to say something but was interrupted by the sound of wheels on metal at the bottom of the ramp.

"Yoo-hoo! Xavier!" A woman in her sixties with a heavily painted face and a sleek red bob waved a bright pink scarf in the air. The scarf clashed with her hair, which, upon further inspection, was an ill-fitting wig. "Can you help me with my luggage?"

"*Oui*, Madame King. One moment." He turned back to me. "Charlotte, there is a conversation we need to have. However, the topic should be discussed in private."

"That sounds ominous."

The smile he gave me was strained. "Is it alright if I come to your cabin later?"

"Of course. You know where to find me. Good ol' cabin 701."

"Are you coming?" Mrs. King stomped her impractical heel on the ground.

"*Oui, madame.*" He grimaced at me and gave a quick wave before jogging toward the woman standing at the bottom of the gangplank with her arms crossed.

What could he want to talk to me about? While I'd be lying if I said I hadn't sensed an air of growing friendliness between us, I suspected I wasn't going to like what he had to say. Nothing about his tone led me to believe it was anything positive. Perhaps because he was *extra* serious.

Our condo, apartment, cabin, berth–whatever one might call a residence on a floating city–had two bedrooms (one for Jane and one for me), two bathrooms, and a decent-sized living room/dining room/kitchen area. My late husband had purchased it as a love nest for his young mistress and their child.

Gabe hadn't passed away because of the crash, his death had been the cause of the accident. A heart attack—a widow-maker someone had called it—had caused him to run the car into a light pole, injuring Kyrie Dawn but sparing the child of even a scratch. The boy, Quinton, had turned one shortly prior the accident and was secured in his backward-facing car seat.

It seemed to me the term *widow-maker* didn't quite tell the whole story, but I'd yet to come up with a descriptor that encompassed the full scope of impact his heart attack and subsequent death had on my life and others. What did one call a mistress after the death of her affair partner anyway? Certainly not a widow.

Gabe's death and the revelations had been made all the more painful by the fact he'd told me before our engagement and throughout our twenty-year marriage he never wanted children. I'd given up that dream in exchange for a life with him, and then he'd gone and gifted it to someone else.

As if losing my husband and discovering his extensive betrayal simultaneously weren't jarring enough, I'd spent the past few months dealing with the lawsuit Kyrie Dawn had filed against me in an attempt to "reclaim" the cruise ship residence which she felt she and her son were entitled to since they'd spent so much time in it. I had to admire her audacity on principle, but my rebuttal was a firm H-E-double hockey sticks N-O.

My attorney assured me her claims were without standing or merit, but so far it hadn't been resolved. I'd even offered her a cash settlement, one I considered more than generous under the circumstances, but she'd refused it. She wanted the floating love nest and would accept nothing less. If she thought I'd let her abscond with one more remnant of the tattered life Gabe had left me, she had another think coming.

THE SHIP SAILED at four that afternoon. The sun was still high in the sky and wouldn't set until about seven thirty.

We'd been greeted by our unit's assigned butler, Windsor Hadwin, who seemed to have an extra spring in his step. He'd visited family and friends back in his hometown of Brighton, England, during the downtime.

Jane took her nap after unpacking, but I was too nervous

about my conversation with Xavier and too excited about the voyage we were undertaking to close my eyes.

I'd also brought along something precious for this particular trip that I couldn't wait to unwrap and explore.

From my purse I withdrew an old book and removed the microfiber cloth swaddling it. The spine was cracked and separated in places, revealing the disintegrating, amber-colored binding glue barely holding the pages together. The cover was a frayed black fabric with one word embossed in gold lettering: DIARY.

When I'd sold my house, I'd gotten rid of most of my belongings as well. The *land condo*, as I liked to call it, didn't have much storage, and the *sea condo* had been fully furnished and decorated by my husband's mistress. Thankfully, she had decent taste.

When I was sorting through the items to sell or donate, I came across a box I'd forgotten I possessed. It contained photos and letters belonging to my great-grandmother Miriam, who'd passed away when I was only eight. I didn't know her well, but I remembered she'd given me my first Barbie doll. She'd worn a pink tutu. The doll, not my great-grandmother.

When I got older, I learned more of Miriam's story. It was a complicated one. She'd married my great-grandfather Johann at only seventeen. By twenty-one, she was a mother. By twenty-four, she'd left her husband and son Karl (my grandfather) and boarded a ship bound for none other than Yokohama.

For years, no one in her family knew where she'd gone.

She sent occasional letters, but correspondence was sparse. She finally returned to Hawaii more than a dozen years later, in 1934, but by then Johann and Karl had moved to Los Angeles. She didn't reenter Karl's life until he was stationed as a naval captain on the *USS Dobbin* at Pearl Harbor in July of 1941.

On December 7, 1941—a day that would live in infamy—Karl had been having breakfast with Miriam at her home up on the hill overlooking the harbor when the Japanese fleet began bombing the *Dobbin*, the *USS Arizona*, and six other battleships. As the attack unfolded, Karl raced down the hill to help his fellow sailors while Miriam watched pilots from her former home of Japan flying over her birthplace, intent on destruction.

My grandfather had once told me she'd called that day one of the most devastating and confusing events of her life. That was saying something, in a long, difficult, and complicated life.

I'd always wondered about her time in Japan but hadn't had the opportunity to ask her about it. And then she was gone.

When my grandfather passed away in 1999, I was given a box of family mementos. Included in the box was Miriam's diary. I hoped finally taking the time to read her own words in her own handwriting would help me finally understand the woman who'd been such a mystery to me my whole life.

At some point Miriam had procured a large sapphire ring, gifted to me by my mother on my wedding day. Miriam had given it to Mom on her own wedding day. I knew I'd never have any children to whom I could to pass it down, but at that time I had felt too ashamed to tell my mother about Gabe's declaration. I'd worn it on my right ring finger for more than twenty years, but it had never given me a sense of her.

Now, knowing I'd be in Yokohama in less than two weeks, the ring had taken on new meaning. So did the diary.

Tucked into its pages were two items.

First was her passport application.

Name: Miriam May Donegan Franke
Age: 24
Stature: Five feet two inches
Eyes: Brown
Place of birth: Hawaii
Declaration: I intend to leave the United States
from the port of Honolulu, Hawaii
sailing on board the S.S. Nanking *on February*
24, 1921
Countries to be visited: Japan
Reason for visit: To be married
Sponsor: Clayton Mathers

The other item was a sepia photo of Miriam wearing sport togs or knickers, a button-down work shirt, knee-high hiking boots, and a wide-brimmed Anouk hat. With her right hand she held a five-foot-tall walking stick, and with the other she held the waist of a man in work clothes and a floppy wool newsboy cap.

The caption at the bottom of the photo read MR. AND MRS. MATHERS CLIMB MOUNT FUJI—AUGUST 19, 1922.

I stared at the face of the woman who'd left behind her family—including her husband and child—to venture across the sea in search of something different for her life, and while I didn't agree with how she'd gone about it, I couldn't help but see my own self in her eyes. It was a strange feeling to be traveling the same path as her, and for similar reasons, but a century later.

Her story fascinated me, and I wanted to understand the *why* of it all. Why did she leave her marriage? Her *baby*. What was in Yokohama and what did she hope to achieve there? Would I experience the same sense of accomplishment and fulfillment when I finally stood on the summit of Mount Fuji as her expression appeared to show in the photo?

If I were to understand her better, I would have to start at the beginning. I opened to the first page.

As I read the diary, part of me kept expecting a knock on the door from Xavier, but it never came.

Soon it was time to get ready for the welcome reception.

"I guess what he had to tell me wasn't so important after all."

"Are you talking to yourself again?" Jane yawned as she ambled out from her bedroom. "What did you mean when you said what he had to tell you must not have been important? And who's he?"

I waved my hand in a dismissive motion. "Oh, nothing. Xavier mentioned he needed to talk to me about something."

Jane eyed me with skepticism. "That doesn't sound like

nothing. Any thoughts on what it could be?"

"None, but the welcome reception is about to start, and I need to take a shower. If he comes by, let him know I'll talk to him there."

Jane plopped onto the sofa and picked up the diary. "What's this?"

"It's Great-gramma Miriam's diary. I thought it was fitting to read about her trip to Yokohama."

The photo fell out of the book and into her lap. She held it up and examined it. "He's a good-looking dude, but he's not *abandon your husband and child to move across the world* level of good-looking."

"I don't think that's how it went, and after reading the first few entries, I'm pretty sure it was more complicated than that."

"Hmm. Probably there's more to the story than we've heard." She set the diary onto the coffee table. "I never knew growing up that there was any tension between Gramps and his mom. It wasn't until later I heard Aunt Gert talking to Mom about it."

"Me neither," I said. "It's like they all decided to play nice whenever we were around."

Jane nodded. "I guess Gramps figured it was better to set aside his own pain for the sake of the greater good."

"Martyrdom was a virtue of that generation. I'm not sure I'm capable of it."

"Me neither. On an unrelated note, is there a theme for tonight? I forgot to look at the itinerary."

"Not that I'm aware. I know tomorrow's dress code is

all-black for Ninja Night."

"Do you think they'll have real ninjas?"

I shrugged. "How will we know?"

"What do you mean? Because ninjas don't carry official ninja badges?"

"Because the word ninja literally means *one who is invisible*."

WHEN WE ENTERED the dining room, we saw some familiar faces and some we didn't recognize. Of the hundred or so residences, many were just one of multiple vacation homes for their owners, so they were often only onboard for a few itineraries per year and the rest of the time the units were left vacant. Some of the owners rented out their units by the trip through a company called Travel the World Experiences and Rental Properties, which Jane so aptly pointed out created the acronym TWERP. That was how we'd been able to secure enough accommodations for our nephew's ill-fated wedding cruise.

Jane and I had been living on the ship for a few months, and we'd begun to get to know several of the regular residents, but each sailing brought with it opportunities to meet new people as well. It was easy to spot the visitors at the welcome reception because they typically stood on the fringes to observe.

The dining room staff were circulating with trays of champagne and light hors d'oeuvres. Jane snagged the last flute of champagne off a waiter's tray as he shimmied behind the bar to restock. He held up a finger to indicate he'd have a glass for me in a moment, and I smiled in return. I didn't recognize him, likely one of the new hires Xavier had mentioned.

"Oh look," Jane said. "It's the four horsewomen of the one-up-pocalypse. I wonder what version of *Keeping Up with the Kardashians* they're playing tonight." She tilted the glass in the direction of four unnaturally blonde women huddled so close a piece of paper couldn't squeeze between them.

They ranged in age from mid-forties to mid-sixties; it came to their combined net worth and average dress sizes, well, there were a lot of zeros between them. Despite being beautiful and wealthy, they displayed latent insecurities through a series of bragging barbs directed at each other and anyone unfortunate—or more so *too fortunate*—enough to be deemed a threat.

Although her back was to me, there was no mistaking the lithe figure of their queen bee, Rhodie Atkinson. Married to Bubba, the great-grandson of a department store tycoon, Rhodie had initially been described to me by another suite owner as a hybrid of Scarlett O'Hara and Coco Chanel...not just their fashion sense, either. Rhodie apparently had a propensity for making snobbish statements with an undercurrent of latent racism.

I'd yet to meet the notorious Bubba. Rhodie was always making excuses for her husband's absence, insisting he was often too busy running his family's company to travel.

Next to Rhodie was Willow Strawbridge, whose style was

garden party ready, year-round. Jane liked to say she was the human equivalent of a mint julep: simple, syrupy sweet, a little muddled, and not as enjoyable as people feigned while trying to be part of the in-crowd.

Willow's husband Simon Strawbridge was a hedge fund manager. A slight, bespectacled man with dark floppy brown hair, in the few encounters I'd had with Simon, my perception of him was he was a wet noodle of a man, with a limp handshake. His strongest quality was the odor of sweet tobacco that permeated his skin, and he was at that moment being accosted in the alcove by an agitated Deacon Beauchamp.

Deacon, a brawny corporate attorney who reminded me of Bluto the brute always trying to steal Olive Oyl from Popeye, loomed over Simon with veins bulging from his flushed neck and forehead. Simon had his hands up and shook his head vigorously in denial.

Deacon's wife, Grace, looked uneasy as she surreptitiously peeked over her shoulder at the kerfuffle in the corner and then at Willow, who was too busy whispering into Rhodie's ear to notice.

When Jane and I had met Grace just after New Year's, she'd introduced herself as "Grace Beauchamp...of the Somerset Beauchamps," like we had any idea what that meant. I wasn't even certain which Somerset she was talking about. For all I knew it could have been Maine, Kentucky, or England. Her pale blonde hair was styled in a *can I talk to your manager* wavy blunt bob that was short at the nape and longer in the front.

The final member of the conclave was Florence Loomis. Florence was thrice widowed and the eldest of the group, but it was nearly impossible to tell that by looking at her. She was nicely tanned, fit, had few wrinkles, and, thanks to Teresa Corazon, the onboard hair stylist, not a strand of gray in sight. Her cleavage gave the impression of surgical enhancement, as did her perfectly upturned nose. She had two tells about her actual age: the sunspots on her hands and the incessant name dropping about her time as a hostess at Studio 54.

Florence made several furtive glances in the direction of Elliot Patenaude, the ship's executive chef. He was holding court near the entrance of the dining room like a celebrity, surrounded by fawning (mostly female) admirers.

"Ma'am?"

The server lifted his tray for me to take a glass of champagne.

"Thank you. We haven't met before, uh," I scanned his vest for a nametag. "I'm sorry, I don't see your name."

He looked down at his chest. "Oh. I must have left it in my locker. I'm Hawk."

"Hawk?"

"Yeah." He blinked a couple times.

Jane, who'd been monitoring the gaggle in the center of the room, focused her attention on the young man. "Did you say your name is Hawk? Like the bird?" She cawed.

Mortifying.

He flared his nostrils. "That sounds more like a crow."

"Hmph. I'm Jane Cobb." She held her glass to her chest

and then tipped it in my direction. "This is my sister Charlotte McLaughlin. We live here full-time now, so you'll be seeing a lot of us."

"I'm not sure I'll be here long." He scanned the crowd. "This isn't exactly my scene. No offense."

"None taken," I said. "It's not really ours either."

He scoffed. "Yeah. Sure."

Jane swigged the remaining champagne and set her glass on the bar. "She's not lying. We're what you might call *nouveau riche*. Well, not me, I'm just along for the ride, so to speak, but Char here only recently discovered she's got money. We aren't bougie."

Hawk appraised me. "How did you not know you're rich?"

"Ehh…" I shrugged. "My therapist calls it willful ignorance. Long story. So, where are you from?"

"I got on the ship in LA. Before that, kind of all over."

"You seem pretty young to be from *all over*." Jane made air quotes.

Haimi Dara, one of the head waiters, made her way to the bar with a tray of empty and mostly empty glasses. Several had lipstick marks on the rim. "Hawk, there are many people awaiting champagne."

I smiled at her. "Sorry, Jane and I have been keeping him."

She fluttered her long dark lashes. "No problem, Mrs. McLaughlin. It is nice to see you." She nodded at Jane. "And you as well, Ms. Cobb."

"Please, Charlotte and Jane," I said. "No need for formality."

"As you wish, Ms. Charlotte." Haimi looked pointedly at Hawk. "Why don't you start near the back and work your way forward. We must make sure everyone is served."

She disappeared into the kitchen.

Hawk finished filling the flutes with champagne and hoisted his tray. "Well, I'm off. Nice chatting with you ladies. I'm sure I'll see you around."

Jane and I watched as he maneuvered through the dining room to those standing near the windows.

"What do you think?" she asked.

I tilted my head. "I'm not sure. He seems polite, but I suspect there's more to him than appears."

"Psychoanalyzing the staff, are we?"

I whirled to face Xavier. "I expected you to come by earlier, but you never did."

His expression soured. "I know, and I apologize, but I had some issues arise that needed my attention."

"Everything okay, X-man?"

I enjoyed watching him cringe at Jane's nickname for him.

"I am handling the situation. Charlotte, it is important that I speak with you, and the sooner the better, before—"

Jane interrupted him with a gasp. "Oh my gosh! It can't be! She wouldn't dare."

I glanced at her and then followed her line of sight. The room was filled with people laughing and chatting, but nothing I saw seemed gasp worthy.

And then I spotted her.

I gasped too.

The satin emerald green and floral print cocktail dress she wore was floor-length but had a side slit that nearly reached her waist revealing one tanned, toned leg. Her strappy nude sandals with a clear band across the toes sported a five-inch Lucite heel. Her blonde hair was swept into a chignon and fastened with a jade and gold hair pin in the shape of sakura cherry blossoms.

She was engaged in what appeared to be an intense conversation with Chef Elliot. Her lips were pursed, and her brows were furrowed as she listened to whatever he was telling her. She looked away from him as if to break the tension. At the moment our gazes connected, her expression was cool and unaffected, but I noticed her mouth twitch.

Kyrie Dawn.

I muttered a string of expletives.

Chapter Two

"WHAT IS SHE doing here?" The hair on my arms stood on end, each nerve ending tingled. An ache started in the center of my chest, pinching and tightening as it rippled outward until every inhalation and exhalation produced a sharp pain.

Xavier put his hand on my arm. "Charlotte, I apologize. I was trying to warn you."

I jerked my arm away from him. "Who let her on the ship? She shouldn't be here. She's not allowed to use the suite. The judge said so."

"She's not—"

He stopped talking when Kyrie Dawn broke away from Chef Elliot and began slinking toward us. A quick scan of the room indicated we were starting to draw the attention of our fellow revelers.

"Hello, Charlotte." Her gaze flitted to my left. "Jane."

Jane harumphed and crossed her arms like a bouncer daring her to engage. I suspected Kyrie Dawn might win that fight due to her youth and profession, but one couldn't discount Jane's advantage of having endured a Gen X childhood. While the children of Kyrie Dawn's generation were coddled and helicopter-parented, Jane and I were practically feral from the ages of six through when we left for college at eighteen.

"You can't be here," I spit. "The injunction bars you from occupying the residence as long as the case is being litigated."

She shifted her chin to the left and bobbed her head. "I know that. I've made alternative arrangements."

I narrowed my gaze. "Meaning what?"

She puckered her lips into a seductive pout. "Xavier, you didn't tell her?"

He shifted his weight from one foot to the other. "I was about to have that conversation."

A flash of betrayal zapped through me. Yet another man had succumbed to the wanton charms of the shameless Kyrie Dawn Wumpenhauer.

"Somebody wanna fill me in here?" I said through gritted teeth.

She moistened her lips. "I work here now."

"What do you mean you work here now?" Jane scoffed. "Resident homewrecker?"

She sucked in her cheeks. "I'm the yoga instructor, of course. That's what I do, remember?"

I gave an incredulous huff as I shook my head. I turned to Xavier and stared at him with my eyebrows raised. Being speechless was not a common occurrence for me, but every word that came to mind was venomous, both to the recipient and my own lips.

I inhaled through my nose and threw a look over my

shoulder. By now, pretty much everyone was watching us. Even Deacon and Simon had stopped their confrontation to observe ours.

"We ought to take this conversation to a private location," Xavier said. "Perhaps to the captain's lounge?"

Kyrie Dawn gave a mewl of assent.

I sucked my teeth and heaved a deep sigh. I flicked my hand in an abrupt *after you* gesture.

Xavier led the way, with Kyrie Dawn on his heels. I brought up the rear with Jane a half-step ahead of me as a buffer.

The captain's lounge was located on Santorini, the eighth floor, one level below the dining room.

Each level of the ship had a different Greek name. The lowest level was actually the third floor, also known as Marina. This was where the crew stayed, including Xavier in cabin 302. Four was called Perseus, which boasted a full theater lounge, casino, a cigar and whiskey lounge, an Italian restaurant, and a Japanese restaurant serving both teppanyaki and sushi called Kuchi Sabishii. On the fifth floor, Capri, was the registration desk, the medical office, the security office, fitness center, full-service spa and salon, a solarium featuring an enclosed pool, and VIP sundeck with an enormous hot tub.

The welcome reception was being held on the ninth level, Mykonos. In addition to the dining room Mykonos held the Azure lounge, a library, and the expedition resource center. At the bow of the ship was an observation deck and aft was a helipad.

The top level, Kalispera (which I'd been told meant good evening in Greek) had a jogging track, a hot tub, two lounge areas (one for sun and one for shade), and a snack bar.

I also found a dead body up there one time.

The sixth (Aegean), seventh (Odyssey), and eighth (Santorini) floors were all residential.

Jane and I had spent a fair amount of time in the captain's lounge during our first cruise amid the murder investigation. I hadn't been in the room since, and it brought with it a wave of anxiety on top of the wave of nausea I already felt being in the presence of my husband's mistress.

I sank into the sofa and immediately felt vulnerable in that position, so I popped onto my feet and positioned myself near the fireplace.

"Are you sure you would not be more comfortable seated?" Xavier asked.

"Nope."

Jane sat in one of the armchairs, while Xavier and Kyrie Dawn took the sofa. I didn't particularly love the sight of them sitting so close. I'd have been more comfortable with a distance of at least three feet, preferably three thousand feet. Times a hundred.

Kyrie Dawn appeared to be frantically texting someone, her brows knit together in a concerned expression.

Xavier watched me warily. If he thought I was going to start yelling, he had another thing coming. I wouldn't give her the satisfaction.

He cleared his throat. "Charlotte, you are understandably upset. I need you to know, I only discovered this a few days ago."

"So, you had nothing to do with it?" I asked.

"I do not do the hiring, only background checks. When this request came to me, it was less of a request and more of a done deal. I was told a full background was unnecessary as she is already well known to staff and corporate."

Jane grunted. "You mean, because my feckless brother-in-law brought her here for his trysts and you all turned a blind eye."

I tried to swallow, but it felt like a marble was lodged in my throat.

"It's none of their business what Gabe and I or anyone else does—" Kyrie Dawn stopped, closed her eyes, and sniffled. Then she continued speaking, her voice softened and cracked. "*Did*. We had a life here, whether you like it or not. I'm going to get our home back if it's the last thing I do!"

I closed my eyes and swallowed once more. The marble had grown to the size of a golf ball. I reopened my eyes and leveled my gaze at her, ready to let her have it, when suddenly the door to the lounge opened.

"Mama!"

I jerked my head to the doorway and spotted Elena, the ship's personal trainer, holding a wriggling toddler at arm's length like he carried the bubonic plague. He managed to squirm out of her arms and ran across the room. He clawed at Kyrie Dawn's legs.

"Mama! Mama! Up! Mama, up!"

Her face softened into a warm smile as she leaned over to

pick up the child and pulled him onto her lap. She brushed his blonde hair from his forehead and kissed it.

"Hi, baby," she murmured. "Did you have fun playing with Elena?"

He nuzzled into her neck and popped his thumb in his mouth. Once again, she brushed his hair from his eyes, and he peeked out at me from under long lashes.

My mouth went dry, my breath caught, and a searing pain ripped through me.

Blinking back at me were the soft brown eyes of my dead husband.

Chapter Three

I TOSSED AND turned all night, unable to sleep. It wasn't the hot flashes, although they didn't help. At one point I was certain I was having either a heart attack or an anxiety attack. Every time I closed my eyes, I saw that little boy with my dead husband's face staring back at me.

Quinton was a beautiful child, no doubt, and yet he represented nothing but pain to me.

At around three A.M., I sat up trying to figure out our precise location and then moved on to google how to get off the ship. There was not enough room for the both of us, much less the three of us. I couldn't spend the next who knew how long dreading walking out my door or around a corner for fear I might run into them.

It was technically April first—April Fool's Day, how apropos—and we weren't due to be near land for a week and a half. Ten days.

I was about to start hyperventilating.

I flopped my legs off the side of the bed and put my head between my knees with the same panicked sense of desperation I'd experienced the time Jane had locked me in our mother's hope chest and then couldn't figure out how to get it open again. By the time our parents arrived home, I'd been in hysterics.

It was the first time I'd felt like a caged animal, but not the last.

The ship had both a submersible and a helicopter. I could charter one that would drop me on some island in the Pacific. I could make a new life there...one where I didn't have to face my heartbreak day in and day out. I'd learn to weave palm leaves into a thatched roof, I'd whittle branches into fishing spears, and eventually the solitude would become less lonely.

The preferable alternative was to get Kyrie Dawn kicked off the ship, but I'd have to navigate that carefully.

When I first came aboard, I'd dealt with the pitying looks of the crew after they found out I was Gabe McLaughlin's widow—both because of his death and because they'd all born witness to his infidelity. Over time, however, the specter of Kyrie Dawn had faded. This became my home, and she was relegated to the past...she-who-shall-not-be-named.

I hadn't considered the relationships she'd formed in her time onboard. She was known and liked enough to be hired. She'd socialized with the residents and made friends with some of the staff, like Elena. That made sense since she was a yoga instructor and Elena was a personal trainer. What made less sense to me was she also seemed to have a particularly strong connection with Chef Elliot.

DESPITE JANE'S ENCOURAGEMENT to face the situation head-on, my anxiety kept me in the suite all day. The weather outside was dreary, so I didn't feel like I was missing out on much. Every time I thought about running into Kyrie Dawn and/or little Quinton, my palms started to sweat.

I spent several hours reading Miriam's diary, hauntingly familiar at times, especially how she described the loneliness she experienced in her marriage to my great-grandfather Johann. I had an intimate understanding of that feeling.

After giving birth to my grandfather, Karl, Miriam's despondent state of mind sounded a whole lot like postpartum depression. Her words were dark and melancholy, appropriately matching my current mood.

It was also fitting that the attire for that evening's dinner—Ninja Night—was head to toe black.

Jane and I arrived at the dining room to find it cloaked in dramatically dim lighting, swathed in black drapes and tablecloths, serenaded by an eerie pan flutist crouched under an artificial bamboo plant. He wore a black *hachimaki*—a headband—imprinted with a red circle on a white rectangle background. The flag of Japan. There were flickering fairy lamps at each table and some rope lighting tucked into the coffered ceiling, but everything else had been turned low or off altogether.

The atmosphere might have been a bit unnerving, but instead the darkness felt like a shield of armor. In my black slacks, black silk blouse, and low black heels, I could be stealthy. Incognito. Nearly invisible.

Oh, the irony. Here I was, desperate to be invisible while

mourning a relationship in which that exact feeling had produced a thousand tiny cuts day in and day out for twenty years, culminating in the final thrust. The death blow. Literally and figuratively.

Jane clutched her *lucky chopsticks* against her chest, eliciting a curious smile from Ulfric Anton, the maître d'. He seated us at a table next to the woman I'd seen wearing a red wig on the docks the day before. Tonight, however, she'd switched to a sleek black bob that coordinated with her black velvet dress. The rest of the chairs were empty.

I jerked my head and thumb toward the tablescape. "See, Jane? I told you there would be plenty of chopsticks."

Jane guffawed and clutched hers even tighter.

"Early bird gets the worm, I always say." The woman traced her fingertips across her decolletage. "I'm Margaret King. I don't believe we've met."

"Not officially. I'm Charlotte McLaughlin, and this is my sister Jane."

Jane nodded at Margaret. "Hello."

Margaret gave Jane and me the once over. Apparently, she wasn't impressed by what she saw. "Are you renters?"

Jane made a disgruntled noise, and I discreetly elbowed her.

"No, I own the suite. 701."

She gave two long blinks and then her eyes flew open. "Oh! McLaughlin. Oh my." She pursed her lips like she just sucked on a lemon. "Mm-hmm."

I could sense Jane tense next to me, but before she could escalate the situation, Ulfric ushered Rhodie Atkinson,

Willow and Simon Strawbridge, and Deacon and Grace Beauchamp (of the Somerset Beauchamps) to the table.

"Margaret! How lovely to see you again." Rhodie leaned down to give her an air kiss before sinking into the chair Ulfric had pulled out for her.

"You as well, Rhodie." Margaret made a show of glancing around. "No Bubba again?"

Despite the dim lighting a visible flush crept up Rhodie's neck and into her cheeks. "I'm afraid not. It's a busy time of year for the company."

Margaret looked down her nose. "Hmm, I suppose so, what with summer coming. Although, I could have sworn you said that fall was his busy season."

Rhodie looked down at her lap as if the business of straightening her napkin required all her concentration. "Yes. He's very busy. Very, very busy."

Margaret turned her attention to the two couples. "Where is Florence?"

"Oh, didn't you hear? She died. Heart attack. RIP." Deacon tapped his fist against his chest, kissed it, and pointed to the ceiling.

Margaret gasped and grabbed her throat. "Whhhaat?"

"April fools!" He pointed at Margaret. "Haaa! Got ya!"

Grace swatted at her husband. "Deacon! That's not nice."

Margaret's shocked expression soured. "Yes. Not funny. Especially since Charlotte's husband died of a heart attack."

All eyes cut to me. So much for my cloak of invisibility. If only I could disappear into the shadows.

Willow clucked. "Poor Florence, bless her heart. She's alive, but she had to bow out tonight. She was feeling under the weather."

Margaret glared at Deacon, who hid a smirk behind his glass of whiskey.

"*Mesdames et Messieurs!* Ladies and Gentlemen! May I have your attention, please?"

Everyone shifted to get a better look at the man standing near the bar with a microphone. A spotlight was shining on him.

"For those of you who do not know me—and let us be real, how could you not—but for those of you who do not, my name is Elliot Patenaude, and I am the executive chef of the *Thalassophile of the Seas.*"

The diners applauded and he bowed.

I noticed he had dark circles under his eyes. It was unusual for a man who often loudly extolled the virtues of his very expensive skincare regimen.

"*Merci. Merci.* I trained at the Culinary Arts Academy at Le Bouveret in Switzerland and have been mentored under the tutelage of the finest chefs in the world, including award-winning sushi chefs, called *itamae*. I have consulted with them to bring you the best Japanese cuisine possible on this voyage. So, please, *bon appetit* or as they say in Japan, *meshiagare.*" Once more he bowed, this time with prayer hands, and the diners applauded.

"One second." Deacon jumped from his chair and made his way over to Chef Elliot, still in the spotlight.

Elliot greeted him with a broad smile and a pat on the

back. Deacon leaned close to whisper something in his ear, and the chef flashed him a mischievous smile. Deacon gave Elliot a jovial slap on the shoulder, and both men rumbled with laughter.

"What was that?" Grace shifted in her chair as Deacon returned to the table.

"Oh, nothing, just a little something special the chef and I are working on." He winked.

She mustered a wan smile before allowing her gaze to drift back toward the chef.

The waitstaff began to serve the first course, miso soup. Haimi placed a bowl in front of Grace, who was still looking in the direction of the bar.

"Grace." Deacon nudged his wife.

She immediately forced a cheerful "Thank you!"

"You should be saying *arigato*." Simon's voice was thin and grating.

"Simon." Willow's sticky southern drawl dripped from her lips. "No need policing other people's manners."

Simon exhaled, causing his shoulders to slump and his glasses to fog.

Margaret blithely observed our tablemates like Andy Cohen at a *Real Housewives* reunion. She raised her glass of sake, tossed the rest of her rice wine down her throat, emitted a satisfied *ahh*, and readjusted her askew wig.

The main course was a bento box filled with all black food. Squid ink noodles, forbidden rice, Japanese eggplant sautéed with black sesame seeds, maki rolls with black rice instead of white, and kuro, a Japanese black curry.

Once the meal was cleared, a drumbeat began to swell in accompaniment with the pan flute. Soon, all we could hear were the drums, and then silence. Seemingly out of nowhere, men emerged from the corners of the room, dressed in black jackets, black pants, black sandals, and what looked like black ski masks, only instead of wool, they were some sort of nylon-like material.

The ninja closest to our table had two sickles in each hand. Another had a long thin stick, about five feet or so. One had a katana sword, and the last had a string with some sort of metal tied to a sickle that he swung around his head.

The man who'd been playing the pan flute switched to plucking the strings of a *biwa*, a short-necked wooden lute.

In the center of the room, the ninjas performed fight scenes using their weapons. The man with the katana sliced a watermelon à la Gallagher with his sledgehammer but slightly less messy. There were martial arts demonstrations.

The lights dimmed further, and the pan flute began to wail a melancholy tune.

"Ladies and gentlemen, or, as they say in Japan, *minasama*," a man's voice called out in an unexpected southern accent mixed with a Japanese affectation. "*Kon'nichiwa.*"

A figure emerged from the shadows with arms in the air, and Jane giggled. Dressed in the same black ninja outfit (minus the mask) a man with persimmon-tinted skin—presumably from too much self-tanner—and long, straight, blond hair sauntered to the center of the room. His expression was comically serious, exacerbated by artificially arched eyebrows giving the appearance of constant astonishment.

Every gesture he made reminded me of an off-strip Vegas magician.

"I am Sensei Machigau." He bowed. "And I am here to demonstrate the ninja weapon of choice. The *fukiyaaaaaaa!*" He thrust a two-foot-long bamboo stick over his head like He-Man with his Power Sword. A stone pendant hanging from a rope necklace swung side to side.

There was a smattering of applause, along with murmurs of confusion. Jane was choking on her laughter. I knocked my knee into hers. She pursed her lips and twisted her fingers in front of them as if locking them.

"Ninjas use many techniques to accomplish goals. From birth they are trained in fighting skills, weaponry, ambush, hiding, espionage, and secret methods that I cannot tell you or I will have to kill you."

He flipped his hair over his right shoulder and gave a smarmy smile as he scanned the crowd, who emitted nervous laughter under his dramatic scrutiny.

"The *fukiya* is an integral part of ninja training. For this demonstration I will use a fifty-centimeter pipe, typical of ninjas. However, in the official sport of *fukiya*, the pipe is more than twice this long at approximately one hundred twenty centimeters. The longer the *fukiya*, the more accurate, but for the ninja warrior, it is more convenient to carry a small pipe, which can also be disguised as an instrument of music rather than death."

One of the other ninjas—I couldn't say which since they were all incognito beneath their cowls—brought out a dart board and set it on a stand approximately twenty feet from

Sensei Machigau.

"We use the *fukiya* with a twenty-centimeter needle-shaped dart." He held an approximately eight-inch thin piece of metal in the air between his thumb and forefinger. "Now, if I were to be sneaking up on my enemy, this dart would have already been dipped in poison, most likely tetrodotoxin from the fugu fish. Because you are all my friends, and excellent tippers..."

He paused for dramatic effect and once again uncertain titters swept across the room.

He cleared his throat. "As I said, because we are friends, I will use no poison on this dart. The goal of shooting a poisonous dart is to hit a vein or artery in order to allow the poison to infiltrate the victim's bloodstream, so the neck is always a preferable target."

The drums and the biwa started up again as the man did some sort of martial arts movements. He pulled a white cloth from his pocket and wiped the end of the blow gun. He then positioned himself with the blow gun near his mouth. As the drums crescendoed, he puffed his cheeks and blew. A dart flew to the target and landed on the bullseye.

The dining room erupted into cheers and applause. Sensei Machigau bowed enthusiastically as he backed himself all the way out of the dining room, wiping the gun as he went.

"Well, that was odd but entertaining," Margaret said as we all turned back to the table. "You know, I heard Sensei Machigau is really Joe Mancuso from Philly."

"What, you mean he's not Japanese?" Rhodie covered

her mouth in feigned shock. "I had no idea!"

"Truly stunning." Jane smirked.

Haimi placed small plates of chocolate mochi in front of each of us.

Deacon rose and pulled his wallet from his back pocket. "I've got a few things to take care of." He removed three crisp one-hundred-dollar bills and handed them to Grace. "Why don't you go play some slots? I'll meet you back at the room in a bit."

Grace took the money and shoved it into her cleavage. "Okay." She watched Deacon weave his way through the dining room and then stood herself. "I'm out. See y'all later."

Margaret popped a mochi in her mouth, slapped the table, and mumbled between chews, "Welp, I'm not ready to call it a night just yet. Think I'll head over to Azure and get myself a drink."

Rhodie feigned a yawn. "Not me. I'm headed for a bubble bath and my comfy bed."

Everyone seemed to take these declarations as a sign the evening had come to an end. We murmured our goodbyes, and everyone headed in various directions.

Jane grabbed two mochis from the table, popped them into her mouth, and began to chew. After a moment she put her hands on either side of her head.

"Ooh oooh brain freeze!"

She squeezed her head trying to massage the headache she got nearly every time she ate anything cold.

She never learned.

"Remember, the trick is to put your tongue on the roof

of your mouth and hold it."

She did as I said, and within a few seconds, heaved a sigh of relief. "Better."

As we got into the elevator, Jane belched and held her stomach. "Something didn't sit right with me."

"Ya think? You practically swallowed two mochi balls whole!"

WE'D ONLY BEEN back in our suite for about thirty minutes when Jane wandered into my room.

"I think I should go down to Capri and grab some antacid. Come with me?"

"Now?"

"It closes in fifteen minutes."

I set my book on the bed. "Fine."

On the way to the sundry shop, I felt a chill wash over me, and my chest constricted. We were approaching the yoga studio.

Why did I allow that woman to affect me?

I inhaled deeply, followed by a cleansing exhale, as advised to do by my therapist whenever anxiety was getting the best of me.

My breathing exercise was cut short, however, when a blood-curdling scream came from within the yoga studio itself. Jane and I exchanged alarmed glances and then rushed toward the door. Xavier burst into the hallway from the security office. He pushed past us with Jane and me on his heels. I snuck a peek around his broad frame.

What in the—

Kyrie Dawn stood over Elliot Patenaude. He was flat on his back with his arms splayed to the side. His eyes were wide open but unblinking.

In her hand was a bamboo blow gun.

In his right carotid artery was a silver dart.

Chapter Four

"KYRIE DAWN, *S'IL vous plait*, set down the weapon and step away from the body," Xavier ordered.

She stared at the piece of bamboo in her hand and then at Xavier. "He's…he's literally in corpse pose." She gurgled a half-wail, half-maniacal cackle at the irony of the positioning of his dead body while in a yoga studio. Her head bobbled on her shoulders like those figurines they give away at sporting events. "If he were standing, he'd be in mountain pose. But of course, he can't stand, because he's…"

She'd lost it.

"Set down the weapon and step away from the body," Xavier repeated. "With your hands over your head. *Maintenant.* Now."

She carefully placed the blow gun on the ground, raised her trembling hands, slowly stood, and backed up several feet. "What is happening?" Her eyes darting around the room. "Is this really happening? This can't be happening."

Xavier crouched next to Chef Elliot and used two fingers to find a pulse on the left side of his neck, the side not pierced by a dart. His head bowed. He was unable to locate signs of life.

He rested his forearm on his left quad and looked up at her. "I'm going to need you to come with me."

She jerked her head. His order seemed to have snapped her out of her state of shock. "You don't think I did this! I didn't even see his body when I came into the room. I nearly tripped over that stick. That's why I was holding it."

Lonnie Irving and Pike Taylor burst into the room. They were Xavier's top security officers.

Lonnie was in his thirties, lanky, with light turquoise eyes and a flaming red crewcut. A swath of freckles dotted the bridge of his nose and cheeks. His complexion wasn't just milky, it was nonfat milk-y. I suspected a strong enough flashlight might be able to see through to his flesh and bones. His "aww shucks" Opie from *The Andy Griffith Show*-like appearance belied his training as a Special Forces officer.

Pike, on the other hand, was tall and broad-shouldered with closed-cropped curly black hair, dark brown eyes, and a deep brown skin tone. He had a serious demeanor worthy of his own extensive military background.

"Irving, Taylor, please escort Ms. Wumpenhauer to the security office. Take her statement. Do not release her until I have had a chance to speak with her."

The two officers moved toward her, and she took a step back from them.

She glanced over her shoulder toward the supply closet. The door was slightly ajar. "Xavier," she said in a pleading whisper, "you know I couldn't have done this."

Pike moved toward her again, and again she took a step back, this time swatting at the air between them.

"Don't touch me! I didn't do anything wrong!"

Xavier put his hands on his hips. "If you assault my officers, you will be spending the night in the brig. As of now, I simply need you to go with them so they may take your statement. Do not make this harder on yourself than it has to be."

She whipped her head back at the supply closet again, and then at me. "I'm sure you're enjoying this." Her caustic tone matched her scathing glare.

I blinked at her. I wouldn't have chosen the word *enjoying* to describe the sensation I was experiencing in that moment. It was that feeling one had when happening upon a scene that was both horrifying and mesmerizing at the same time. I couldn't look away, no matter how awful it was.

"Nobody's enjoying this, Kyrie Dawn." Jane countered her acidity with equal vigor. "A man is dead. Murdered. By someone on this ship. In the middle of the ocean."

Her nostrils flared, and she jutted her chin in a defiant pout. "Fine. But I need to come back here afterward to get my...stuff. Also, I go by K.D. now."

She looked at me expectantly, but I said nothing. I had no intention of calling her by a nickname. We weren't friends. We weren't buddies. What was the Japanese word I'd learned? *Nakama*. We were definitely not *nakama*.

Lonnie and Pike each placed a hand on her back, but she shimmied them off. Xavier gave her a look of warning as they shepherded her from the room then turned his attention to Jane and me.

"You cannot be in here." He shooed us toward the door.

"This is a crime scene."

"Is there anything we can do to help?" I asked.

He gave a disgruntled sigh. "I have sent a message to Dr. Fraser. However, he has not answered. I need him here as soon as possible. Could you go to his room, 318, to see if you can rouse him?"

Jane opened her mouth to make what I was certain was an inappropriate joke, but I yanked her arm toward the doorway before she could say anything we'd all regret.

"Will do."

As we hustled toward the elevator, Jane grumbled, "You never let me have any fun."

"I don't think Xavier is in any mood for your truck stop humor."

"We'll never know now, will we?"

At the far end of the hall of Marina level, we found a cabin marked 318 and tapped quietly in case his wife Becca was sleeping.

No answer. We knocked again.

Jane put her right ear against the door. "I can hear someone in there."

The door opened, and Jane nearly fell into the room. Becca had a dazed, disheveled appearance. Her eyes widened as Jane came flying at her.

Jane grabbed the doorjamb and pulled herself back into the hallway. "Sorry, Becca."

"Whoa! What's happening? Is there an emergency?" In addition to being Dr. Ian Fraser's wife, Becca was also the ship's nurse.

"Xavier sent us down here. He's been trying to get ahold of Ian. Is he here?" I crooked my neck to look past her, but the living room was dark.

"Yeah, we were already in bed. He's in full snoring mode. He didn't get a ton of sleep last night." Becca ran her fingers through her graying hair. "Such a dummy."

"Ian?" I asked.

Becca laughed. "No, Elliot."

Every hair on my body stood on end. "Chef Elliot?"

"Yeah. Apparently since we're headed to Japan, he's decided to teach himself how to prepare and cook this particular type of Japanese food. I guess you're supposed to have special training to make it. He never even learned to make teriyaki in culinary school, but he thought he could do some dish only the most prestigious chefs know how to do properly. He's hired a temporary crew for this trip to help the chefs from Kuchi Sabishii do all these specialty dinners, but you know Elliot, he's all about the ego and the glory. He wants to have some exclusive meal just for a handful of the high rollers with this rare fish that's poisonous if you make it wrong. Only problem is, he tried to learn on some dark website, and I guess he ended up making himself sick when he practiced it last night."

Jane and I exchanged open-mouthed expressions.

"What? What's wrong?" Becca asked.

"I don't suppose you know the name of this fish," I asked.

"Can't remember. Ian could tell you." She leaned back and looked to her right. "Oh, here he comes."

He shuffled into view. "Jane? Charlotte? What are you doing here so late?"

Jane looked at her phone. "It's only ten thirty."

"Oh yeah, well." Ian yawned. "I only got like three hours of sleep last night."

"I was just telling them about that fish that made Elliot sick," Becca said.

Ian waved a frustrated hand. "Ugh. That guy. I guess one of the residents talked him into preparing a dish he had no business making. Japanese chefs go through years of rigorous training and testing in order to be qualified to even handle the darn stuff. In a lot of places, it's illegal to buy it or serve it without certification."

"What was it called?" I asked.

"Pufferfish. I think the Japanese call it fugu."

Jane and I exchanged another shocked glance.

"I told him he was nuts to do it," Ian continued, "but he swears he was doing it the right way. He even has a special bucket for all the guts. He's gonna toss it overboard so no one will accidentally be exposed to the toxins."

"Ian," I began, "how did he get sick? Did he eat some of the fish?"

He shook his head. "He said he was cutting it up while watching a tutorial video on how to prepare it and some of the liquid from the liver squirted onto his mouth. He wiped it off, but then his lips started tingling and he panicked. He called me because he was dizzy and nauseated. I got there to take his vitals; his BP was 150 over 90. Elevated, but not life-threatening. I gave him an IV and activated charcoal to flush out his system, and he seemed to improve so I let him go to his room. I'll tell you this, though, if any more of that tetrodotoxin had made it into his body, he'd be dead right now."

I groaned. "Interesting you should say that."

As SOON AS we told Ian why Xavier had sent us to fetch him, he threw on a robe and followed us back upstairs. Jane and I tried to enter the yoga studio with him, but Xavier blocked us, so we hovered in the hallway trying to eavesdrop.

As Ian examined Elliot, he called out his findings while Xavier took notes.

"I've got to tell you, Xavier, if this dart was dipped in tetrodotoxin before injection like ninjas used to do, this was a terrible way to die," Ian said in a mournful tone. "Just brutal."

"Can you elaborate?"

"Well, after he left the medical office at about three this morning, I did a little research on the pufferfish he'd been working with. The liver, which is what he was working on when he got some of the excretion on his mouth, is quite toxic, along with the ovaries, eyes, and skin. Apparently, the liver is also considered a delicacy—one that has been outlawed in Japan since 1984—and there's an appeal to some in taking that risk. Someone onboard offered to pay Elliot a significant sum for the opportunity to eat the liver. I guess there was going to be a small group willing to take quarter-sized bites."

"Sort of like Russian Roulette, but with food," I said.

Xavier threw an annoyed glance over his shoulder.

"Sorry." I slunk back from the doorway before he kicked us out of the area altogether.

Ian nodded. "Russian Roulette. Except the odds are worse. With Russian Roulette you've got a one in six chance of getting shot. With tetrodotoxin, you've got a hundred percent chance of experiencing unpleasant symptoms at best, and in many cases, instant death would be a relief in comparison to the alternative."

"Which is?" Xavier asked.

"Like Elliot found out, it starts with tingling lips. Then the victim starts having trouble breathing as muscle paralysis sets in. Soon, they're being asphyxiated, but they're still entirely conscious. Awful."

At his description, I got lightheaded. Poor Elliot. He was boorish and patronizing and had the reputation of being a bit of a lothario among the wealthy women of the ship—both single and married—but no one deserved to die like that.

Jane looked at me. "You don't think Kyrie Dawn is capable of inflicting that kind of cruel death on someone, do you? I mean, she's not my favorite person, and it wasn't my husband she was cavorting with, but do you believe she's a killer?"

"I don't know her well enough to know what she's capable of."

"What was that?" Xavier scanned the room.

"What was what?" Ian asked.

Xavier held up his hand for silence.

A tiny whimper was barely audible above the sound of air blowing through the ceiling vents.

"There. Did you hear it?" Xavier jerked his head back and forth.

"Mama?"

He moved to the supply closet and opened the door. Out toddled little blonde Quinton, past the dead body, and straight to Xavier.

He waved his arms in the air. "Up! Up!"

Son of a—

Chapter Five

XAVIER LOOKED DOWN at the boy with a perplexed expression and then at me as if to say *help!*

My mouth went dry. "I'm pretty sure he wants you to pick him up."

"I do not know how."

I scoffed. "Are you seriously trying to tell me you don't know how to hold a small human? Come on now."

He grimaced at me and then attempted to soften his face for Quinton, who was now trying to crawl up his leg. He reached down and released the tiny pudgy fingers from his Perma Press pants. Quinton began to whine and rock his upper body back and forth, as if he could propel himself into Xavier's arms with enough momentum.

Xavier squatted and enveloped the boy in his arms. Quinton immediately grabbed onto his neck. He lifted him and stood upright, staring into his tiny face with awe and a little fear.

"What now?"

"You've got him. If you can hold a revolver steady, you can hold a toddler," I said.

"Revolvers are less...*ondulant*. Less wiggle." Once again,

he looked at me as if he wanted me to rescue him. "Charlotte, *s'il vous plaît?*"

I shook my head. "Sorry, buddy, this is all you. You can't expect me to hold my dead husband's love child because his mother is busy being questioned regarding the death of a man over whom she was found holding the murder weapon."

"But you have the experience I do not."

A gurgle escaped me, half scoff, and half whimper. "Why, because I'm a woman? I'm the youngest of three. I have no children, thanks to my selfish dead husband who told me he never wanted kids. My pseudo-parenting experience started when my nephew Andy was five, could walk, talk, and was potty-trained."

Xavier shot a look at Jane, who held up her hands in mock surrender.

"Whoa, whoa. Don't look at me either. I have even less experience with kids than Char. I lived two states away from Andy."

Quinton poked his little chubby finger up Xavier's nose. "Oof!"

Quinton giggled, and Xavier looked at him in astonishment.

"Oh, do we think that is funny?"

Quinton poked him again, and again Xavier said, "Oof!"

More giggles.

A broad smile swept across Xavier's face, transforming it. I'd never seen him look that joyful. As a matter of fact, he rarely smiled. As Quinton made another attempt at his nostril, Xavier blocked his hand and poked his index finger into Quinton's neck to tickle him. Quinton giggled once more and flung his head backward until the top half of him was hanging upside down.

"Wheee!"

Xavier's glee was replaced by visible panic. "Careful!" he yelled as he rushed to put his hand underneath Quinton's head.

"This is the strangest murder scene I've ever attended," Ian muttered.

Xavier glanced down at the body of Chef Elliot and immediately shielded Quinton's eyes. "You are right. We should move away from here." He attempted to wrangle the wriggling toddler and headed our direction. "Hold still."

"Good luck with that," Jane said. "That's like telling a tornado to stop spinning."

Quinton snuggled in Xavier's strong arms. The sight hit me like a blow to the gut. It wasn't a betrayal, but somehow it still felt like it. Maybe it was just because Quinton represented betrayal to me. A terrible thing to say about an innocent baby, but true, nonetheless.

I thought I'd come to terms with my childlessness years before, but there was no preparing for the resurgent pain that came with looking Gabe's son in the face, along with myriad emotions brought to the surface about what I'd given up.

Even though Quinton was the embodiment of my husband's unfaithfulness and the reminder that it wasn't that Gabe hadn't wanted a child, but that he hadn't wanted one with me, I couldn't hate a baby. I didn't even dislike him.

Frankly, until this moment, I had believed I could compartmentalize my feelings and banish any thoughts about him from my mind.

That was impossible to do when his fluffy blonde head released a torrent of adorable giggles as Xavier swung him around in circles, a different angle of them showing in each mirrored wall panel like a kaleidoscope of cuteness.

Quinton was here.

In my new space.

With my handsome new friend.

Xavier collapsed onto one of the yoga mats. "Phew, I'm tired. Are you tired?" he asked Quinton.

Quinton nuzzled once more into Xavier's neck, eliciting another smile from the stoic Frenchman.

Our gazes connected, and his smile was replaced by something more familiar.

Pity.

"Char." Jane put her hand on my arm.

I shrugged her off. "I gotta get some air." I fled from the room and down the hall toward the security office. My intention was to blow past it, but just as I reached the doorway, Pike came through.

"Oh, sorry, Mrs. McLaughlin. I didn't expect anyone to be outside the office at this time of night."

"It's okay. I was just going to get some air."

I peeked into the room and saw Kyrie Dawn sitting in a chair next to Lonnie's desk. Her face was red and splotchy, and her hands fidgeted in her lap. She glanced up and caught sight of me.

"Charlotte! Come in here. *Please.*"

I wanted to run, but my feet felt like they were glued to the industrial carpet.

"Charlotte."

Her plea was quieter this time, and I felt a crack in the ice encasing my heart. Her eyes were wide open and red-rimmed, filled with terror.

Pike grimaced at me.

I chewed on my lower lip and then my upper lip. I puckered them into a sour pout and pulled them all the way into my mouth like I was toothless. A comical sight, to be sure. I sighed. I sighed a second time. I sucked in my cheeks and then puffed them out.

All the while, she stared at me with an expression of hope. I sensed Pike's intense gaze out of the corner of my right eye and Lonnie's from the corner of my left eye. No one said a word.

Smart men.

I closed my eyes and breathed. I reopened them and took one tentative step toward her. Her eyelids fluttered with surprise. I had no idea if my inner conflict was visible on my face, but every part of me was in turmoil, lightheaded, and on the verge of hyperventilation.

I took another step, and her expression filled with gratitude.

I hesitated. I didn't want her to feel relief. I wanted her to feel the same agony I'd felt since the day I learned of her existence.

I was nearly inside the office when the sound of toddler

joy echoed down the hall. I closed my eyes once more, said a quick prayer for strength, and reopened them.

I took one more step, and Pike gently closed the door behind me. He probably feared I'd escape if he didn't.

I eased into the seat next to her like I had a broken coccyx.

"Charlotte, I need your help. It looks really bad for me. I'm not sure they're going to let me out of here tonight."

"What do you want from me?" My stoic demeanor was intended to cover up for the chaos I felt just below the surface of my placid façade.

"If they don't release me, I need someone to watch Quinton." Her voice broke. "I wasn't supposed to bring him on the ship. I didn't tell the person who hired me that I have a kid. I thought I could get away with it since it's only a couple classes a day. He's asleep in the yoga studio closet. He'll be scared if he wakes up and I'm not there."

"He's awake."

"What?" She stood abruptly, but Lonnie gave her a warning glare, so she quickly sat back down. "Where is he?"

"He's with Xavier. He's fine."

"I know it's a lot to ask—"

"Then don't."

She blinked rapidly as tears formed. "I don't have any other options. There's no childcare on the ship, and it's not like I can hire someone to come watch him. We're in the middle of the Pacific Ocean. We won't see dry land for a week and a half."

"What about all the friends you made onboard while you

were playing house with my husband?"

She winced but didn't defend herself. "They're acquaintances not friends."

"What about Elena?" I asked. After all, the personal trainer had brought Quinton to her at the captain's lounge.

"She's got the maternal instincts of a potato. I had to pay her two hundred dollars just to watch him for an hour last night. That's why she brought him to the captain's lounge. She said if I didn't come get him soon, she was going to set him up at a slot machine with a bucket of nickels. Doesn't she know those are choking hazards for babies?" she wailed.

"I'm pretty sure she was joking. Those machines don't even take coins," I said.

She huffed. "Abandoning a baby isn't a joke!"

I shot a look at Lonnie, whose lips were pursed and his face was the color of a stewed tomato from holding in laughter.

I rubbed my lips together and separated them with a pop. I inhaled. "What exactly are you asking me to do?"

"He's a very good baby, I swear. You'll hardly notice—" She stopped as if she recognized my rising irritation. "Charlotte, will you please take care of Quinton until I'm released from here?"

I turned to Pike. "How much longer will she be here? Fifteen minutes? Twenty?"

He shrugged his broad muscular shoulders. "Dunno."

I shifted back to face Lonnie and cocked my left eyebrow. He shook his head. "We're doing the initial questioning, but Mesnier will want to talk with her.

Shouldn't be more than a few hours."

"A few hours!" I pulled my cell from my pocket. "It's nearly eleven now as it is!"

The door opened, and Xavier walked into the room holding Quinton. An unpleasant smell wafted in behind him, followed by a grimacing Jane.

"Mama!" Quinton leaned toward Kyrie Dawn.

"Someone needs a *couche changée*." Xavier placed Quinton in her lap.

She squeezed him in a bear hug followed by a barrage of kisses. "I love you, love you, love you." She looked up at Xavier. "Did you bring his diaper bag?"

"Oh, *non*, I didn't see it." He turned to Jane. "Did you?"

"Huh unh." Jane shook her head no.

"It was in the closet. Ooh, you really are a stinky boy."

Xavier pointed at Pike. "Will you go and check the closet? Tell Dr. Fraser I will be back soon."

Pike gave a small smile, and I wondered if he was relieved to be escaping the smelly room.

She looked up at me with baleful eyes. "Please, Char."

Jane peeked around Xavier to address me. "I'm sorry, what is she asking you?"

"She's asking me—and by way of the fact you live with me, she's asking *us*—if we would take care of the baby."

Jane's gaze widened.

"Just until I'm done here," Kyrie Dawn said.

"You got a lotta nerve, lady," Jane said.

"I promise you, if I had any other option…"

Jane grunted. "How about you keeping your toned little

tush on land where it belongs?"

"I can't do anything about that now, can I? What, you want me to jump overboard and swim back to Seattle?"

"You going overboard isn't the worst idea I've ever heard."

"Jane!"

"Come on, Char, don't let her manipulate you. It's not your responsibility to take care of her kid because she's gotten herself into hot water."

"I know it's not."

Jane gave a smug smile of victory. Kyrie Dawn's shoulders slumped.

"But it's not Quinton's fault either."

"What are you saying?" Jane looked at me like I'd sprouted a second head.

"I'm saying it's the right thing to do. We'll take care of Quinton."

Tears sprang from Kyrie's eyes, and she gushed, "Oh, thank you so much, thank you Char; thank you, Jane. He won't be any trouble, I promise, and I'll come get him as soon as I can! I'll make this up to you, I swear!"

I nodded. "Oh, you will. You'll make it up to me."

She nodded vigorously.

"One more thing."

"Anything."

"Don't call me Char. Only family and friends call me Char, and you're not either of those things."

Chapter Six

"**I** CAN'T BELIEVE you agreed to this."

"Me neither."

Jane and I stood in Kyrie Dawn's cabin and surveyed the array of baby gear.

"Do you even know how to change a diaper?" Jane asked.

"Ehh. I mean, I've done it before, but not for a long time. How about you?"

She held her hands in the air. "Not a chance."

We'd left Quinton with Kyrie Dawn so she could change him, but inevitably we would have to get our hands dirty, so to speak.

"It's quite a fall from grace for her," Jane said.

"Being accused of murder?"

"No, slumming it down here with the regular folks instead of up in the suite."

Kyrie Dawn had been assigned a studio cabin on the third floor with the rest of the crew. In contrast to my suite on the seventh level—that she'd so meticulously decorated—her new space was cramped and utilitarian.

Jane and I packed a bag of clothes, extra diapers, toys,

blankets, sippy cups, and the portioned meals she'd stocked in the fridge.

"This is a lot for a few hours." Jane eyed one of the meal containers.

"What if it's longer?" I asked. "What if she's detained for days?"

Jane shuddered. "Don't put that thought out into the universe. We should grab the stroller. I'll feel better if he's strapped in." She grabbed the stroller and started trying to open it. "The last thing we need is to lose someone else's kid."

A lump formed in my throat. "Gabe's kid."

Jane paused her attempt to open the stroller. "Yeah," she said. "Sorry, Char."

I shrugged and swallowed the tears threatening to rise up my throat.

We tossed the stuff into the stroller and locked the door behind us we got back to the security office, Quinton was sound asleep, sucking on his thumb with his head on Kyrie Dawn's shoulder.

Her face said everything her grief wouldn't allow herself to utter. *Take care of him. He's my world. I'm scared. Can I trust you?*

When she spoke, her voice cracked. "Did you get his Pandy like I asked? It's his favorite."

Quinton's most prized toy was an animatronic dancing red panda. She'd told us he kept it with him at all times. Jane had accidentally pushed its nose, and it began screeching an obnoxious rap about letters and numbers while its hind feet frenetically tap-danced. Whoever designed it definitely didn't have kids or held some sort of grudge against parents.

"We did. And his blue blanket."

She gave a solemn nod. "Okay."

Jane removed the items from the stroller to make room for the sleeping child, but Kyrie Dawn didn't move.

"Madame, they will take good care of him." Xavier's voice was soft and compassionate.

Her fingers tightened their grip on his body. "Why can't he just stay with me? He's asleep. He won't bother anyone."

Xavier shook his head. "I am sorry, but we must follow protocol."

Her expression reminded me of Dumbo's mom when he was taken from her, and it felt like someone was taking a hot poker to my heart. No matter how I felt about her and what she'd done—to me or to Chef Elliot—her love for her son was painfully evident.

She squared her shoulders and lifted her chin. She inhaled and exhaled. She pursed her mouth several times. Finally, she rose to her feet and carefully placed the boy in the stroller. She pulled a blue striped blanket from the bag we'd packed and draped it across his little body, limp from exhaustion.

She turned her head as if the sight of him was too excruciating to bear.

"You know how to reach us," I murmured as I slowly pushed the stroller holding my husband's child out of the room and away from his mother.

The cruel irony of the situation was not lost on me, but I

took no pleasure in it.

Once inside our suite, I collapsed onto the sofa. Tears streamed down my face. Jane sat next to me and held my hand while I cried.

I cried because of all the losses I'd experienced in the past several months.

I cried because of my dead husband.

I cried because of his betrayal.

I cried because of the things I'd given up for a marriage that had turned out to be filled with lies.

I cried for the babies I never had, and for the one he'd had without me.

I cried because Gabe should have been there to take care of his child, and I cried because I was now burdened with the responsibility, even if temporarily.

I cried for the little boy who'd lost his daddy and was on the verge of losing his mother.

I cried because I thought I'd found a refuge from the pain, but it had pursued me onboard.

When I'd exhausted every last tear in the reservoir, I felt something unexpected.

Relief.

I hadn't realized how much I'd been holding in, and the release of it all was cathartic.

Jane squeezed my hand. "Feel better?"

"I actually think I do. I guess I needed a good sob fest."

She glanced at Quinton. "Should we just leave him there?"

"I think so. No point in disturbing him. You head to

bed. I'll take the first shift, and you can take the next one."

"You sure? I can wait up with you for a while."

"We don't know how long she'll be down there, and we don't know how long he'll sleep. We should take turns getting rest."

Jane yawned. "Okay. Holler for me if you need help."

Quinton made tiny whimpers as he slept. It reminded me of a puppy.

"I have a feeling you'll be hearing his hollers long before mine."

Jane stood and squeezed my shoulder. "'Night, Char."

"Night."

Soon, the only sound in the suite was the quiet wheezes of the baby's breathing. Occasionally, he rustled under the blanket, but then he'd settle down again.

I was tired, but fear of something happening to him on my watch kept me awake.

Until it didn't.

In my dream, a firetruck siren was wailing. After a few moments, I realized the sound wasn't only in my dream but coming from somewhere in the darkness of my living room.

"Char? You awake?" Jane's voice called from her bedroom.

"I am now."

Quinton had rolled onto his stomach and was attempting to get up on his hands and knees in the stroller. He was crying at the top of his lungs.

I reached down to pick him up, and he immediately clung to my arms, the wetness on his cheeks brushing against my skin.

"Shh," I cooed. "It's okay. You're okay." I bobbed around the living room in what I hoped was a soothing motion and not a jarring one.

He found his thumb and began to suck. With his mouth now full, he was no longer crying, but he was still making noises that sounded like a struggling car engine.

I hummed a few random notes, which somehow morphed into "Problems" by Ariana Grande.

"You hoo hoo!" I sang as quietly as possible.

His moaning subsided, and soon all I could hear was the sound of him sucking and an occasional passing of gas.

I bounced on my toes over to the balcony door. Peeking through the curtains, I saw nothing but the black expanse of the Pacific Ocean at night. I shifted from bouncing to swaying, still humming under my breath. After a few minutes, I sat on the sofa and tucked a pillow under my elbow to support my arm, which was cradling his little blonde head. I stroked his hair and bent down to sniff his head, inhaling the scent of baby shampoo and a little bit of sour milk.

Was it possible to physically explode from two contrasting emotions colliding inside a person?

Elation and heartache. *Kaboom!*

Anguish and joy. *Kerblam!*

Like an old episode of *Batman. Thwack! Zlonk!*

Quinton's shuddered sigh was followed by the fluttering smile of a blissful dream. Myriad expressions crossed his sleeping face, followed by drop of liquid sliding down his cheek. I glanced up at the ceiling to see if something was leaking from above, but it was dry. I swabbed my damp neck with my fingertips, brushed my jaw, and swiped the remaining tears from my cheek.

Resignation and resolve. *Kapow!*

No matter how I felt about her, this little boy needed his mother, and whether I wanted to or not, I needed to exonerate Kyrie Dawn.

Chapter Seven

"CHAR," A VOICE whispered in my ear.

"Mmm."

"Char, coffee."

I opened my eyes to find Jane hovering over me. Sunlight streamed into the cabin.

"What time is it?" I kept my voice low to not wake the baby sleeping on my chest.

"Seven. Windsor just delivered a pot of French press."

As gently as I could, I laid Quinton on the sofa and eased myself off of it. My neck was kinked like an off-brand Slinky. I stretched my arms above my head and yawned. I stumbled into the kitchen where I found the coffee service ready for pouring.

"How did last night go?" Jane sipped from her cup.

"Other than the screaming fit at three, he slept the whole night." I poured my coffee and added creamer. "I need to tell you something, and I need you to keep an open mind."

Jane narrowed her gaze at me over the brim. "What?"

"Promise."

She scowled. "Now I don't want to promise because I'm worried that I'm not going to like it."

"You might not."

She sighed and rolled her head forward for me to speak.

"I think we should help her."

"Who?"

"Kyrie Dawn."

"We are helping her. We're babysitting her kid while she's in the hoosegow."

I laughed. "She's not in the hoosgow. And I don't just mean last night. I mean we need to help her get out of this jam she's gotten herself into. We need to prove she didn't kill Elliot."

Jane blinked three times. "Okay, first, I think Xavier will have something to say about that. Second, why should we lift a finger to help that homewrecker who's been *literally* trying to steal our home?"

My attention went to sleeping Quinton. "For him."

"Oh my gosh, did you fall in love with that baby last night?"

I shrugged. "I guess I did."

Jane waved her hand dismissively. "Oh, for the love of—"

"Jane, smell his little neck! It's like heaven."

She pinched her face. "No thank you. I don't find sweaty necks to possess a pleasant smell. Come to think of it, I always thought it was weird that people put baby's breath in their bouquets. Who wants to catch a whiff of sour milk and pureed peas along with their roses?"

"Like the great poets of Outkast sang, most roses smell like poo-poo anyway. And baby's breath flowers don't really smell like anything at all, except maybe a musty attic."

"You're making my case for me."

Our conversation was interrupted by a knock at the door.

"Windsor again?"

Jane shrugged. "I didn't request any other service."

I ran my hand through my hair. "I'm not in any condition to receive company." I peeked through the peephole. Oh, man. "It's Xavier." Fudge.

I rooted through my purse until I found a pack of gum. I shoved a piece in my mouth as I opened the door.

"It's a bit early, don't you think?" I chewed furiously while smoothing down my hair.

"This is not a social call."

He looked like he hadn't slept much, judging by his red-rimmed eyes and uncharacteristically mussed hair.

"Did something happen?"

"May I?" He followed me inside.

"We need to keep our voices down. The baby is still asleep."

Quinton's diapered bottom was arched in the air.

Xavier's grimace softened. "How did it go last night?"

I stifled a yawn. "Parenting is a young person's game."

"I can imagine." He rubbed the back of his neck. "That is what makes this so difficult."

He was stalling. Not a good sign.

Jane tsked. "Spit it out already!" she stage-whispered.

"I will not be able to release Kyrie Dawn this morning."

Not great news, but not terrible, so why was he hemming and hawing? "Well, when will you be able to release her?"

"I'm not sure that I will."

I wanted to ask what he meant but suspected I didn't really want to know the answer.

"Our initial investigation has revealed significant evidence pointing in her direction as Elliot Patenaude's killer, and we are officially holding her on suspicion of murder." His stiff demeanor made him seem like a stranger.

"What evidence?" Jane crossed her arms.

"I cannot divulge everything, but you are already aware she was found in possession of the blow gun, as you discovered her standing over his body, holding it."

"Yes, and she explained that. She picked it up from the ground. She said she nearly tripped over it, and she didn't even see his body when she entered the yoga studio." I succeeded in keeping my volume down for the sake of Quinton, but panic raised my pitch three octaves. "She claims it had to have been Sensei Machigau."

"Hers were the only fingerprints found on the weapon," he said.

"The killer was probably wearing gloves!"

Quinton stirred.

"Possibly, however, there was no sign of forced entry into the studio, which she admitted herself she keeps locked. I am not trying to argue with you. I do not want this to be the case any more than you do. I also do not enjoy the fact that yet another murder has occurred on a ship I have been employed to patrol and keep as a safe environment. However, the evidence is strongly suggesting things are as they first seemed."

"What about the DNA from spit? It's a blow gun. There has to be spit on it."

"Dr. Fraser swabbed it, but it did not seem to yield any results. He will be sending the sample, along with everything else, to a lab for further investigation."

"Who's going to watch this baby if his mother is in boat jail?" I asked.

Xavier gave me a pointed look.

"Uh, no. That was never the deal. This was just for one night. I'm not watching him indefinitely."

"*We* are not watching him indefinitely," Jane chimed in. "I live here, too."

"She does not have many options."

This couldn't happen. "You understand what you're asking of me, right? You get how cruel this situation is."

He nodded. "I have an inkling, and I am sorry you are in this predicament. I do not know of any other solution."

"Put her on house arrest, like you did with Andy," Jane offered.

"After the situation with your nephew, we tightened our protocols on how to deal with suspected murderers until we can deposit them in the proper jurisdiction for prosecution. One of the protocols is that anyone suspected of high crimes must be detained in the security office until or unless they have been cleared or are being transferred to another facility to await their day in court."

"Then let her keep Quinton with her."

"Jane!" I was horrified at the thought. "We're not sending that baby to jail."

"Not to mention, I could not allow that anyway. It is a violation of the Athens Convention, the Geneva Convention, and frankly, I am appalled you would even suggest the idea."

There was a good chance he was making all of that up, but I knew Jane didn't know enough to argue.

She threw up her hands. "You're right, of course you're right. I just didn't give up my life to move onto this ship and become a nanny for the love child of my twit of a brother-in-law...R.I.P."

"I understand how you feel," I said. "I do. But he's a baby, and we are the closest thing to family he's got right now, so we're gonna just suck it up and deal with it."

Quinton stirred again and whimpered. I sat next to him and rubbed his back as he wriggled himself awake. He sat up, blinked several times, looked at me, and then furrowed his brow. He caught sight of Jane, and his mouth pulled into a trembling pout. He then looked at Xavier and his eyes opened wide.

He looked back at me. "Mama? Mama?"

"Mama will be here soon." I glared at Xavier. "As soon as Auntie Char solves a murder."

Chapter Eight

XAVIER HADN'T PARTICULARLY appreciated my promise to Quinton that I would solve Elliot's murder, but then I didn't appreciate being forced to caretake for my husband's love child either.

After he left, I changed Quinton's diaper and made a bowl of his oatmeal. If I had to guess, less than fifty percent of his breakfast actually made it into his stomach. The rest had dribbled down his chin or was raspberried back at me and into my face. He seemed to find that quite amusing.

Jane wandered in from her shower and took in the sight of us. "Having fun?"

"Your turn."

"Oh no. I already showered." She picked up the diary from the coffee table. "Find anything interesting?"

"Our great-grandfather was kind of a jerk."

"I figured, considering he married his sister's teenage stepdaughter and then after a nasty divorce, abandoned the kid to his step-grandmother slash aunt's care."

"I didn't think I'd feel empathy for Miriam because I can't imagine leaving my baby." I glanced at Quinton, who had stuck his entire fist into his bowl. "I can't even imagine leaving someone else's baby."

"Char…"

"What?"

"This is a potentially messy situation. Keep your wits about you. Don't let an estrogen surge cloud your brain."

"There's no *potentially* about it. It's messy."

Quinton slammed his oatmeal-coated hand on the table. "Gah!"

"Yes, messy like that."

He gave a toothy grin.

"Oh boy," she said. "So, what's the plan for today?"

"I think we should start talking to people, trying to get a feel for the situation, both above and below deck."

She scrolled on her phone. "It says tonight is Sushi and Sake Night down in Kuchi Sabishii."

"Can babies eat sushi?" I asked.

"Siri, can babies eat sushi?"

"Yes," said the electronic voice coming from her phone. "They love it. Just don't give them wasabi."

"Well, there you go." She laughed. "Sorry, Q, no wasabi for you!"

He blew a raspberry. "For you!" He jabbed his chubby little finger at Jane, and she pretended to bite it. This caused him to erupt in a full belly laugh, so she kept doing it until his laugh became forced.

"Now you're just faking it." She caught me watching her. "Don't say it."

I held up my hands in mock surrender. "I'm not saying a word, *Auntie* Jane."

"PANDY!" QUINTON MADE grabby hands at Jane.

Jane rummaged in the diaper bag. "Shoot, I forgot Pandy."

The elevator doors opened.

"I'll go back and get him. Where should I meet you guys?"

"We should start at the yoga studio. I'm guessing Xavier has it locked so no one can mess with the crime scene, but maybe there are clues nearby that he missed."

Jane was already heading back to our room. "Okay, see you in a minute."

Despite the tragic events of the previous night, the lobby on Capri seemed to be business as usual. Residents and guests streamed past us, likely on the way to the fitness center, the beauty salon, and the solarium. One woman I didn't recognize told me my son was adorable. Quite the ego boost for a woman in the waning cycle of perimenopause.

"This is unacceptable!" Margaret King pounded on the reception desk. Today's wig appeared to be from the Dolly Parton collection. "And don't give me that *we're looking into it* baloney. I've paid too damn much money to have my space invaded by common thieves."

Lexi, the petite hospitality manager, smoothed her short strawberry blonde hair and managed a shaky smile. "Mrs. King—"

"Ms. King! I didn't burn my bra to have the beneficiaries of my efforts turn around and jam me back into the box of patriarchy."

Unless it was a training bra she burned, I highly doubted Margaret was old enough to have participated in any supposed bra-burning events of the late sixties.

She snagged Xavier as he rushed past.

"What are you doing about the robbery?"

"Madame, I was told the only thing you have discovered missing thus far are of a minor value. Perhaps you have simply misplaced them?"

Her heavily rouged cheeks flushed further. "Look at this!" She grabbed both sides of her fluffy blonde mane. "Does this look like the appropriate hairdo for zazen?"

"I do not know this zazen."

"Zazen. Japanese meditation. It starts in an hour in the yoga room, and my yoga wig is nowhere to be found!"

Yoga wig? I learned something new every day. Quinton gurgled his bemusement. Or so I surmised. Maybe he just had gas.

"Unfortunately, madame, that will not be possible. The yoga studio is off-limits due to the murder."

"Murder!" She squeezed his arm, digging in her red stiletto nails.

He winced. "*Oui, madame.* And I am very busy with that pressing matter, so I must go." He extracted himself from her clutches.

Margaret whirled to face Lexi. "First robbery, and now murder? This place is going to hell in a handbasket. You people better get it together or I will sue!"

As she stomped away, Quinton waved. "Bye-bye!"

The kid was really starting to grow on me.

On the door of the yoga studio, someone had posted a makeshift cardboard sign with "Yoga studio closed until further notice" scribbled in permanent black marker. I nudged my shoulder against the door. Locked, as expected.

"Mama," Quinton cooed.

"Yeah. That's your mama's work. She's not here right now, but we're gonna figure out what happened and get her back to you. I promise."

A woman brushed by me wearing a tan Burberry trench and oversized sunglasses like Holly Golightly in *Breakfast at Tiffany's*. The only thing missing was a scarf and a chignon.

"Grace?"

"Oh, uh, hello, Charlotte. How are you?"

She couldn't tell how I was doing by my new sidekick and the dark circles under my eyes? "I've been better."

"Yes." She pushed up her glasses and sniffed. "Elliot's death is quite a shock." She leaned closer and whispered, "I hear they're saying it's *murder*. He was stabbed or something."

Or something. "Just out of curiosity, where were you last night after dinner?"

"Out of curiosity, huh? Right. I know all about how you and Jane played Miss Marple on the Alaska cruise."

Ouch. Miss Marple? Sure, Nancy Drew was a stretch, but elderly Miss Marple? So much for the ego boost I'd gotten from people mistaking me as Quinton's mother.

"If you recall, Charlotte, Deacon gave me cash to play slots. I'm sure there are cameras all over the casino that can verify that's where I was."

Jane rounded the corner from the elevator and came to a screeching halt at the sight of us. "Whoa, Columbo!"

"I was leaning more toward McGruff the Crime Dog," I said.

Grace cinched her coat. "It's supposed to rain today."

"Then why the sunglasses?" Jane handed Quinton the binky, which he promptly stuffed into his mouth.

"There may be sunbreaks."

"Indoors?" Jane scoffed.

Grace pushed the sunglasses tighter onto her face. She was hiding something.

I shifted from one foot to the other and caught a glimpse of bruising around her left eye.

"Grace, are you okay?"

"I'm fine." She took a step back.

"Who did that to you?"

She sealed her lips into a straight line.

Jane, who didn't have my point of view, craned her neck. "Who did what?"

Grace shielded her face and lowered her head. "Nothing. I have to go."

"What was that about?" Jane asked as Grace hustled down the hall.

"It looked like she had some bruising around her left eye."

"It's gotta be that roided-out husband of hers. I thought for sure I was going to see him assault poor Simon at the welcome reception. I wonder what made him so mad."

"Guys like that don't usually need much of a reason," I said.

"Deacon should be at the top of our suspect list. He's clearly prone to violence."

"I guess that means we should have a list."

Jane shoved her hand into the diaper bag and pulled out a notepad and pen. "Already ahead of you."

She scribbled at the top of the first page SUSPECTS and on the second page MOTIVES. "Okay, so Deacon is a suspect, and his motive is?"

"Uncontrollable rage?"

She bobbed her head. "Could be. What about jealousy? Elliot was a ladies' man, right? Maybe Deacon found out something was going on between Grace and Elliot. Late-night cooking lessons that led to something more scandalous?"

"Wouldn't that make all the husbands and boyfriends suspects?"

"I guess."

"Not to mention, female rivals for his attention and affection," I added.

"Good point. Have you heard any specific rumors about who he might have been involved with?"

"No, but I know who might have heard the rumors, and the last time I saw her she was marching off in search of her missing wigs."

Chapter Nine

AFTER SEARCHING THE fitness center, the library, and the solarium, with a short break for a diaper change and a snack, we finally located Margaret in the Azure lounge sipping a neon green beverage from a tall glass.

"May we join you?" I asked.

She eyed Quinton as she slurped from her straw. "Should you have a baby in a bar?"

"I'm not aware of any age limits in here."

Jane slid in next to her. "We were hoping you might be able to help us out."

"I don't babysit."

I took the seat closest to the stroller. "We're not asking you to babysit. We need intel."

Margaret ran her tongue across her teeth. "What makes you think I have the information you're looking for?"

In my experience, women like Margaret responded best to flattery, but it couldn't be too obvious. "I heard you've dabbled in fortune-telling. Now, I'm not one to judge the merits of the craft, but I do know it takes a keen wit and an innate ability to read people."

Margaret chewed on a piece of ice. "This is true, I was

born with the gift. For example, I know you've got the hots for Inspector Clouseau." She raised her eyebrows until they disappeared beneath the blonde bouffant wig.

Who? Inspector Cl—wait. "Xavier? Are you talking about Xavier Mesnier?"

She grunted a laugh. "No need to pretend with me. I see all."

Jane nudged me under the table with her foot. "Very astute. Although, I'm not sure Char has come to terms with those feelings quite yet. Give her time."

Margaret gave me a knowing nod. "You'll realize it eventually. So, who is it you want dirt on?"

I swallowed my protest. "We're not sure. Do you recall any rumors about who Chef Elliot might have been seeing?"

She finished her drink with a loud slurping sound and frantically waved at Cortes, one of the ship's bartenders. A stereotypical surfer dude in both looks and accent, Cortes barely looked old enough to be served alcohol himself. He shared bartending duties with a charming Irishman named Egan.

Cortes cupped his right ear.

"Another Shochu melon spritzer, please," she called across the lounge. "Do you ladies want anything?"

"I typically wait until after lunch to start drinking."

Hopefully, Margaret hadn't picked up on Jane's sarcasm.

"I'm okay," I replied.

"That's all," she called.

Cortes flipped his sandy brown bangs away from his warm brown eyes and gave a thumbs-up. "You got it," he said with the requisite surfer fry in his voice, like Spicoli from *Fast Times at Ridgemont High.*

Margaret returned the thumbs-up. "So." She slapped her hands on her lap. "You want to know who Elliot was boinking."

"I wouldn't put it in those words exactly."

"You'll have to forgive Char. She's a bit of a prude."

No point in arguing that, although I didn't appreciate Jane exposing me to Margaret.

"Not me. I've been divorced since early in the Bush administration—senior, not junior. That day, I ripped the shoulder pads out of all my blazers, traded my beige BMW in for a red Buick Reatta—you're gonna have to take my word for it, that car was sexy—and spent several months following the Rolling Stones Steel Wheels tour around the world. That's how I ended up in Japan the first time. They played ten shows at the Tokyo Dome."

"You were a groupie?"

She gave me a smug grin. "Honey, don't knock it 'til you try it."

Cortes nodded as he set a fresh cocktail in front of her. "Duuude." He glanced down at Quinton who'd begun to doze off in the stroller. "Awww. Little dude."

"Can we get back to Elliot?" I asked.

"Elliot figured out pretty quickly that there were a lot of lonely rich women onboard looking for a boy toy. I don't think he necessarily went looking for it. They came looking for him, and he took advantage of the opportunities presented."

"Were any of them married?"

Margaret sputtered her drink. "Married?" Her laugh was harsh. "Yeah, they were married. I'd say 90 percent. I think he preferred it that way."

"Why?"

Jane slapped her forehead. "Oh, Char."

"What?"

"My dear naïve sister. Think about it. Married people have more to lose, so they'll keep the affair a secret. If he's juggling multiple women, he *needs* them to keep it to themselves, otherwise they'd all find out about each other, and then he'd have a mess on his hands."

"Okay, but I'm guessing fraternizing with residents is against company policy also, so he'd be able to give single women a reason to stay quiet as well."

"But single women would also be more likely to want a legitimate future with him. A real relationship. Married people don't have expectations of their affair partners because they rarely intend on leaving their spouses. Single people don't have that hindrance."

Margaret tipped her glass toward Jane. "She's right."

"You seem to know an awful lot about this, Jane."

"It's common sense."

That had better be all it was. Jane knew what Gabe's affair had done to me, how it had messed me up. "Can you give us any names of these mostly married women?"

Margaret narrowed her gaze. "What exactly are you planning to do with this information?"

Must tread carefully. Wouldn't want to spook her, but

also didn't want to misrepresent the situation either. "We're assisting Xavier in solving Elliot's murder. His killer is on the loose, and none of us are safe until we find them."

"And?" Her left brow jumped and hid beneath her bangs.

"And…we believe jealousy is the most likely motive. Either the husband or boyfriend of one of his mistresses, or one of the women themselves."

"Should I be offended you don't consider me one of his paramours?"

"Oh no." Jane clucked. "That's not it at all."

"We just don't think you'd be insecure enough to kill him out of jealousy. You seem more evolved."

Margaret's eyelids grew heavy like a satisfied kitten after a bowl of warm milk. *Gotcha.*

"Very true. I believe the concepts of monogamy and exclusivity are outdated, from a bygone era when we still bought into the idea you could fully belong to another person." Margaret glanced at Quinton. "Those who don't get with the modern ideas of love, romance, and sex are destined to find themselves heartbroken."

Whether she intended it or not, her words stung.

Jane must have sensed their impact because she said, "Oh, I don't know about that. Lots of people find their forever love."

"Have you?" Margaret's green eyes bore into Jane.

"Well, I-I mean, I've never really wanted to settle down. I like my freedom."

"Exactly." Margaret tapped the tip of her nose. "Anyway,

for the record, I did not have sexual relations with that man." She laughed. "I'm sure I could have, but I didn't."

Was she stalling? "You're not going to give us names, are you?"

"I don't typically peddle in gossip because I prefer to keep the juicy tidbits for myself. I collect the information for use at opportune moments, when I can have a little fun with it."

"You mean like alluding that Rhodie's excuses for her husband's absence aren't as she claims?" I had picked up on the exchange at dinner. Rhodie had squirmed.

"For example."

Hello, cat that ate the canary. "Was Rhodie involved with Elliot?"

Margaret sucked her teeth and smacked her lips. "I have no direct evidence of a relationship. I can tell you, Bubba and Rhodie have a *don't ask don't tell* kind of relationship, if you know what I mean."

It was her second Clinton administration reference in so many minutes, and I knew exactly what she meant.

I also knew who we needed to look for next.

Chapter Ten

RHODIE ATKINSON SAT perched at the edge of a gold velvet chair in the library, her ankles crossed beneath her. She held a hefty book in front of her with rigid elbows crooked at a 45-degree angle. At first glance, she looked like a statue of Miss Manners, but then her arms began to sag under the weight of the novel. *Ulysses* by James Joyce, an eight-hundred-page behemoth.

She wasn't actually reading. That much I could tell by her eye movement. She'd stare blankly for a few minutes, and then turn the page.

I didn't blame her. *Ulysses* was considered one of the most difficult stories to slog through. But why was she pretending to read at all?

"Rhodie?"

"Oh, Charlotte, hello. Jane." As she set the book on the table, she did a double take at the sight of Quinton. "You've got K.D.'s baby?"

I refused to acknowledge the nickname. "She's being detained for questioning in Chef Elliot's murder."

"I heard she was found standing over the body. Poor thing. I empathize with her. No one likes to be a romantic castoff."

"You think they were involved?" Jane asked.

"Well." She brushed imaginary crumbs from her lap. "It wouldn't surprise me. I kept warning Elliot one of these days he was going to mess with the wrong girl." She sighed. "I wish he would have listened."

"Were *you* ever involved with Elliot romantically?"

She bristled at my question but quickly recovered.

"Of course not. I'm a married woman."

"Happily?" Jane probed.

Rhodie pursed her lips. "That's a rude question."

I sat in the chair opposite her. "Kyrie Dawn claims she didn't kill Elliot. We're trying to figure out who might have. At the end of dinner, you said you were going back to your room for a bubble bath and then bed. Did you see Elliot?"

"Not that I recall."

"How about anyone else?"

She tapped her red-painted lips with her fingertip. "I'm not sure. I mean, I'd had a few drinks, and I didn't realize at the time a murder was occurring, so it's not like I was taking notes or anything."

"Did you go straight back to your room?"

Rhodie snapped her head in Jane's direction. "Oh, I get it. I'm an outsider. An interloper. It must have been me that killed him. Is that it?"

Not how I ever would have described her. "In what universe are you an outsider?"

She jutted her chin. "I'm just a girl who was pretty enough to snag a dumb rich husband. That's what they say behind my back."

"I don't think they—"

"Of course they do! I'm not like *Grace Beauchamp of the Somerset Beauchamps*." She affected her voice to sound like Thurston Howell from *Gilligan's Island*.

Jane laughed. "Okay, so instead you're Rhodie Atkinson of the Savannah Atkinsons."

"I'm Rhododendron Tuppence Atkinson of the Peepers Gorge, West Virginia, Tuppences. My maiden name literally means two pence, as in, we didn't have two pence to rub together when I was growing up. I left home for Savannah the moment the clock turned midnight on my eighteenth birthday, and I never looked back."

I took in her navy pantsuit, her strand of pearls, her leather designer shoes with matching handbag, her perfectly coiffed hair, and her gleaming white veneers. I reflected on all my earlier impressions of her as the confident—arrogant, even—queen bee of her social circle. Her entire life was a performance, a tireless campaign to hustle for acceptance. It was a façade to mask deep insecurities and an abiding belief she didn't belong.

"I get it."

"How could you?" she spat at me. "You're one of them."

"I'm not."

"Charlotte, you own one of the bigger apartments on the ship."

"You mean the love nest my dead husband bought for his mistress"—I glanced at sleeping Quinton—"and their child with money I didn't know he had? I was a part-time librarian, Rhodie. I clipped coupons while Gabe was on here traveling to exotic locales while being served champagne by a butler."

She slumped in her chair, finally giving up the mannequin pose. "It's exhausting, isn't it?"

"What is?"

"Playing the game."

"I don't play the game," I said. "I don't even know the rules."

"We're all playing the game, whether we want to or not."

Jane folded her arms. "We know your husband rarely joins you onboard. It wouldn't be surprising if you wanted some company."

"I wasn't having an affair with Elliot Patenaude. Contrary to popular belief, my marriage is sound. I love my husband, and this arrangement works for us."

I believed she was telling the truth. About that, at least.

"What about the others?"

Her laugh was bitter. "You want me to risk what I've built by throwing my friends under the bus? Not gonna happen. What I've got going on here is a house of cards."

"Look at him." I pointed at the stroller. "His mother may go to prison for a murder she didn't commit. His father is dead. Can you really live with yourself if this kid becomes an orphan because you didn't want to face social backlash?"

Her eyes flashed. "Help me understand this. You're trying to exonerate the woman who ruined your life and you're angry with me because I won't help you?"

"She didn't ruin my life. She doesn't have that kind of power over me. But the kid needs his mother."

"Look, I sympathize. Really, I do. But if your plan is to expose my friends' secrets in order to not have to raise your husband's illegitimate child, you're on your own."

"He's not illegitimate." I pounded on the armrest. "No human being is illegitimate. He didn't ask to be born into this mess."

Quinton whimpered, and Jane rubbed his back.

"Funny how you're so keen to protect your friends, but they won't do the same for you." I shouldn't have said it. Instantly, I regretted it, but at the same time I wanted to see what unnerving her would reveal about Rhodie and her *sisters' golden hair.*

Rhodie reared back like she'd been struck. "What are you talking about?"

Jane gave me a look of warning, but I was in too deep to stop. "You think we came looking for you on a whim?"

Rhodie's lower lip trembled. "You're bluffing."

I shrugged. "Maybe."

She blinked as if scrolling through all possible scenarios of who might have cast aspersions her direction. She must have landed on someone, because her expression hardened.

"That witch!"

"How do you feel like that went?" Jane didn't mask her disappointment in my approach to Rhodie's stonewalling.

"I feel fine about it." I dropped the diaper bag on the kitchen counter of our suite.

She cocked her left eyebrow. "Do you?"

I popped the lid off one of Quinton's microwavable toddler meals. This one was cheese and spinach ravioli. "She clearly had an idea of the person she believes put us on her scent."

"Yes, but I'm sure she believes it's one of her close friends, not Margaret, because that's the impression you gave her."

"Hmm. Did I?"

"You know you did."

"Did I take advantage of her insecurities to stir up dissent among that group of women? Sure. Do I feel a little guilty? Maybe a little. But that illegitimate comment really hacked me off."

"Hacked you off? I haven't heard that phrase since Mr. Tuck's U.S. History class my junior year. Remember him? He used to say that all the time."

"Of course, I remember him. Best teacher I ever had."

"I get that she riled you up, but being unkind and poking at someone's vulnerabilities isn't like you."

I shut the microwave and pressed the start button. Quinton woke up with a wail, so I picked him up and popped the binky in his mouth. As I bounced him on my hip, he stared up at me with those familiar brown eyes, searching my face.

"This is probably pretty confusing for you, huh?"

He sucked on the pacifier, which squeaked as it rubbed against his tiny front teeth.

"Right now, my priority is getting this little boy his mother back. Once that's handled, I'll have a long call with my therapist to work through all my other issues."

Chapter Eleven

J ANE, QUINTON, AND I arrived at Kuchi Sabishii at about a quarter after six for Sushi and Sake Night. Upbeat J-pop music blared from the speakers and the diners seemed to be in great spirits. The regular dining room was closed for the evening, so Ulfric, Haimi, and the new server, Hawk, were on hand to assist the restaurant's regular staff.

Seated about ten feet from the entrance was the peroxide posse, although the vibe was less than congenial. Grace passed a tray of sashimi to Deacon. He took it without acknowledgment like it was a collection plate and they were strangers sitting next to each other in a church pew. Willow and Simon chewed quietly, intently focused on their meals. Florence Loomis was intent on adjusting her bosom, seemingly unaware of the withering stare Rhodie was shooting her direction.

"Well, don't they look more disgruntled than a sumo wrestler on a diet."

"Oh!" I jerked my head back. "Margaret. I didn't see you sneak up on us."

Tonight's wig was medium length, curly, and auburn, a la Julia Roberts in *Pretty Woman*.

"I don't sneak. You were just too engrossed in that pitiful scene. Any idea who or what put the bee in their bonnet?"

I made a dramatic grimace.

"Oh." She chuckled. "You're the apiarist."

"In Char's defense, she only rattled the hive of the queen bee. I've no idea why the rest of them look like that."

"Well." Margaret grabbed the handle of Quinton's stroller. "Let's go find out."

Rhodie turned her glare from Florence to us as we approached the table.

Florence's eyes were puffy and red-rimmed, and her blonde hair was disheveled.

"May we join you?" Margaret's question to the table held an unspoken dare to refuse.

"Of course," Grace murmured. She patted the area around her left eye, the one that had looked bruised earlier in the day.

Makeup covered a multitude of sins, apparently.

I sat next to Grace, with the stroller wedged between Jane and me. Margaret squeezed in next to Florence.

"What's good?" I asked.

"The rice." Grace scrunched her nose. "I don't like fish, raw or otherwise."

"How would you know, dear? You've never tried it," Deacon sang through gritted teeth.

"Pass the *sake*," Margaret practically shouted.

Simon held up his index finger. "Actually, *sake* actually means any alcoholic beverage, so when you ask for *sake* in Japan you should be more specific."

"Pass the *sake*," she repeated. "Wine."

"Actually, rice wine is a misnomer, because it's actually brewed like beer—"

Willow placed a hand on her husband's arm. "Simon, honey. Let's try to limit the use of the word *actually* to once per conversation."

"*Actually*," Rhodie said, "how about we talk about the concept of loyalty?"

Deacon grunted. Grace shifted in her seat. Margaret chuckled.

"Florence, you've lived much, much longer than the rest of us."

Florence scowled at Rhodie. "What's that supposed to mean?"

"It means you have more life experience than the rest of us. Haven't you found in your many, *many* years that loyalty is a valuable characteristic in friendship?"

"Rhodie, if you have something to say to me, spit it out," Florence said.

Rhodie cast a sour glance my way. "Maybe you can talk to Charlotte. You two seem to be sharing all sorts of secrets these days."

"Rhodie, what in the heck are you talking about? Charlotte, do you know?"

"Don't play coy." Rhodie stood and threw her napkin onto the table. "I don't need this. I don't need any of you." She stomped out of the restaurant.

Florence's expression was one of sullen bafflement. "What was that?"

Jane's disapproving stare bore through the side of my head.

I shifted in my seat. "She may have inferred from something I said that one of you gave me the impression she'd had an entanglement with Elliot Patenaude."

Florence slammed her hand on the table. "And what exactly did you say to give her this impression?"

"Gah!" Quinton squealed.

Jane pulled him from the stroller onto her lap. He banged his hands on the table like Florence.

"Wait, Rhodie was having an affair with Elliot?" Willow turned to Grace. "Did you know about this?"

Grace clenched her jaw. "I did not. Is this true?"

"Hold up," Deacon said. "Is that what you're saying, Charlotte? That Rhodie was hooking up with Chef Elliot?"

"I'm not saying that. Jane and I are just trying to aggregate as much information as possible about what Elliot was up to—and with whom. We had a chat with Rhodie this afternoon."

"So why does Rhodie believe I've been spilling her secrets?" Florence flared her surgically altered nostrils at me.

"I may have implied someone had pointed us in her direction. But I never named names, so I'm not sure why she thought it was you."

"Hmmph."

Xavier appeared in the doorway of the restaurant. He spotted me and waved me over.

"One sec," I said to the table, thrilled to have a reason to escape.

"It appears I interrupted an intense conversation." Xavier's mouth tipped slightly to the right.

"I may have stirred the pot a bit, trying to shake something loose. Any updates?"

"I told Kyrie Dawn that I would have you bring the boy to see her."

He didn't use her nickname. Good. Relief usurped any guilt I might have felt about my pettiness. "Okay. And?"

He put his hands on his hips. "Yes, there are updates; no, I cannot share them with you. It is an ongoing investigation."

"Just give me something. Anything." My attempt at cajoling came across more like begging.

He blew out a sigh. He wanted to tell me. It was in his eyes. I just needed to be patient.

"There was a hair."

"A hair?"

"On the body."

"I figured. Where on the body?"

"Someplace it should not have been."

I should have known he'd be mulish about revealing information. "So not his?"

"No."

"How do you know?"

"It was blonde."

Kyrie Dawn was blonde.

Rhodie was blonde.

I turned back to look at the table. All the women seated were blonde, except Jane and Margaret.

Come to think of it, I had no idea what color Margaret's hair *actually* was under all those wigs.

Chapter Twelve

K YRIE DAWN SMOTHERED Quinton's face with kisses. "Oh, I missed you, I missed you so much!"

He giggled under the barrage. "Mama! No, Mama, no kisses."

It wasn't like I believed for one second that Jane and I were a substitute for Quinton's own mother, which I didn't want to be anyway, but still the sight was an important reminder of why our task was so essential.

"Were you a good boy?" She nuzzled into his neck. "Ooh, you're gonna need a bath soon."

That sounded like a chore I was not equipped to undertake.

I stepped out of the room to give them some privacy. Jane had gone back to the suite.

Pike was at his desk, looking at his monitor. His chin rested on his palm and his eyes were heavy with boredom.

"Why so serious?"

"I'm looking at hours of security footage from all the cameras. There are so many, and yet somehow there are no good angles of the yoga studio."

"So, you're looking at the closest ones?

"I'm looking at everything. Mesnier wants me to look for any unusual activity, not only around the time and location of the murder, but every camera onboard since passengers began arriving on Sunday afternoon."

"What have you found so far?"

"A whole lot—people definitely seem to have forgotten there are cameras throughout the ship, judging by some of the things I've seen—but nothing that stands out to me as pertinent."

I stood over his shoulder. Housekeeping staff were dusting the registration desk and surrounding areas.

"This is tedious. Maybe if you increased the playback speed, it wouldn't take so long."

"I tried that, but the boss says I might miss something. He says I'm only allowed to do double speed."

The next footage that appeared was of the gangplank.

Jane came into frame, straining like she was dragging an entire building behind her. She stopped once to wipe her brow.

Oh no.

"You can fast forward this part. I was there, so I know nothing happened."

Pike sat up and grabbed the mouse. "Oh, I'd say this scene should be slowed waaay down. Wouldn't want to miss anything."

My face appeared at the bottom of the screen. I looked constipated as I pulled my luggage. I covered my face. "Let me know when it's over."

"Well, well, what do we have here?"

I removed my hands. "What?"

He gave an impish grin and sat back. I moved closer to get a better look.

He'd frozen the screen on a shot where Jane and I trudged up the gangplank with our heads down. Xavier was at the top of the ramp watching. He was smiling. Not a mocking smile. Not a condescending smile or a forced smile of greeting. He was looking at me and smiling like he was glad to see me.

The door opened, and both Pike and I jumped.

"Are you interfering with my investigator?" Xavier asked.

I moved between him and Pike's computer. "Not at all."

"Hmmph." To Pike he said, "Anything?"

"Uh, nope, uh…wait. This may be something."

I whirled to look at the screen. It had better not be embarrassing footage of me. Xavier joined us behind Pike's desk.

The reel was of the loading area. Chef Elliot was pacing, checking his phone.

My heart stung at the sight of him less than forty-eight hours before his death.

Someone off-camera must have caught his attention, because he looked over his shoulder. He glanced around the area as if to see who might be watching him. He strode out of view. For several minutes, the footage showed no activity. Then Elliot came back into view, carrying a small ice chest by the handle. With his other hand he held a bucket. He set the bucket down and held his cell phone to his ear. He said something unintelligible—too bad I didn't know how to read lips—and then wedged the phone into the crook of his neck, picked the bucket back up, and disappeared into the loading bay.

"What do you think that was?" I asked.

"He was obviously trying to keep whatever he was doing on the down-low."

Xavier stroked his scruffy chin. "I suspect that was when he smuggled the fugu onboard. Little did he know, he was setting up his own demise."

"XAVIER, CAN YOU please slow down? My legs are shorter than yours. I can't keep up."

"Well, then, perhaps you should not have followed me."

"And miss you discovering evidence? Not a chance."

We were headed for the kitchen in hopes of locating the cooler and the bucket Elliot had ferreted onboard. Technically, it should have been called the galley, but that evoked images of some greasy, rusty spot below deck where a cook named Lobster Legs Louie stirred a giant pot of whatever had been dredged from the bottom of the sea, whereas this was a state-of-the-art chef's kitchen that produced gourmet meals.

I'd left Quinton with his mother, who was grateful for the additional time. Xavier hadn't exactly invited me to go with him, but he hadn't expressly denied me either.

"You just don't want to admit I make a good partner."

He paused briefly but began walking again. He held up his finger. "You are not my partner. You are a resident of this ship, and it is my job to investigate this crime and keep you and the other passengers safe."

"I'm a good problem solver."

"Yes…"

"And you enjoy my company."

"Not always."

"So you admit it. Sometimes you do."

"Sometimes."

He had his back to me, but I could hear the smile in his voice.

He unlocked a door, and we entered the main kitchen, which was off the regular dining hall. Since there hadn't been a meal served upstairs tonight, it was dark and empty. He flipped on the light. There were no dirty dishes, no overflowing trashes, no employees.

On the counter was a box of light blue latex gloves. He pulled out two gloves and handed one to me.

"Put this on. Do not touch anything without it. I prefer you do not touch anything at all, but just in case."

I set down my phone as I wrangled the tiny glove over my wide hand. My nose itched, and I attempted to scratch it with my forearm. The smell of the glove reminded me of my freshman year in college when I worked at a greeting card store. I'd spent most of my shifts blowing up balloons, and the scent gave me a little PTSD, particularly when I thought of the graduation rush. I'd spent hours making bouquets until the helium got to me and I nearly passed out. "I think I might be allergic to latex." I rubbed my nose again.

"Maybe if you stopped touching your face."

I gave him the stink eye, but he had his back to me.

He took one side of the kitchen, while I scoured the other. It was the most organized space I'd ever seen. Each drawer was labeled and partitioned. The pantry contained stacked cans and a variety of clear containers marked with their contents. Metal trays held potatoes, onions, or tomatoes. There was a whole section of dry pasta.

Huh. I figured he would have made everything from scratch, including the pasta.

"I'm not seeing anything. I'm going to check out the walk-in fridge."

Xavier, his head inside a cupboard, mumbled his assent.

I unlatched and opened the heavy steel door. I was immediately hit with cold air. "Whoo! It's chilly in here." I rubbed my right arm with my ungloved hand.

I slipped through the PVC strip curtain and into the main part of the fridge. Metal trays like I'd seen in the pantry were well-stocked with fruits and vegetables. Meats had their own section, separated by type.

"I had no idea cruise ships stocked so much whipped cream," I called. "There must be three hundred cans in here." I picked one up and shook it.

Should I? I glanced at the door. "Xavier?"

I waited a beat. Nothing.

I pulled off the lid and hovered the nozzle over my mouth just as he popped his head through the plastic curtain.

"Were you calling for me?"

Dang it. Caught. Heat crept up my neck and into my

cheeks. I replaced the lid and set the bottle back on the shelf. "Uh, it was nothing."

"Charlotte?"

"Hmm."

"What were you doing?"

"Investigating."

"Investigating how much whipped cream you can fit into your mouth?" He walked all the way into the fridge.

"Something like that," I mumbled. I shuffled over to the seafood section, hoping the cold would quell my blush. "What does a puffer fish look like when it's fileted?"

"No idea. I only know what it looks like in photos. Spiky. Bulging eyes."

"The stuff of nightmares."

"*Exactement.*"

I crouched down used my gloved hand to slide a box of prawns on a lower shelf out of the way. "Xavier."

"*Oui.*"

"Look."

He crouched next to me and peered deep into the shelf. Hidden behind other items were an ice chest and a bucket similar to what we'd seen on the security footage.

"Madame Charlotte, I do believe we have located the source of our poison."

And that's when the door to the fridge slammed shut.

Chapter Thirteen

"THIS IS NOT good." Xavier pushed against the door, to no avail.

Not good? I was freaking out and he nonchalantly said *this is not good.* Nonchalance. It had to be a French invention. The ability to act like being trapped in a cold storage refrigerator was no big deal had to be genetic. There was no other explanation.

My mouth went dry.

He tried the door for a third time, as if it might magically unlock. It didn't.

"That door is so heavy. How did it shut so easily?" My teeth chattered. It had to be below 40 degrees.

"I fear it did not shut of its own accord."

"You think someone purposely locked us in here?"

He grimaced and looked at his cell phone. "No reception. I cannot believe I left my radio. I know better."

I reached for my own phone, patting all my pockets. Dang. "I left mine on the counter out there. Someone will come find us eventually, right?"

"Eventually."

Ominous. "Any idea how long before hypothermia sets

in?"

"No, and I prefer not to find out." He banged on the door. "Hello! Can anyone hear me?" He banged again.

"I really wish I'd worn a jacket." I wrapped myself in a hug.

Xavier removed his blazer. "Come here."

"I can't take that. You'll freeze."

"You are already shivering, and we have not been in here for ten minutes yet." He flung the jacket around my shoulders and enveloped me in his arms.

We swayed as he insulated me within his embrace.

All the movies I'd seen where two people had to use body heat to stay warm had made it look so romantic. It wasn't. My joints ached and my dry mouth—caused by fear and adrenaline—had made my breath turn. It turned out, facing death wasn't great for the libido.

"Now I understand why people retire to warm climates. The older you get, the more cold temperatures revive old injuries. My left wrist feels like I broke it last week, not forty years ago."

"I know what you mean." His chest rumbled in my ear. "My body is reminding me of the many bones I have broken in my life."

"How many?"

"Hmm, well, I believe it is less than a dozen, but not much less."

"Geez, did all that happen in the military?"

"Many, but not all."

"Always a man of mystery."

"Is that how you see me?"

I leaned back enough to see his face. "Well, I've managed to get tiny bits of information, an overheard rumor here and there, but not a lot. I know you're from France, and I know you have some sort of Special Forces background, but other than that, I know nothing."

"I know little about you as well."

I scoffed. "You knew more about my life than even I did, and for quite a while. You knew about Gabe buying a residence here. You knew about Kyrie Dawn. And Quinton."

Don't give me the pity look. Please don't give me the pity look.

His gaze softened, and his brow furrowed. His light brown eyes rippled with sympathy.

Sigh. And there it was.

"Charlotte, I am sure there is much more to your life than your husband's poor judgment. But we can talk about that another time. Here, let us sit, and I will tell you some things about myself."

We slid to the floor and leaned against the shelf containing packages of various raw meats. He pulled me close to his side his broad frame protecting me from the cold. I could get used to this feeling. Warm, secure, safe, even in the midst of danger.

I inhaled the scent of him, catching a whiff of his body odor. It wasn't stinky but natural. No cologne or deodorant fragrance. Was this what pheromones smelled like?

There was also a hint of peppermint.

"What do you want to know?"

"Well, let's start with your broken bones."

He laughed. "The first time I broke a bone," he said, "I was playing football. Soccer, as you call it. I was goalkeeper, and I saved a penalty kick...with my forearm."

"Ouch. How old were you?"

"Nine."

"Geez! Where did you grow up?"

"I come from Nimes, a city in the south of France."

"Like Nice and Cannes? Are you a fancy Frenchman?" I teased.

"I think you know I am not fancy." He chuckled. "Even the one thing we are famous for is not fancy."

"What's that?"

"Denim. The fabric used to make jeans. It comes from the phrase *de Nimes*, or from Nimes."

"Whoa! I never knew that."

"*Oui.* As for Nice and Cannes, those places are about a three-hour drive from Nimes, and no, I would not say my hometown is anything like them. No beaches, very few celebrities."

"Bummer." I wriggled my toes, which were starting to go numb. "I've always wanted to lounge on the French Riviera."

"*Oui.* Bummer." It was strange hearing him use slang. "When I was eighteen, I was conscripted to join the *service nationale*. While my term was for only twelve months, I reenlisted for another four years. I had planned to move on at the end of that term, however I was put into the *Division Daguet* at the onset of the first Gulf War conflict. From there

I joined the GIGN."

"GIGN?"

"*Groupe d'intervention de la Gendarmerie nationale.* It is what you might call Special Forces but operating mainly in France."

"How long were you a part of that?"

"A very long time."

Hmm. Vague. "You told me you broke many bones, the first playing goalie—"

"Goalkeeper."

"Goalkeeper was your last broken bone?"

"Five years ago. I broke my left hand." He held it up for me to examine. His knuckles bore white scars, and a raised purple scar streaked across the top of his hand.

"How?" I traced the jagged line with my fingertip.

For a few moments, the only sound in the walk-in was the hum of cooling fans and the sound of his heart beating against my ear.

"I punched a wall."

Unexpected. I glanced up at him, trying to read his expression. "What made you angry enough to punch a wall?"

"I received very bad news."

I waited for an explanation, but he didn't give it. The urge to pry was strong. I opened my mouth and shut it. His reticence to share the details indicated a boundary. Our burgeoning friendship was at risk if I violated it. I pouted internally but didn't push the topic.

I released his hand. "I'm sorry."

"Why?"

"I'm sorry you received such upsetting news it resulted in you breaking your hand."

He sighed and his shoulders sagged with what seemed like relief. Maybe he was glad I wasn't going to press him on the issue. "Thank you."

I rubbed my hands together. "Do you think anyone will come for us?"

"Yes, of course."

He enclosed my hands in his. I nestled into him as much as I could. His warm breath blew on the top of my head. Neither of us spoke for what seemed like several minutes but probably was only one or two. It felt intimate, but not in a sexual kind of way, more like a *we're in a fight for survival together* kind of way.

"This would be a really good time for a hot flash," I muttered.

He burst into laughter, his whole body shaking.

"I'm just saying. They never come when they're actually useful."

"That is certainly unfortunate for us."

A click at the door caused both of us to jerk upright.

"Hello?" called the voice.

"Pike!" I jumped to my feet. "We're in here! Don't let the door shut, it locks."

Pike poked his head through the slit in the curtain. "You all okay in here? How did this happen?"

Xavier lumbered to his feet. "We can discuss it once we are able to feel our extremities."

"HELP ME UNDERSTAND this." Pike tapped a pen on his desk. "You believe someone locked you in the cold storage on purpose?"

Xavier handed me a steaming cup of tea. "*Oui*, I want you to check the security footage."

"I've looked at so much security footage tonight, my eyes are starting to cross, but I can try."

"Why would someone want to lock us in there? Were they trying to scare us or kill us? Maybe they just wanted to stop us from finding something. And how did they even know we would be there? Since the dinner service was at Kuchi Sabishii, that place wasn't even used tonight."

"I suppose the answer to that lies with the who." Xavier sipped from his own mug. "Good news. I am starting to feel my fingertips."

"My hands are so numb; I can barely hold this cup."

When we'd arrived back at the security office, I'd checked on Quinton, who was soundly sleeping on his mother's stomach. Kyrie Dawn was lightly snoring as well. No point in waking them up yet.

"So here are the two of you walking down the hall," Pike said. "Actually, Xavier is walking, and you appear to be chasing him, Charlotte."

"I wasn't chasing. He just has a longer stride than I do."

"You also seem to be arguing."

"About the fact he was moving too quickly for me. Also, I wouldn't call it arguing. More like a spirited conversation."

"Ah! I think I found your culprit. Check it out, sir." Pike shifted his monitor to show Xavier.

Xavier set his cup on the desk. "Well, well."

I joined them behind Pike's desk. Frozen on the screen was a suspicious-looking man ducking into the kitchen.

It was Deacon Beauchamp.

Chapter Fourteen

"IT WASN'T ME." Deacon folded his arms. "Ask my wife."

Grace sat next to him wringing her hands. The concealer she'd layered around her left eye had worn off enough to reveal a hint of violet and chartreuse. "It couldn't have been Deacon. He's been here with me since dinner."

"There you go. It couldn't have been me who locked you in the freezer."

If Deacon thought he'd be able to talk his way out of this, he was mistaken.

"Walk-in refrigerator," I corrected.

"Whatever. Wasn't me. I was here with my wife." Liar. The imperceptible twitch at the corner of his mouth told a different story.

"*Monsieur* Beauchamp, we have video evidence to the contrary. We know you were out of your suite tonight."

That too.

"Oh, uh, you know what? Now that you mention it, I guess I did go out briefly to, uh, get a book from the library. That must have been when the cameras caught, uh, saw me in the hallway up on Mykonos."

"Is that so?"

Get him, X.

There was an added satisfaction that not only was Xavier about to nail the person responsible for our near-death experience, but a suspected (by me) wife beater as well. Deacon deserved everything he had coming to him.

"Yes. I forgot. I was having trouble sleeping. Isn't that right, honey?"

He patted Grace's thigh and squeezed. Not gently, either.

She winced her way into a strained smile. "Oh, silly me, I forgot. It was my suggestion, actually. I find reading to have quite the somniferous effect."

For a moment Deacon forgot about the script. "Somni-what?" The derision dripped from his words.

She bowed her head and watched her hands smooth her lap.

There was more to Grace than I'd realized. How many times had she shrunk herself, dumbed herself down so that Deacon could feel superior to her?

"Somniferous. Now that's a fifty-cent word. I'll bet you're great at crosswords, Grace."

She returned my smile with a shy one of her own.

Deacon grunted. "Yeah, she's always doing those things. Such a waste of time." He mouthed *somniferous* and pinched his brows together.

It was Xavier's turn to look confused. "Fifty cents? What does money have to do with anything?"

"Never mind." I waved my hand dismissively. "So, what

did you get, Deacon?"

"Huh?" Seemingly still stuck on the vocabulary word, Deacon had lost track of the conversation.

"I believe Madame McLaughlin is asking which book you chose from the library."

"Oh, I, you know what? I didn't find one that looked interesting."

"There are hundreds of books in the library, from classics to contemporary. And you were unable to find anything to suit your interest?" Xavier leaned forward.

"Nope."

"I suppose that is why you were seen roaming the halls without a book." He tilted his head, his gaze like a laser beam, as if Deacon were a bug under a microscope.

He shifted under the scrutiny. "Exactly."

"And what were you looking for in the galley?" Xavier tilted his head the other direction.

"I wasn't... I didn't... I came back here."

"Yeah, after you nearly turned us into Popsicles!" I squealed.

Xavier threw me a glance that I read as *hush*.

"Officer Taylor has already lifted prints from the door and handle. As you know, purchasing a unit on this ship requires a full background check. Your prints are on file, so I recommend if you have anything to explain, now would be an opportune time."

Pink crept from below Deacon's collar and up his neck. He made a blustering sound. "This is ridiculous. I shouldn't be treated like a criminal in my own home!"

"You wouldn't be treated like a criminal if you didn't act like a criminal!" I glared at him.

"To be clear, *Monsieur* Beauchamp, I am investigating the refrigerator incident in connection to the murder of Chef Elliot Patenaude."

Grace sank into the sofa.

"I didn't kill anyone!" Deacon shouted.

"What did you do, monsieur?"

The more worked up Deacon was, the calmer Xavier's demeanor became. It was a master class in getting a pig to squeal.

"You should tell him." Grace gently placed her hand on his arm, her voice barely above a whisper. "It'll get worse for you if you don't."

Deacon shot her an angry look, and she recoiled.

"What do you need to tell me?"

Deacon cleared his throat and thrust his lower lip into a pout. "I wasn't trying to hurt anyone. I swear."

Xavier pulled a notepad and pen from his coat pocket. He clicked the pen and looked at Deacon expectantly.

"I was headed to the kitchen when I saw the two of you go inside."

"Why were you going in the first place?"

"I needed to get something."

"Something that belonged to you?"

"Sort of. Not exactly." Deacon squirmed. "Elliot had specially ordered something for me, but he...died before I could get it from him."

"Fugu."

Deacon's gaze widened. "How did you know?"

"It is my understanding that fugu is a dangerous fish to handle. Highly regulated."

"Yeah, but Elliot had a guy who could get him one."

"Do you know who the man is?"

"Nope, he just said he got it. We were going to have a private dinner here. Only a select few ever get the chance to try it, and I was gonna be one of 'em."

"You know how dumb that is, right?" I asked. "He had no business preparing that fish. You could have died if he did it wrong."

Deacon's flushed cheeks paled to a sallow shade of green that looked a bit like the bruising around his wife's swollen eye. "He said he knew how."

"He YouTubed it, Deacon," I said.

A flash of something that looked a lot like wistfulness flashed across Grace's face. Had she hoped her husband would succumb to his foolish endeavor? *Pride goeth before destruction and a haughty spirit before a fall.* I suspected she was counting on it.

"So, you were going to the galley to retrieve the fish?" Xavier crossed his legs and bounced his foot.

"Mm-hmm."

"Anything else?"

"Like what?"

"You tell me."

"He told me he'd fileted the fugu and we were all set for the special dinner. It was supposed to take place tonight at midnight. I figured since everyone was already expecting it..."

Xavier blinked at Deacon. "You don't mean to tell me you were going to try to cook the fish yourself and serve it to other passengers?"

"Are you out of your mind?" I couldn't help my outburst. "It's poison! Poi. Son."

His sheepish expression turned defensive. "Look, in retrospect, it wasn't the most brilliant idea I've ever had, but we were all set, and all my buddies back at the Somerset Country Club said they didn't believe I was gonna do it. I had to do it. They'd never have let me live it down if I didn't go through with it."

I thought I heard Xavier mutter the word *crétin* under his breath.

I smacked my forehead. "Hey, dummy, you were never gonna live it down if you did go through with it. You were *literally* not going to live it down because you'd have killed yourself and all of your guests."

Xavier cleared his throat, a signal for me to let him handle the conversation. "Who was to attend this soiree?"

Deacon shifted his posture and jutted his chin. "I'd rather not say."

Xavier briefly closed his eyes and inhaled. "You understand that you are not doing yourself any favors here. Cooperation, as your wife said, will benefit you in the long run."

"I'm no snitch."

Xavier closed the notebook and retracted the pen. He uncrossed his legs and tucked the notebook back into his inner pocket. He put the pen in his inner pocket. He placed his hands on his thighs and stood.

Relieved, Deacon deflated into the cushions. His brow arched and a tiny smile formed at the corner of his mouth.

Smug S.O.B.

"Deacon Beauchamp, I am placing you under arrest for the attempted murder of myself and Charlotte McLaughlin."

Deacon's face fell faster than the stock market on Black Monday.

Got 'im.

Chapter Fifteen

"WAIT, SO THEN what did Deacon do?" Jane hung on each and every word of my retelling of the night's events.

"He may have peed a little. He didn't say a word after Xavier announced he was placing him in custody."

"Did he say why he trapped the two of you in the cooler?"

"No, as soon as he realized how much trouble he's in, he shut his trap. My guess is, he knew we were about to find the bucket of fish guts and he panicked."

Across the room, Quinton rustled in the portable crib.

Jane lowered her voice. "Is there room for two suspects in boat jail?"

"I guess. But get this. Xavier had the gall to bring up Andy's house arrest."

"What do you mean?"

"I mean, he implied perhaps that was a preferable solution for Kyrie Dawn."

She furrowed her brow. "If that's the preferable solution, why doesn't he do that? Then Quinton could stay with her."

"You don't understand. He wasn't saying she should be

locked in her room. He meant she should serve her house arrest here." I stabbed the arm of my chair with my fingertip.

"You've got to be kidding."

"I wish I were."

"For such a smart dude, that's pretty clueless."

"Pretty much what I told him."

"Does he believe Deacon killed Elliot?"

"Hard to say. Deacon's motive is unclear, because he needed Elliot to make the meal. But they were doing something illegal, so maybe something went wrong between them. Maybe Elliot decided it was too dangerous and refused to follow through. Plus, who else besides Deacon knew Elliot had the fugu, which is most likely his cause of death? Of course, that doesn't explain the blonde hair."

"What blonde hair?"

"Oh, I didn't get the chance to tell you. Xavier pulled me aside after dinner and told me that a single blonde hair was found on Elliot's body."

"Whoa. Like a woman's blonde hair?"

"He didn't say, but that's part of the reason he's still holding Kyrie Dawn."

"There are a lot of blonde women on this ship, including the four we had dinner with tonight."

"My thoughts exactly, but only one of them was found standing over the body."

"Setting aside personal history, do you believe she did it?" Jane asked.

"I don't know what to think. Part of me wants to talk to her, try to understand her relationship with Elliot. Part of me would rather jump off the balcony."

"I doubt Xavier would even let you."

"Talk to her or jump off the balcony?"

"Either. But mainly, talk to her."

"After tonight he might."

Jane leaned forward. "Did something happen while you were trapped? Did you, uh—" She raised and lowered her eyebrows. "You know."

"No! Nothing like that."

"Don't sound so offended. No one would blame you."

"It wasn't like that. It's just...he talked to me about his life. I feel like we bonded."

"Any juicy tidbits?"

"Even if there were, I wouldn't tell you. Not my story to tell."

"Well, that's no fun." Jane yawned and peeked into the crib. "I'm exhausted, but I'm guessing you are too. I'll keep my door open tonight in case he starts fussing so you can get some sleep. I say tomorrow we start systematically interviewing the blonde brigade, see if one of them has any insight."

"I probably need to set the record straight with Rhodie, let her know Florence didn't point me in her direction or say she was having an affair with Elliot."

"You definitely should do that."

"She didn't deny it, though."

She considered my words. "You're right. She didn't. In fact, the way she worded it, sounded like she believed Florence had betrayed her trust, which sounds more like a revealing of a secret rather than spreading a false rumor."

"Speaking of Florence, did you notice anything unusual about her tonight?"

"Like what?"

"She seemed sad."

"About Elliot?"

I shrugged. "Maybe. I don't know. Just a sense I had."

"Well, after you make things right with Rhodie, we can track down Florence and see what's going on. Also, I checked the itinerary. Tomorrow night's dinner theme is sakura blossom, and I don't own a single item of clothing that's pink, so I need to pop into Aphrodite's Boutique at some point."

"It's ironic, isn't it?" I said.

"What?"

"Maybe ironic isn't the right word—apropos, poignant, perhaps—but it's stunning to me that two days after Elliot's murder, we'll all be dining in pink clothing, surrounded by sakura blossoms."

"I'm not following."

"I once read a book—I wish I could remember which one, but it was many years ago—throughout which the sakura was a prominently featured metaphor. In Japanese culture, the sakura blossom is a symbol of both life and death, beauty and violence. It's the embodiment of the idea that life is fleeting."

"IT'S LIKE A vat of Pepto Bismol exploded," I said.

Quinton cooed his amazement at the dining room, swathed in pink lighting, fabric, and sakura cherry blossoms.

"Well, one thing is crystal clear," Jane said.

"What's that?"

"Pink is *not* everyone's color."

"Good evening, ladies." Ulfric wore his usual black tuxedo, but his cummerbund and bowtie were the shade of bubble gum.

"Hi, Ulfric. Any chance we can be seated again with the flaxen faction?"

"The flaxen wha—" He scanned the room and when his gaze landed on the table with the four wan blondes—plus Margaret wearing something akin to cotton candy on her head—his confusion morphed into a regretful smile. He wagged his finger at Jane. "Ms. Cobb, you will get me in trouble one of these days."

Grace glowered as we approached the table. "You have a lot of nerve coming here tonight. My husband is in jail because of you."

As Ulfric pulled out my chair he made a subtle noise that, with one sliding note, said *ooh, someone's trying to start something.*

"Grace, your husband has been detained because he tried to freeze two people to death, including the head of ship security—and me."

I was tempted to add something about the fact she should be grateful he was locked up and not using her as a punching bag, but that wouldn't do anything other than embarrass and hurt her, not to mention make her an uncooperative witness.

"He says he wasn't trying to freeze you, only stop you from finding out about the fugu."

"The fugu was in the cooler with us."

"I'm not saying it was a well-thought-out plan. Clearly, he panicked."

Simon draped a pink napkin across his lap. "I for one am relieved he's locked away. I didn't appreciate him threatening me. He's prone to violence." He drummed his fingers nervously on the table.

This was news. "He threatened you? How? When? Why?"

He pointed to the alcove where I'd witnessed an irate Deacon get in Simon's face.

"At the welcome reception?"

"Yes, on our first night back onboard." His gaze flicked to Grace, who was intently straightening her silverware. "He accused me of some pretty unsavory things."

"Such as?"

He adjusted his glasses. "It's not for me to say."

Why was he being evasive if Deacon had threatened him? Protecting him was a strange move. "Okay, then how did he threaten you?"

He picked up a chopstick and spun it with his left hand like a baton. "He told me he would kill me."

Willow's hand flew to her mouth. Margaret clucked. Quinton threw his sippy cup on the floor.

Grace paled but stayed focused on straightening her already perfect table setting. She didn't defend her husband.

She didn't refute the possibility he was capable of such a threat or following through with it.

Jane leaned down to pick up Quinton's cup. "Here you go, buddy." She eyed Simon, but he was too busy keeping his chopstick routine going to notice.

Why did Jane's face look so odd?

"There you have it." Florence's face was flushed, and her chin quivered. "Deacon has killer mentality. I hope he rots in prison for it."

"Florence!" Grace cried. "How can you say that? That's my husband you're talking about."

"A man is dead, Grace. Maybe Deacon didn't mean to kill him. Perhaps his temper got the best of him." Florence paused. "You'd know more about that than anyone."

Grace stood and threw her napkin down like a gauntlet. Her glare could have sliced through diamonds. "That's low, and you know it."

"That's the truth."

"Oh, you want to talk about truth, Florence?" Grace's laugh was hollow and tinged with bitterness. "Because you're such an honest, authentic person, right?"

"Grace…" Florence's plea held a note of warning. She rose from her chair and leaned on the table with both hands. "Don't do this."

"They need to start serving popcorn as an appetizer at these meals," Margaret said.

"What is she talking about?" Rhodie asked Florence.

Florence flinched but said nothing. She and Grace were in a standoff, arguing in silent scowls.

Grace must have decided to end the stalemate with a kill shot. "Florence is just upset because she had a closer connection to Elliot than she wants to admit."

"Grace, please."

Willow sat up straight. "Florence? Were *you* having a relationship with Elliot? Was anyone *not* involved with Elliot Patenaude?" Her cheeks were crimson.

"Oh, she was having a relationship, all right." Grace smirked. "Just not a romantic one. Right, Florence?"

Florence inhaled, her nostrils flaring.

"Come on, Florence, no need keeping the secret anymore," she taunted.

Grace was being cruel in a way I hadn't thought she was capable. Florence was clearly in distress from the looming revelation.

I stood with my hands out. "Cease fire. This is unnecessary."

Grace's upper lip curled. "I think it's quite necessary. My husband is being held on suspicion of murder, without clear motive. What stronger motive could there be than protecting a forty-year-old shameful secret, eh, Florence?"

"I shared that with you in confidence." Florence's shoulders slumped.

"Would you like to tell them, or shall I? 'Cause it's gonna come out tonight."

Florence swallowed. "Please, Grace."

"Charlotte, don't you think Xavier would want to know that Florence had ulterior motives coming onboard the *Thalassophile*, and they were directly related to Elliot

Patenaude?" Grace sneered.

"I believe he would. Yes." I glanced at Florence, who had dropped her chin in resignation. "Are you saying you know what these motives are?"

"I do. Florence used to know Elliot a *long* time ago, but she wanted to keep that secret." Grace scoffed and scanned the table. "You think you know someone, until you discover the kind of person they really are."

"Why would she need to keep knowing him a secret?" Jane asked.

"Because he was her son, and she abandoned him."

Chapter Sixteen

A LL HELL BROKE loose after Grace's revelation about Florence and Elliot. Rhodie yelled at Grace for being so cruel. Willow sat shell-shocked while Simon watched Florence like she was a pot of water on the verge of boiling. Florence threw her napkin on the table and stormed out of the dining room. Margaret and Quinton seemed to be the only ones at the table who were enjoying the chaos.

Someone needed to rein things in. "Grace, how did you discover that Florence is Elliot's mother?"

Grace sniffed. "Apparently, that's not my story to tell."

"Oh no you don't," said Rhodie. "You don't get to blow the lid off her secret and then act all noble, like you care about honoring her privacy."

"I shouldn't have said anything," Grace mumbled.

"No, you shouldn't have, but you did. Now spill it."

"You don't have to be so harsh, Rhodie." She flared her nostrils again. "I overheard them arguing."

"When was this?" I needed to remember every detail to share with Xavier.

"The night of the ninja dinner. That's why Florence didn't come. It wasn't that she was sick, it was that she was a blubbering mess."

"What did you hear?"

"He was being awful to her. She was saying that she needed to explain, and he told her he didn't want to hear it. He felt betrayed, not only because of what she'd done when he was a baby, but because she'd befriended him under false pretenses. He'd shared private information with her because he thought she was someone he could trust, but really, she was the women responsible for his trust issues in the first place. He said she was a pathetic old woman and that everything about her was fake. Actually, he said faux, but I know that means fake." Grace paused, possibly waiting for kudos on knowing the translation of one French word that never came. She cleared her throat. "Anyway, before he stormed off, he told her he never wanted to see her again and he hoped she fell overboard."

"Yikes," Simon muttered. "That's a crushing thing to say to a mother. She must have taken that quite hard."

"Oh, she did. I helped her back to her room, and that's when she told me the whole story."

Everyone at the table leaned forward, except Quinton, who was playing with a spoon.

"Apparently, Florence was an exchange student in the late seventies or early eighties. She spent a school year in France. Early on, she met a man, and he swept her off her feet. He was older, handsome, sophisticated. A diplomat of some kind. He was also married. She found out she was pregnant, he told her he was going to leave his wife and marry her after the baby was born."

"Did he?" Willow asked.

"No. It turned out it was a scheme. Maybe not the whole time, but once she got pregnant. You see, the man's wife wasn't able to have children. They had tried for years with no luck then Florence became pregnant; they offered her a cash payment to walk away. She was scared to tell her parents what happened, and she knew she couldn't raise a kid alone. She took the deal. While Florence was still recovering from the birth, the man and his wife filed two sets of paperwork: one to get full custody and one to get Florence deported back to the States. I guess because this guy was so well connected, they got quick approval for both. She was back home within days."

"Bless her heart," Willow clucked.

"Earlier, you made it sound like she abandoned Elliot. She was a child herself, and he was a grown man who abused his power to get her kicked out of the country. That's not exactly abandonment." I crossed my arms.

"She did, though," Simon said. "She took the cash in exchange for the kid. What else would you call it? No wonder she wanted to keep that secret, and no wonder Elliot was angry."

"Was this her first contact with him?" Jane asked.

"No. Maybe that was part of the reason he was so mad. She's been sailing on this ship on and off for months. She offered to be his patron, help him open a restaurant. He thought she was being nice. I know he confided in her—she was quite proud of the fact she'd become his confidante—although she didn't tell me specifics. I guess she thought they'd developed enough of a rapport and it was time to tell him the truth about being his mother. She was wrong." Grace pursed her lips. "I just think it's rich for her to be judging Deacon when she's got plenty of skeletons in her own closet to answer for."

Oh really. "Not quite the same scenario. One was a teen, most likely taken advantage of by a grown man, and the other is a grown man who locked me in the cold storage like a side of beef."

Grace's indignance was confusing, considering the man she was defending had more than likely given her a black eye.

Simon stood. "Well, this has been yet another eventful meal. Willow, remind me to bring antacid next time."

She nodded, gave everyone an anemic wave, and followed him out of the dining room.

"Rhodie, can I speak with you for a moment?" I asked. "In private?"

Once we were in the alcove where Deacon had threatened Simon, she said, "What's this all about?"

"I want to apologize for giving you the impression one of your friends had implied a romantic relationship between you and Elliot."

"Why did you?"

"I was trying a divide and conquer approach. To see if I could exploit the cracks in your friendships and find out who might have been involved with Elliot's death. I know it wasn't cool."

"What makes you so sure it was one of us? There could be any number of people on this ship who had a vendetta against Elliot."

"True, but so far no evidence has led to anyone else."

"Except K.D."

"Yes, there's a lot of evidence pointing toward Kyrie Dawn. I have to ask, Rhodie, *were* you involved with Elliot? Romantically? When you got mad at Florence, it seemed like you were upset because you felt she'd betrayed your trust, not made up a lie about you."

"It's humiliating."

"That you had an affair?"

"Hah! That would be less humiliating."

"I'm confused."

"I didn't have an affair with Elliot."

"Okay…"

"I *tried* to have an affair with Elliot, but he rejected me."

Ouch. "I'm, uh, well, sorry seems like a strange thing to say under the circumstances, but I can imagine that was a difficult thing to experience."

"I'm sure you think poorly of me, especially because of Gabe and K.D."

Kyrie Dawn. Her name was Kyrie Dawn. K.D. was reserved for singer-songwriters and former Seattle Supersonics basketball players. (R.I.P. Sonics.) "Yes, it's true that discovering Gabe's affair was a painful thing for me. However, I recognize that infidelity is most often a symptom of problems in the marriage, not the cause."

A tear streamed down her cheek. "I'm so lonely. Oh, gawd, Charlotte, my husband can barely stand to be in the same room with me. He acts like everything I say is dumb or uninteresting. He has no interest in the things I like to do, traveling, for example, and he'd rather spend all his free time at the club." She hiccupped. "I knew Elliot had a reputation as a ladies' man, that he often wooed the wealthy women on the ship. Bored wives like me."

"Real Housewives of the *Thalassophile*?"

She gave a weak smile. "Something like that. Last September we sailed to South Africa. I tried to get Bubba to come with me. He said he'd rather drink varnish than be stuck on a boat with a bunch of old biddies for three weeks. I guess I'm considered an old biddy to him these days. Probably why he doesn't lay a finger on me anymore."

This was sounding familiar. I'd wager a hundred bucks Bubba had some hot young thing like Kyrie Dawn to keep him company while Rhodie sailed the seven seas. I suspected Gabe and Bubba were cut from the same cloth.

"One night I got tipsy and called Bubba, asking him to fly out to South Africa to join me on the safari. He laughed and hung up on me. Elliot found me crying out on the sundeck. He took me to his room. He let me blather on and wiped my tears. I don't know what came over me, I just kind of lunged at him. I guess I caught him off-guard, so he fell backward, and I tumbled with him."

"Romantic."

"Hardly. He was so mad. He screamed at me and asked what the hell I thought I was doing. I told him, he laughed." She buried her face in her hands. "Laughed at by two men in less than fifteen minutes. How does one recover from that? Maybe Elliot could see through my debutante persona, and he felt I was beneath him."

"And you shared that with Florence?"

She dragged her fingers down her cheeks. "I ran into her in the hallway. She saw how upset I was and invited me in for tea. I told her everything. About my childhood, my remaking of my image, my marriage, and Elliot's rejection."

"What did she say?"

"Mostly she just listened. She said she'd smooth things over with Elliot, tell him to cut me some slack since I wasn't sober." She blew out a breath. "I can't believe she didn't tell me that she's, his mother. She had the perfect opportunity to share that with me. I was being vulnerable, and meanwhile she was holding this massive secret."

My mind jumped to my grandmother's diary and all the secrets she held. "I've come to realize than when people are in survival mode, they only think about what they need to say or do to get them through from one crisis to the next."

Chapter Seventeen

B Y THE TIME Rhodie and I returned to the table, the only ones left were Margaret and Grace.

"The baby started fussing, so Jane went to put him down for the night. You ladies work everything out?"

Margaret had a glint in her eye that I resented quite a bit, considering she was the one who had spilled the beans that perhaps something had happened between Rhodie and Elliot.

Come to think of it, how *did* Margaret know there was something there, even though it hadn't...come to fruition, so to speak?

"I guess," Rhodie said. "I'm going to bed. Anyone remember what tomorrow night's theme is?"

"Hokkaido Night," I said. "Everyone is supposed to wear lavender."

Margaret clucked. "I had the perfect wig to wear, too, but it's vanished without a trace."

Grace groaned. "I'll have to borrow something. I don't own a single item of clothing in lavender. I look terrible in any shade of purple. Washes me out."

"Most people look dreadful in lavender," Margaret

mused. "Like a zombie, all gray."

"You mean they look dead?" Rhodie grimaced.

Margaret straightened her pink wig. "Yep. Lucky for me, I'm not one of them."

MARGARET MAY NOT have been someone who looked dead in lavender, but Florence was.

Literally dead.

According to Xavier, Florence's body was found by housekeeping just after eleven the next morning. She was wearing a lavender silk robe, undone to reveal her naked, surgically modified form. Around her neck was the robe's silk tie.

"Do you think it's, uh, do you think she did this or did someone do it to her?" I asked.

Jane, Quinton, and I had rushed to the security office as soon as word began to spread around the ship.

Xavier exhaled a weary sigh. "I do not know, Charlotte."

"She was very upset last night, you know." She'd been embarrassed, certainly, but was embarrassment a reason to end your own life?

"What do you recall about her state of mind?"

"Well, she was definitely having a hard time even before the big reveal. Her eyes were puffy."

"I noticed that, too," said Jane.

Xavier held up his hand. "Big reveal?"

"Wait, you don't know?"

His scowl indicated he did *not* know.

I smacked my forehead. "I was going to tell you last night, but then I got into an intense conversation with Rhodie about her trying to have an affair with Elliot— unsuccessfully, I might add—and then we got to talking about tonight's dinner theme and, well, I forgot."

An unblinking stare. A slight twitch of the nose. He was mad. Furious, even. I had to get him the information before he combusted.

"*FlorencewasElliot'smother!*"

"Florence was—" he repeated slowly. "Florence was Elliot's mother? No, that cannot be. It would have shown in the background check."

"Probably not," Jane said. "He was raised by his father in France, and that man's wife. Florence was just a teenager when she had Elliot. The guy was a married diplomat, pulled some strings. He got the baby and Florence got deported with a briefcase of cash."

"And what was her purpose in coming here? Reunion? Revenge?"

"I can't see her taking revenge, and even if she did, it would be against his father. I think she genuinely wanted to be in his life."

"Rewind, *s'il vous plaît*. To the beginning."

Jane and I tag teamed telling him Florence's story. The pregnancy. The relationship she developed with Elliot. The argument witnessed by Grace the night of his murder. Florence's obvious grief and guilt, along with her shame after the secret was revealed at dinner.

"So, now he is dead and her secret has been revealed, so she takes her own life? Is that your theory?" Xavier leaned back in his chair. "I know it sounds crass, but it would be better for you if she were murdered. That would go a long way toward exonerating K.—"

"Don't you dare," I growled.

"Kyrie Dawn."

Smart man. "How soon will you know cause and manner of death?"

"Dr. Fraser was never supposed to be a forensic pathologist. He has basic training in it, and after last fall's…situation, he has been doing some online classes, but this is not his area of expertise. Although, since you ladies have come onboard, he is getting quite a bit of on-the-job experience. Why do you suppose that is?"

"Bad luck?" I shrugged.

"Yours or mine?"

Brat. "Both?"

"Probably. He will do his best to get as many answers as possible while the scene is fresh so that he can pass along his findings as soon as we dock in Kushiro."

"So, you can't release Kyrie Dawn?"

"I'm debating. Knowing her as well as I do—" He stopped as soon as he caught a glimpse of my face. "Which is not well, but I've had enough interactions with her that I find it difficult to believe she's a danger to others. That is why I was hoping you would consider another arrangement like we had last year with Andy."

"Aww, come on, X-man. You can't expect Charlotte to

bring Kyrie Dawn into our home," Jane said. "That's too much."

"I can only imagine the difficulty. I am simply trying to find a solution where you take custody of her so that she can be with her child."

It *was* too much. All of it. Would this be the thing that finally broke me? "We'll do it."

"What? Char, no!"

"Quinton needs his mother. And I don't think she killed anyone. She certainly didn't lock us in the freezer, and she can't be responsible for Florence's death if it turns out to be something other than suicide."

"You don't have to martyr yourself."

"I'm not. I've weighed the pros and cons, and I feel like this is what we should do."

Jane flung up her hands. "I need some air. Come on, Q, let's go find you a snack."

"Nana! Nana!"

"Yeah, we'll get you a banana."

"Nana! Bye-bye!" Quinton waved Pandy.

Xavier rubbed the back of his neck.

"Have you slept? You look awful."

"*Merci.*" He suppressed a yawn. "What is it they say? No rest for the wicked?"

"More like no rest because of the wicked. I know you can't officially say, but what do you really think happened with Florence?"

"Difficult to say. What you have told me—about her being Elliot's mother—makes me question whether, because he was cruel to her, she perhaps killed him and then herself out of guilt and grief."

I hadn't really thought about that. "I guess it's possible. Let's say she didn't kill herself. Let's say someone killed her."

"Okay."

"What would the motive be?"

"That is a question to which I wish I had an answer. My first thought is the same person who killed Elliot also killed Florence and for the same reason."

"Because that is the most logical or because you don't want to consider the possibility of two killers onboard?"

"Both. It's complicated by the fact Deacon is clearly capable of nefarious and violent actions, and there is quite a bit of evidence against K.—Kyrie Dawn."

"You know he's abusing his wife."

"I have suspected as much."

"And you haven't done anything?"

"In many ways, my hands are tied. I have not witnessed him assaulting her, and when I have inquired, she has told me that is not the case."

"It's fascinating to me, how a woman could appear to have it all, be full of strength, and yet put up with a Neanderthal husband who uses her to take out all his frustrations with the world."

"It is a complex situation, certainly. She is angry with me for detaining him, although she is getting respite from his tirades."

"Maybe she's worried that the longer he sits in there, the angrier he'll be. So, what about Kyrie Dawn? Are you gonna let us babysit her?"

"Of course. It was my idea. I believe it will be helpful in a number of ways."

What was he up to? "Is there something I need to know?"

"What do you mean?"

"I mean, is this part of a larger plan?"

His mouth twitched. "My job is to keep the passengers and crew safe. I am working tirelessly to do that, regardless how it may appear considering current circumstances. I will use all options available to do that."

"Including using her as bait?"

Bull's-eye. Deer caught in the headlights. He glanced over his shoulder in the direction of the room where she was being held. "I will be keeping a close eye on the situation."

It was an interesting conundrum. I didn't feel particularly protective over Kyrie Dawn, but I could easily go mama bear when it came to Quinton. Or to be more accurate, step(ish)-mama bear. Not to mention, if Kyrie Dawn was bait, and she was staying with Jane and me, then we were all in potential danger.

"Give me until after dinner tonight."

"What are you up to?"

Skeptical. I didn't blame him. "I just need some time to prepare."

This time he didn't suppress his yawn. "I do not have it in me to try to figure out what you are up to, but please do not get yourself into a situation from which you need rescuing. Again. I am already exhausted and overwhelmed."

"Maybe you should take a nap."

"Both my cots are taken up by murder suspects."

"I meant in your room."

Immediately, I pictured him in bed. *Don't picture him in bed. Don't picture him in bed.*

I'd only seen Xavier's room once, during our cruise to Alaska when my nephew nearly got sent away for murder. It was the nicest of the staff cabins, other than the captains' suites.

I fluffed my shirt to get some air circulating.

He eyed me with a puzzled expression. "Where did you go just now? Your face flushed and your eyes darted around like you were telepathically rearranging the furniture."

"Hot flash," I mumbled.

Lonnie Irving entered the office in time to save me from further probing. "Dr. Fraser wants to speak with you."

Xavier gave me one more sidelong glance. "Are you sure you're alright?"

"Mm-hmm. Hot flash," I repeated. "They're the worst."

Lonnie looked at me like he didn't know whether to be concerned or amused.

"What time will you be back to pick up Ms. Wumpenhauer?"

"I'd say around nine. It depends on which of the platinum platoon decides to throw a fit at dinner."

"Clever."

I shrugged. "I'm running out of nicknames. I'm down to the bleach bunch—"

"Nice," Xavier said with a smile.

"The sandy syndicate and troop towhead."

"What is happening here?" Lonnie asked.

"Just my way of staying marginally sane. Can I talk to Kyrie Dawn really quickly?"

Xavier nodded and indicated for Lonnie to unlock the door for me.

She popped her head off the pillow when I walked into the room. Her eyes were red, and her cheeks were wet. "Oh, hi, Charlotte." She swiped her tears. "Is everything okay with Quinton? Is he here? Can I see him?"

"He's with Jane. But I have good news. Jane and I have offered to take you into our suite under house arrest so you can be with him."

It was like the sun had come out. Her face lit up and the tears flowed freely. "Oh Charlotte, thank you so much." She stood and opened her arms. "Can I—can I give you a hug?"

Oh hell no.

But before I could object, her well-toned arms were around me, squeezing me like I held the last bit of toothpaste. She smelled like eucalyptus and cinnamon. I felt oversized to her petite frame. Oaf-y. Like Shrek with Fiona, in princess form.

"You can't imagine what this means to me. My heart has literally been breaking every moment I've been away from him. I try not to think about it, but it's always there."

I refrained from correcting her use of *literally*. "We'll come by and get you after dinner."

Gah, I needed to get out of that room as fast as possible and away from whatever those odd, inexplicable emotions I was experiencing that felt strangely like fondness. For Kyrie Dawn.

Chapter Eighteen

"WHAT'LL YOU HAVE this afternoon, Mrs. McLaughlin? A mojito? How about a strawberry colada? Sake?" Cortes scooped ice into two glasses.

I'd yet to run into Jane and Quinton, and she wasn't returning my texts. Was she mad that Kyrie Dawn was going to stay with us, or because she thought I was doing it out of guilt and manipulation rather than choice?

"I'm all sake-ed out, and I don't think I'm in the mood for anything fruity. Today calls for a serious drink."

"I gotcha, I gotcha. Lemme finish up these other drinks and then I'll take care of ya." He grabbed a crystal glass from beneath the counter. "Tough day at the office?"

"You could say that."

"I hear ya." Slumped over the bar next to me and nursing a double something on the rocks was the inimitable Sensei Machigau. Up close and without the dim lighting, he was at least ten years older than I previously thought. In the daylight, his spray tan was even more egregious. His forehead and eyes had been so heavily Botoxed, his expression was frozen in amazement with a hint of terror. His shoulder-length bleached hair looked like cornsilk left in the sun too long. He was dressed in a brown *gi* with a black belt. He wore the same stone pendant hanging from a brown rope necklace that he had during his demonstration. Up close, it looked like the yin yang symbol, which I found confusing, considering that was Chinese, not Japanese.

I held out my hand. "Sensei Machigau, my name is Charlotte McLaughlin. I enjoyed your performance the other night." Not a lie. I enjoyed the cheesiness of the spectacle. It was beautifully, fantastically over-the-top.

He grunted but didn't take my hand. "Well, I hope you enjoyed it, because it was the last performance I'll ever do." Swig. Gulp.

"Why's that?"

He looked at me like I'd just asked him if I could borrow his belt. "Becaauusse"—he said the word with six slurred syllables instead of two—"one of my blow guns and darts were used to kill Elliot." The duh was implied. He took another big gulp of amber liquor.

"Did you know Elliot well?"

His gaze narrowed. "You a cop?" The more he drank, his Sensei Machigau persona slipped away, and, in its place, Joe from Philly began to surface.

"Not a cop. Just a concerned resident."

"Do any of us really know each other? Really?"

Great. Philly Joe was morphing into Philosophy Joe. Phillyosophy Joe, as it were.

Cortes topped the drink he was making with a maraschino cherry and a lemon peel and slid it in my direction.

"Thanks. What's it called?"

"I call it the Cortesazerac. It's like a Sazerac, only instead of rye whiskey I use tequila. And lots of it." He winked.

The wink did nothing for me.

I'd long ago come to the grim determination that after fifty, most winking men—at least the ones younger than me and even marginally attractive—were more likely to be buttering me up for a good tip than looking for a good time.

My first sip was warm with a hint of bitter. "Not bad."

"Thanks. I'm always experimenting, trying to find new ways to do old stuff. I thought I was gonna get my own bar, but since Elliot—" He trailed off into a deep frown.

Sensei Machigau held up his glass. "R.I.P. Lelliot." He swigged the remainder of his drink and slammed the glass on the counter. He wriggled his left index finger above the glass, but Cortes ignored him. After a moment he gave up and rested his cheek on the bar.

"What do you mean?" I asked Cortes. "What about Elliot?"

"Well, his sugar mama was gonna fund his restaurant. I was gonna get full run of the bar. That's why they hired Hawk, to replace me. Not now, though." Cortes flung a rag over his shoulder.

"Oh, I'm sorry. And now she's...gone too. Poor Florence."

"Huh?"

"Oh, I guess I figured you would have heard. Unfortunately, Florence Loomis was found dead in her cabin this morning."

"Whoaaaa. That's too bad." He furrowed his brow. "But what does that have to do with the restaurant?"

"Because Florence was the one funding Elliot's restaurant."

I didn't expect his befuddled expression. "Nah, I think you got your facts twisted. It wasn't that lady. It was another one."

"Which one?"

"I can't remember her name. But she wears a lot of wigs. Oh look, she's over there."

On the other side of the Azure lounge, Margaret was draped across the sofa like a Botticelli Babe. She caught the two of us staring at her, and I could swear I saw her mouth utter, "Uh oh."

"YOU LIED TO me."

"I most certainly did not." Margaret crossed her arms.

"You said you had nothing to do with Elliot Patenaude."

"No, I said I wasn't *sleeping* with Elliot Patenaude. That's not the same thing."

I should have known she was the type to parse the truth in order to serve her own agenda.

"Cortes called you Elliot's sugar mama."

"Only in the sense I was giving him money, not sugar."

"Tell me about the restaurant."

"Maybe you should sit. You're a little wound up, Charlotte. You know what you need? You need a good old-fashioned roll in the—"

"Hey! We're not talking about me. We're talking about your involvement with a murder victim. Information that you withheld."

"Oh, pshh! I didn't withhold anything. It was an open secret that Elliot was looking for funding to open a restaurant in Tampa. He was hitting up everyone who might be able to give him an infusion of cash. Fusion Globale he wanted to call it, global cuisine with a French flair. It's one of the reasons he took the job onboard. He wanted opportunities to hone his skills in all types of food from across the world. Between his unique concept and his good looks and charm, he believed he would become the next celebrity chef."

"Wasn't he already an award-winning chef?"

"He was. Highly trained, highly esteemed. But he set his sights on being the French Bobby Flay or Gordon Ramsay. A household name."

"Did he approach you or did you approach him about getting involved?"

"Neither. It was him." Margaret pointed in the direction of the bar, which was now empty. "Oh, I guess he left."

"Who left?" I scanned the lounge.

"Sensei Michigan or whatever he's calling himself."

"Wait. Sensei Machigau was involved with Elliot's restaurant?"

"He wasn't just involved. He was his partner."

I glanced back at the bar. Was Sensei Machigau—or Philly Joe or whatever his name was—was he drinking because his business partner was dead or because of a more nefarious reason like guilt?

One thing was certain. He was not who he pretended to be.

Chapter Nineteen

"H E'S GOT BLOND hair."

"I realize that, Charlotte, and we have interviewed the sensei. Seeing as it was his weapon used against Elliot, of course we interviewed him."

I couldn't tell whether Xavier was more irritated or exhausted.

"But did you ask him about the business arrangement?"

"I did not, seeing as how I did not know about it until this moment, and he has not volunteered that information."

"That's suspicious, right? That makes him a prime suspect."

"Everyone is—"

"Yeah, yeah. Everyone's a suspect."

He put his index finger to his chin. "Would you rather I rush to judgment?"

"Of course not."

"I will speak with Sensei Machigau again."

"Thank you."

He checked his watch. "It is almost dinner."

"Are you trying to get rid of me?"

"Actually, I was thinking I may join you if that is alright.

Your table seems to be the source of much intrigue."

"What about talking to the phony sensei?"

"I suspect he will make an appearance at some point during the evening."

"I'm not sure the rest of the gang will be thrilled to have the head of security at our table, but I have a feeling it will be fun."

He gifted me with a rare grin. "Then let us have fun together."

"WELL, BUDDY, THIS is probably our last dinner out together." Jane gave Quinton's hand a squeeze.

He squealed in response.

"You're actually choked up about this," I said.

"No, I'm not." She cleared her throat. "I have a piece of popcorn lodged in my uvula."

Liar. I figured I'd let her off the hook, though. She'd spent most of the day wheeling Quinton around the ship, exploring every nook and cranny. By the time I finally got back to the room, both of them were passed out on her bed, with some preschool show featuring a cartoon porcupine singing about the trials and tribulations of making friends when you're covered in quills.

She'd begrudgingly accepted the fact that after dinner, we'd be bringing Kyrie Dawn into our suite.

"Mesdames."

I turned to face Xavier and audibly gasped.

"This is the color of the evening, is it not?" He scanned the room. "Or perhaps I have chosen the wrong shade."

Instead of his navy wool sweater or his standard suit, Xavier was wearing gray slacks and a rich purple polo that wasn't standard lavender but one I'd always understood to be called "old lavender." Instead of a cool, grayish tone, his shirt was closer to mauve. *No one looks good in lavender*, Margaret had said. Boy, was she wrong. The contrast of his light golden-brown eyes and swarthy complexion with a color that reminded me of the Rocky Mountains at sunset was so striking all I could do was stare at him and hope my tongue wasn't hanging out.

Jane whistled. "You made the perfect choice, X-man. Don't you think, Char?"

"Mm-hmm."

Ulfric appeared with a broad smile. "Xavier, what brings you here tonight?"

"I was hoping to dine with these ladies…and the small gentleman."

Ulfric leaned forward and lowered his voice. "Normally, I'd say the tables are too full, but they've lost a couple. Frankly, they're dropping like flies."

"I am aware. I have one of them lying in cold storage and the other locked up."

"Right. Right. Sure. This way, please."

I hadn't considered what happened to bodies on ships. Even the previous fall, I hadn't thought to question where they had been taken following examination by Dr. Fraser.

"Do you put dead bodies in the walk-in fridge?" I whispered. I hadn't noticed anyone when we'd been locked inside, but perhaps Elliot had been moved there afterward.

He leaned closer, smelling like a wooded hike in the rain. "No. We have a designated spot. With so many retirees onboard, it seemed prudent."

"Ah." It made me feel better, knowing I wouldn't be eating dishes prepared with meats that had hung next to corpses. I'd hate to find out later someone thought it was okay to store biohazards next to a cheese wheel.

The table was draped in pale purple satin and organza, with an enormous floral display of lavender flowers in the center.

"Wow, this is pretty." Jane pushed the stroller into the space next to her chair.

"It smells like my mother," Simon muttered. He wore a gray suit with a bowtie I'd have called more periwinkle than lavender.

"These lavender cocktails are yummy." Willow slurped a clear liquid with tiny bits of flowers floating in it.

Everyone at the table froze when Xavier pulled out a chair.

"To what do we owe this pleasure?" Margaret purred.

I stared at her wig, trying to understand what I was looking at. Apparently, since the purple one had been stolen, she'd taken the pink wig from the night before and soaked it in something in attempt to turn it purple. Kool-Aid perhaps? It had only marginally worked, with splotches of various hues ranging from aubergine to thistle and everything in between. It was tie-dyed.

"Xavier has been working so hard, I figured he could use a nice dinner." *And he wants to spy on you all.*

"Isthat so?" Margaret strung the first two words together into one. She dragged her fingertip around the rim of her martini glass and gave him the look of a predator stalking its prey.

"Mmm. What is the cocktail of the night?" The sooner I diverted attention from Xavier and what he was doing there, the better. Not to mention, Margaret's flirtation had my hackles up and I didn't want to have to throw down, but I would if I had to.

Rhodie, in a spectacular purple revenge dress—although what she was seeking revenge for, I had no clue—cradled her glass. "It's called Lavender Chi. Chi means lifeforce."

"I mean, what's in it?"

No one seemed to know. Willow shrugged and slurped, but then spit out a flower bud.

"Oh, Haimi." Margaret grabbed our server as she rushed past.

"Yes, Mrs. King?"

"What's in these things?" She dinged her glass with a knife.

"The cocktail of the evening is Lavender Chi. It's made with Empress gin, Yuzu, simple syrup, lime, and soda water. Oh, and of course, sprigs of lavender."

"I don't know if I like drinking something that's usually found in soap," Jane said.

I wasn't convinced either. "Would it be boring if I just stuck with a glass of cabernet?"

"No," Haimi said just as Margaret said, "yes."

"Shouldn't you be out investigating or something?" Grace asked Xavier. "I'd prefer you solved the case so I don't have to spend the rest of this trip alone."

"Unfortunately, while your husband may not have committed murder, he most definitely locked Madame McLaughlin and me in the refrigerator. He will not be released prior to our docking at Kushiro, at which point he will be transported back to the United States for possible prosecution."

She pouted. "Well, that's just great."

"Bless your heart, Grace," Willow said. "It'll be okay. You can hang out with Simon and me. Right, honey?"

Simon adjusted his glasses. "Of course. I must admit, it's kind of nice not worrying about being shoved into a corner to have my life threatened. No offense, but things are definitely less blustery around here with Deacon gone."

"Oh, I'm sure none taken." Margaret rolled her eyes and sipped her drink. "You know, Grace, if I were you, I'd take advantage of this time flying solo."

"I don't even know how to do that."

"If I may," Xavier said. "Monsieur Strawbridge, what did you mean by having your life threatened?"

Oops. Had I forgotten to mention that to him?

"The night of the welcome reception." Simon's hand shook as he adjusted his glasses. "Frankly, I'd rather not think about it too much. It was quite upsetting."

"Oh brother," Margaret mumbled under her breath.

Not enough under her breath, apparently.

"You weren't there, Margaret." His tone was whiny. "You don't know."

"I was there, Simon, I just wasn't at your table. I was mingling."

"Oh, Simon, grow a pair." Grace slammed her hand on the table.

"That's not nice," Willow said. "Grace, where are your manners?"

"It's fine, dear."

Xavier observed the antics of our table like an exhibit at the zoo. "Monsieur Strawbridge, why was he threatening you?"

Simon sucked his teeth. "I don't want to cause anyone any trouble."

"Would you prefer I bring you in for an official interview?"

Oh, Xavier was playing hardball, was he? I was here for it.

Simon seemed to debate his answer. "I'm sorry, Grace. I have to tell him."

Grace jerked her head, her eyes and mouth wide open. "What are you talking about?"

Simon chewed his words before speaking them. "Deacon thinks you've been messing around, and he believes it was with me."

A rumble came from Xavier.

"Oh boy. Dinner and an impromptu show," I whispered into his ear. "This should be fun."

All the color drained from Willow's face. "What did you

just say?"

Simon covered his wife's hand. "It's not true. Of course it isn't."

If a look of fury could cause someone to combust, Simon would have burst into flames. Grace's cheeks were magenta with rage and, I suspected, embarrassment. "Of course it isn't true," she sputtered. "Why on earth would he think I would debase myself by having an affair with *Simon*." She spit out his name like three-day-old sushi.

"Gee, thanks, Grace. You flatter me too much."

"I don't think she means it personally, honey." Willow squeezed Simon's hand. "She'd be lucky to have an affair with you. Any woman would."

"That's the oddest compliment I've heard in a while." Margaret sipped her cocktail.

"You know what I mean. I don't want him to have an affair, obviously. I just know he's sexy and women are going to find him attractive."

Margaret began to cough and slap her throat. "Lavender. In. My. Gullet!"

Jane whacked her on her back three times. Rhodie passed her some water. Quinton mimicked her, forcing coughs.

"Oh, stop, now." Jane's reprimand to him was gentle. "You're fine. Here, have a cookie."

Quinton grabbed the cookie and sucked on it.

"I tried to tell you," I whispered to Xavier.

"You did not do it justice. Is it like this at every meal?"

"Pretty much."

"It's funny." Rhodie plucked lavender buds from a stem.

"I don't see how any of this is funny," Grace retorted.

"No, it is. Because anyone who's paying attention knows you're not having an affair with Simon."

"Thank you, Rhodie." Grace sniffed. "But I still fail to see how it's humorous."

Rhodie continued plucking the flowers one by one. "We all know you were having an affair with Elliot."

Grace sputtered. "How dare you!" She lunged across the table at Rhodie.

Xavier jumped to his feet, but not before Grace got a handful of Rhodie's hair.

"Let go!"

"You take that back!"

"Too late, cat's out of the bag! I'm not telling anyone— ow—what they didn't already know."

Xavier pried them apart, but Grace managed to get one more yank on Rhodie's head. "Enough. You are grown women acting like children."

Quinton yipped.

"He's not talking about you, buddy," Jane said. "You're a good boy."

"Good boy. Good boy," he repeated. He bounced Pandy on the table. "Good boy."

"I would like to speak with both of you in my office. Now." Xavier grabbed Grace by the arm and waved at Rhodie to stand.

"Can I sit in?" I asked.

He gave a resigned sigh. "Fine. But you will be quiet."

I zipped my lips and tied them off with a twist.

"I MUST SAY, Madame Atkinson, I am frustrated that you did not bring such an important piece of information to my attention."

Rhodie shifted in the chair. "It wasn't my story to tell."

I nearly choked on my incredulity, and Xavier gave me a warning glare. I pantomimed an apology.

"So, what made you decide to share tonight?"

"I dunno. I think part of it was she was being so rude. Like, you're gonna sit there and bash on poor Simon, on your high horse, when you know full well you were playing kiss the cook behind your hubby's back."

"Do you have evidence of this, or is it an assumption?"

"If you're asking if I'm holding onto her soiled undergarments, then no."

Xavier briefly closed his eyes. "That was not exactly what I had in mind. Tell me how you came to believe this was happening. Did you witness an encounter?"

"Everyone knew what Elliot was like. Well, the women, at least. It was a known fact that he preferred the company of married women in particular. Somehow, he believed it was less complicated that way. Of course, there were rare exceptions. Anyway, one day I saw Grace sneaking out of the stairwell. I was in the casino, and she was coming up the back way from the third floor barefoot, with her heels in her hand. I just knew she'd been in his room."

"*How* did you know?"

"Because." She huffed and blew her hair out of her face.

"It's the same route he had me take."

"You were also involved with Elliot Patenaude?"

I timidly raised my hand.

He exhaled. "*Oui*, Charlotte?"

"In the mayhem of the past couple days, I might have failed to mention to you that Rhodie shared information with me about her relationship with Elliot."

He tightened his mouth. "Is that so?"

Rhodie nodded. "I did tell Charlotte. I'm sure she was only trying to protect me from embarrassment."

She gave me too much credit. I'd simply forgotten.

"Embarrassment over your affair?"

"No. He rejected me. And then he sent me up that same back stairwell so that no one would see me."

Xavier tapped his pen against his lips. "This was your only proof of Madame Beauchamp's illicit relationship with him?"

"Well, yes, but more than that…I saw the look in her eyes. I knew that look. Shame. Guilt. If you look closely, you'll see a lot of women on this ship walking around with that same expression. You think you'll feel exhilarated. This handsome, charming man has *seen* you. Maybe you haven't felt seen in years. Your husband spends more time at work or at the club—country, not dance—than he does at home with you. Your children see you as a means to an end, not a person. Men stop whistling and instead walk past like you're not even there.

"So, when this man tells you you're beautiful, makes you feel desirable, visible—it's an intoxicating thing. But eventually you realize he's nothing but a trawler, dredging the ocean floor for whatever he can pick up and then throw back when he's done, and the whole experience loses its luster, ya know?"

"May I ask, did he say why he rejected you?"

She sat quietly, then her eyes began to well with tears. "He said I was too needy. Too clingy. That the situation would get too messy for his taste. Do you know how humiliating it is to be told you're undeserving of affection because you want it too much?"

Ouch. I felt bad for Rhodie. I understood how she felt on many levels. My only consolation was that I'd been neglected in my marriage so long, it had become normalized. In the waning years I no longer even yearned for more. Couldn't be disappointed when you set expectations low to begin with.

"Can you tell me the names of any other women onboard who might have gotten involved with Elliot?"

"None that I'm 100 percent on. Other than K.D."

"K.D.," he repeated. "You do not mean Kyrie Dawn?"

"Of course I do. Are you telling me you never saw them flirting? Gabe hated Elliot for that very reason. Ask the staff. I heard from several people they suspected Elliot was actually Quinton's father. I doubt that's true, but I'm sure Gabe caught a whiff of the rumors at some point. Frankly, if he were still alive, he'd have been my first suspect."

Chapter Twenty

I T WAS A strange sensation, hearing someone speak about your dead husband's jealousy for his mistress. Gabe in particular. He'd never once said anything to indicate he was jealous because of attention I received.

One night on my way home from the library, I stopped to get gas. A man approached me. At first, I was nervous, unsure whether he was going to ask for spare change or if he was on something and wasn't in his right mind. It turned out to be neither. He'd said he'd been selling flowers when he spotted me. He handed me a rose. I tried to refuse, assuming he wanted payment. I told him I had no cash. He'd shaken his head and said it was a gift. "A beautiful flower for a beautiful woman." And then he walked away.

When I told Gabe about it, he'd laughed.

"What's so funny?" I asked. "I thought it was a nice gesture."

"He probably saw how tired you look and thought you needed an ego boost."

"Most husbands might feel a bit threatened if a handsome *younger* man was complimenting their wives and giving them roses."

He'd held up his hands in mock surrender. "Oh no, are you gonna leave me for the gas station rose guy?"

He'd gone back to watching the nightly stock report.

But he'd been jealous about Kyrie Dawn's interactions with Elliot. Was there anything to them? Maybe she was just flirting to get a rise out of Gabe. Elliot couldn't have been Quinton's father, could he?

Xavier must have sensed I was not doing okay, because he sent Rhodie out to sit with Grace. He told Lonnie to keep an eye on them, lest another catfight broke out.

"Charlotte, are you okay?"

"Hmmm, you know, I've been better."

"This complicates things."

"What do you mean?"

"For Kyrie Dawn."

"Because there were rumors that she was romantically linked to Elliot?"

"For starters."

"You were here. Did you ever hear anything like that?"

He stared at me for a moment. "I tend to avoid the gossip mill."

"You probably shouldn't. That's where you learn all sorts of things."

"Do you want to talk about this?"

"What's there to say? My dead cheating husband went bonkers over rumors about his mistress and the now-dead executive chef. He obviously didn't kill him."

"That had to have been painful to hear."

I waved my hand dismissively. "Just another nail in the

coffin of what I thought was a decent marriage," I said. "So to speak."

"Did you?"

"Did I what?"

"Did you think it was a decent marriage?"

I'd never thought about it before. "It was my only one, so I didn't have anything else to compare it to. He was a good provider, although how good I had no idea. We rarely fought, we enjoyed going to the theater and museums together..." Pathetic. Even I could hear it. "I guess I kept my expectations low."

"You deserved more than decent." His light brown eyes deepened.

I shrugged. "That ship has sailed."

"Literally." He smiled as he picked up the receiver on his phone. "Cortes, it is Xavier Mesnier. *Oui. Oui.* I have a question for you." The corner of his mouth tipped into a smile. "I know I promised I would try it, but as you may have heard, I have been preoccupied with the deaths of two people. *Oui.* My question is, what do you know about rumors of a relationship between Kyrie Dawn and Chef Elliot?" He waited as Cortes gave his answer. His left brow cocked. "Is that so? Mm-hmm. *Oui. Oui.* I will. *D'accord. Merci.*" He stared at me, stupefied. "Wait here."

He was gone for about three minutes. I chewed my cuticles, like I always did when I had nervous energy. He returned with Kyrie Dawn in tow.

You've gotta be kidding me. Despite having been technically incarcerated for days, she looked beautiful and well-rested. Her hair was shiny, recently washed, and her skin was clear. She certainly didn't look like she was wasting away. If a person was going to be detained anywhere, a cruise ship was the way to go. Instead of three hots and a cot, she had three feasts and percale sheets.

"Where's Quinton?"

"Jane has him," I said. "They're finishing dinner."

"Am I being released?" she asked Xavier.

"Not exactly. Some things have come up, and I need to ask you about them."

"Okaaay?"

"I know you have spoken to my officers about this in detail, but I would like to go over it again. What was your relationship with Elliot Patenaude?"

"As I said before, Elliot and I were friends."

"Not more than that?"

"No! Why are you asking me this?"

"How did Monsieur McLaughlin feel about your...*friendship* with Chef Elliot?"

She stole a glance at me. "Does Charlotte need to be here?"

I clasped my hands in my lap. "Is there something you're uncomfortable talking about in front of me?" *Squirm, baby, squirm. Let's see who's more uncomfortable.*

"I just thought—well." She exhaled. "If you insist."

I gestured for her to go ahead.

"Yes, Elliot and I were flirty. It was our way. It never meant anything. Gabe, however, knew about Elliot's reputation, and he was worried something was brewing between us."

"Would it surprise you to hear there have been rumors circulating for some time that Monsieur McLaughlin is not the father of your child, but rather Elliot Patenaude?"

Kyrie Dawn's face morphed from abject horror to hysterics. "Are you kidding me?"

"I am not."

She jerked her head to look at me. "Is this your doing? To punish me, you're spreading lies about me and my child? That's pretty low, Charlotte."

I'm low? *I'm* low? The woman slept with my husband for years, made a baby with him (Allegedly. Purportedly), and she had the audacity to call me low? I didn't need a DNA test to know Quinton was Gabe's. Just looking at him, I was 100 percent sure. I could have put the issue to rest, but instead I put all my energy into suppressing the urge to put her in a chokehold.

"Madame McLaughlin had nothing to do with this. I have heard it from multiple sources."

"Your sources are wrong."

"Let me paint a picture for you. A young woman gets involved with an older man—"

Kyrie Dawn scoffed. "Just because you don't approve of some of my choices doesn't mean I'm a murderer."

"Agreed. Allow me to continue. The man provides a nice lifestyle for the woman, but he will not commit. After all, he already has a wife. He cannot spend holidays with her. He cannot introduce her to his friends or his family, his work colleagues. She is unhappy, so he takes her onboard a luxury cruise ship, where they develop a new social circle and are able to be public with their relationship without fear of recourse. How am I doing so far?"

"That's about right."

This was like torture for me. I'd expended a lot of energy avoiding thoughts of their life together.

"Their life at sea is idyllic, at first. Inevitably, the push and pull between his real life and his fantasy life become too much of a strain."

"I resent the implication his life with me wasn't real."

"He leaves her to return to his responsibilities—"

Hold up. "So, she's the fantasy and I'm the Sturm und Drang?"

"I did not say that. He leaves her by herself for weeks on end. Ultimately, she gets lonely and turns to the ship's lothario for comfort."

"No!"

"But then she discovers she is pregnant, and she is unsure who the father is—"

"No!"

"But it does not matter, because now she has leverage in her relationship with the older man. She tells him she is going to have his child. Fast forward twenty months and the man unfortunately passes away. Now his wife knows about her and the child. No more fine dining, no more cruise ship suite. No more child support—"

"In my defense, I didn't even fight the twenty-five percent his will allocated to her and the baby."

"So generous," Kyrie Dawn mumbled. "Like it wasn't all

Gabe's money. He earned it."

I dug my fingernails into the armrest. "Washington is a community property state. Fifty percent of our net worth belongs to me. His wife." I bit that last word in half.

"May I finish?" Xavier asked.

Kyrie Dawn and I both bobbled our heads.

"Without a father for her son and the financial support he provided, the woman looks to the other possible father, hoping he will step up and play the role. But he refuses. He denies paternity and tells her he wants nothing to do with her or her child. This makes her angry. Perhaps angry enough to jab a poisoned dart in his neck."

After a moment of silence, Kyrie Dawn begins a slow clap. "Oh, bravo, Inspector. Look at you. You solved the case. Only one problem. None of it is true."

Xavier's desk phone rang. "Yes? Alright." He returned the receiver to its cradle. "I will be back shortly. Wait here."

He left us in his office, with the door open. I worried that if I looked directly at Kyrie Dawn, I might scratch her eyes out.

Pike's voice carried from the other room. "Can you believe it?"

This time I did make eye contact with her. We both glanced at the door. I jumped up, but she was quicker. We collided at the doorway, each of us trying to squeeze through. Rhodie and Grace observed us in fascinated silence. Xavier and Pike turned away from Pike's computer monitor to see what the hubbub was about. I wriggled free first, and she was right on my heels.

"I said to wait in my office."

"What did you find?" I asked Xavier.

Kyrie Dawn pushed ahead of me. "Is it about the case?"

Xavier straightened and put both hands on his hips. The area where his wedding ring had once sat on his finger had faded until it was barely visible. One of these days I had to ask him about it. This wasn't that day.

"Madame, did you not think it pertinent to my inquiry that you argued with the victim shortly before you were found standing over his corpse?"

Her mouth fell open. "I—"

Pike pressed Play. Security footage showed Kyrie Dawn approach Elliot in the hallway near the dining room. He was wearing all black, just as he had the night of the ninja demonstration. Elliot seemed to rebuff her attempts to have a serious conversation. She moved toward him, but he brushed her off, laughing. She tried once more, with her hand on his upper arm, and he removed it. He leaned in close and said something to her before marching off. All we could see was the back of her, but her head hung low. She swiped her cheek.

"It's not what it looks like," she said feebly.

Rhodie and Grace had joined us at the monitor.

"It looks like you had a big fight with Elliot right before he died." Rhodie clucked. "Seems like something that should have been disclosed."

"That's not all." Pike clicked on another tab and pressed Play. "This is just a few minutes later."

I couldn't tell the exact location, but Sensei Machigau

was standing in the hall holding a blow gun. He twirled it in his fingers. Kyrie Dawn approached him. We couldn't see her entire face, but we could see her profile, and she was batting her eyelashes. She placed her hand on his forearm and gave him a huge smile.

I pursed my lips at her, and she awkwardly bared her teeth in return.

On the video, Sensei Machigau recoiled from Kyrie Dawn's touch and flipped his long blonde hair over his shoulder. She laughed. She moved her hand to his pecs and leaned closer to whisper something in his ear. Whatever she said made him grimace.

She wrapped her hand around the blow gun. His eyes opened wide, but he allowed her to take it. He watched as she examined it intently, rolling it across her palm. I couldn't quite put my finger on his expression, but he didn't really seem to be enjoying the experience. She still had it in her hand when they walked arm in arm offscreen.

"Where's the next shot?" I asked. "Where did they go?"

Pike was grim-faced. "There isn't one. Not that I've found so far."

"Where did you go?" I asked her. "You were literally holding the murder weapon right before Elliott was killed."

"I didn't know it was right before Elliot was going to be killed or I wouldn't have touched it!"

"Come on! What were you trying to pull?"

She gave an exasperated sigh. "I thought I could flirt my way into his good graces. I'd heard he was an investor in Elliot's restaurant, and Elliot was trying to cut me out.

That's what we were arguing about. But I gave it back to Sensei Machigau. You can ask him!"

"Kyrie Dawn, you are no longer a person of interest in the murder of Elliot Patenaude."

"Wait. I'm not? Oh, thank gawd."

"You are officially a suspect, and I am placing you under arrest."

Chapter Twenty-One

"WHAT'S GOING ON out there?" Deacon shouted from behind a locked door.

"Deacon? Baby, it's me. Grace!"

"Grace? What are you doing here?"

"Long story. But Kyrie Dawn is getting arrested for Elliot's murder."

"I knew it! Now can you release me, Mesnier?"

"Quiet, please." Xavier escorted Kyrie Dawn back into his office. "Charlotte, you will not be taking her back to your suite tonight. I need to take a full statement from her, and—" He glared at her. "Judging by her lack of transparency and cooperation thus far, I suspect it will take a while."

"Xavier, please. I need to be with my son."

"You should have thought of that before you impeded my investigation." He turned to Rhodie and Grace. "You two as well. I do not have time to talk with you tonight. I will reach out tomorrow. Please make yourself readily available. And Charlotte—" He rubbed the back of his neck. "I know you were not expecting to still be watching the boy tonight."

"It's fine. Of course it's fine."

"Don't I get to see him?" Tears poured from Kyrie Dawn's eyes. "You said I would get to see him!"

"It will have to wait until the morning. Now, follow me. You have much to explain."

After he shut the door, Grace, Rhodie, and I stared at each other, shell-shocked.

"What's happening now?" Deacon called.

We ignored him.

"Ladies." I bobbed my chin and walked out of the security office.

"I WAS STARTING to wonder if you were ever coming back," Jane said in a hushed tone as I walked into the suite.

"Me too." I flopped onto the sofa. "Where's Quinton?"

"He's asleep in the portable crib in my room. Where's Kyrie Dawn? I figured you'd bring her back with you."

I explained the whole story in detail, just the way Jane liked it. I told her about the conversation with Rhodie, and then about the rumors that Kyrie Dawn and Elliot were having an affair. I told her about the security footage and the state of things now that she'd been seen arguing with Elliot and schmoozing Sensei Machigau.

"She was literally fondling his blow gun?"

"Yep. And then they moved off-camera."

"This looks really bad for her."

"It does." I perused the room. "It really hurt hearing Xavier talk about her life here with Gabe."

"I can only imagine. That's the kind of thing that if you dwell on it too long, it might sink you."

"It feels that way." The wall phone rang. "Who could be calling us at this hour?"

"I don't know, but grab it before Q wakes up."

Too late. Whimpers came from Jane's room.

"Ugh, you grab the phone, I'll go get him," she said.

"Hello?"

"Charlotte?"

"Kyrie Dawn?"

Jane's gaze was wide as she returned with a sleepy Quinton. He rubbed his eyes.

"Xavier said I could call you." She'd been crying. I could hear it in her broken voice. "I need to ask you a favor."

"Okay."

She hiccupped. "I think I'm in really big trouble. I need a lawyer."

"I thought you had a lawyer." The shark who tried to fleece Gabe's estate—and me—for nearly every dime.

"I have a civil attorney. I need a criminal one."

"You want me to find you a lawyer?"

"See if there's someone back in Seattle who'd be willing to represent me by video conference. I need help."

I sighed. "Okay, I'll look into it in the morning. Goodni—"

"There's one more thing. Another favor. It's a big one. A really big one." She was choking on her sobs.

"If I can."

"Promise me."

"I'm not promising anything until you tell me what this is about."

"I need you to promise me that you'll take care of Quinton."

"I am. We are."

"No. I don't mean now. I mean, if I get sent away, there's a good chance he will end up in the system. Tell me that you won't let that happen."

"I'll find a family member—"

"There's no one."

"Not your mom or dad? Siblings?"

"I have," she hiccupped again, "no one."

"What exactly are you asking me?"

"I know you're a good woman, Charlotte, and I know you wanted to be a mother, but Gabe didn't want to have kids."

"How did you—"

"Take care of my son. He doesn't deserve any of this. Give him a good home and a good life."

Before I could respond, she hung up.

Jane waited for me to say something, but the words escaped me. Stunned. Incomprehensible.

"She wants you to get her a lawyer?" Jane bounced around the living room with Quinton resting against her chest.

"Yes."

"That shouldn't be too hard. So why do you look like she just demanded you climb Mount Fuji in the buff?"

"She asked me—us—to take custody of Quinton."

Chapter Twenty-Two

J ANE AND I sat in silence, staring at Quinton as he lay on the sofa sleeping.

What cruel joke was the universe playing on me? I'd put the idea of raising my own child out of my mind a long time ago. Now I was possibly going to be raising my husband's love child? On a boat?

That wouldn't do. We'd have to ditch our plans to sail the seven seas and instead settle down back on land. I'd probably need to sell my condo. It was only a two-bedroom, and Quinton would need his own room. Besides, I never considered the school system when I purchased it. Would it be hard to get him into a good preschool? I'd seen so many shows and movies where parents had to jump through hoops to get their kids into the best schools.

"We've got to figure this out," Jane said. "Pronto."

"Agreed. What have you heard about Bellevue Public Schools? They might be better than Seattle."

Jane jerked her head back. "What are you talking about?"

"Schools. For Quinton. We might as well start thinking about that now. It will be here before we know it."

"Charlotte. *Charlotte.* Have you taken leave of your senses? We're not raising Kyrie Dawn's baby. We need to figure out how to exonerate her."

"What if she's not exonerate...able? That's not a word, but you know what I mean. The evidence is stacking up against her."

"Do you think she killed Elliot? Really?"

"I don't know. Even if she didn't, she wouldn't be the first inno—she wouldn't be the first person to go to prison for a crime they didn't commit."

"You can't bring yourself to say it."

"What?"

"You can't bring yourself to say she's innocent, even if you don't believe she's a murderer."

I wanted to defend myself, but she was right. "I'm not gonna lie, Jane. Part of me wonders if this is some sort of cosmic prank, and part of me wonders if this is karma trying to right some wrongs."

"You can't possibly think that infidelity deserves a punishment of life in prison with no possibility of parole."

I shifted my chin. "I don't know, but maybe karma does."

Jane blew out a long sigh. "I can't speak for karma, or the universe, or God, but I can tell you this: this little boy doesn't deserve to suffer for the sins of his parents. We have the ability to help him recover the last semblance of normalcy his little life can have. And one more thing."

"What's that?"

"I don't *want* to be a parent. I'm in my fifties. I like my freedom. I like sleeping, and not having to worry about someone sticking their finger in an electrical outlet or eating laundry detergent. I like being able to read a book for hours or stay out late having drinks and talking about interesting topics with other adults. I don't want to watch cartoon kids whining about not knowing how to tie their shoes or puppets singing dumb songs about vegetables."

"I thought you were enjoying your time with him."

"Sure, but only because I know it's temporary. I'm too old and worn out to chase him around much longer. Do I like the kid? He's great. He's sweet. He's adorable. But he's not mine, and I'm glad about that."

I covered my face. "I can't stomach the thought of him going into foster care."

"Me neither. That's why we've got to find out who the real killer is."

She was right. In my gut, I knew it. "Okay, first thing tomorrow morning, Operation Save Quinton's mom from Recrimination shifts into high gear."

"It's an acronym. SQUIRM."

"Technically it would be SQUIFMR, but close enough."

JANE AND I rarely went to the dining room for breakfast. It was open every day from seven until ten A.M., with extended hours on weekends and holidays for brunch, but we typically ate in our suite. Sometimes we'd have Windsor bring us a tray of pastries and fruit, but mostly we made it ourselves.

Today, however, we needed to mingle with people, get a

feel for what anyone might have seen or heard, and begin to piece together the puzzle of what happened to Elliot, and possibly Florence.

Operation SQUIRM in full effect.

We arrived just after eight, and the restaurant was only a quarter full. We weren't the only ones who preferred a slow morning in the suite.

Hawk waved at us from the bar. "Want a mimosa?"

"I'm going to the cereal bar to get Q a handful of o's," said Jane. "And then I'll get us a table."

"Sounds good." I headed toward the bar. "Hey," I said to Hawk. "Long time no see. It's been, what, since Sushi and Sake Night downstairs three days ago? I was starting to wonder if you'd jumped ship."

"Nah. I'm just fillin' in here and there. They aren't quite sure what to do with me. I was supposed to take over for Cortes when he left, but I guess that's dead in the water." He paused. "Heh. I made a joke, but I didn't mean to."

Not a very funny one under the circumstances. "Speaking of Elliot's death, have you seen or heard anything that might be related? Sometimes you see an interaction, but you don't realize it's important. Hindsight gives a new perspective."

"Ain't that the truth." He finished pouring several flutes of champagne and orange juice. "Lemme think. I worked the welcome reception, and that's when you had your, uh, scuffle with K.D."

I bristled at her nickname. "It wasn't a scuffle. I didn't expect to see her here. She wasn't supposed to be here."

"You definitely looked surprised. She looked pretty smug about your reaction."

"You saw that?"

"I see a lot. Probably more than people want me to see."

"That's exactly why I wanted to talk to you. What else did you observe?"

"Let me take this tray of mimosas out, and I'll come right back."

He hustled around the bar and began to offer the drinks to diners. Jane waved him off. She was playing some sort of game with Quinton and a pile of cereal. He was giggling, and her eyes sparkled as she watched him.

The idea of taking on that level of responsibility was daunting. No doubt. But I couldn't help thinking that she was enjoying it more than she let on, and we could do it together—the parenting thing—if we had to.

"I did think of something," Hawk said when he returned from his rounds.

"What's that?"

"You know those blonde ladies you always sit with?"

"Yes. The ashy association?"

"Huh?"

"Sorry. I've been making up names for them."

"Oohh." He laughed. "Because of their hair. What else have you come up with?"

"I was thinking of the cream contingent and the butter batch, but I think that's just because I'm hungry."

"Could be. Anyway, I saw one of them having a *moment* with the chef that first night. The one with the short hair."

Grace. "What kind of a moment?"

"I'd seen them making long eye contact a few different times, and then after you left with Mesnier and K.D. to hash out your beef, she came up to him and whispered something in his ear. He was over there." Hawk pointed at the hallway that led to the restrooms. "So, he wasn't really visible to most people, but I could see him from the end of the bar where I was cutting up limes."

"What was it about their encounter that stood out to you as more than just two people talking?"

"When she walked away, I saw he was holding her hand. She looked over her shoulder at him and flashed this thousand-watt smile and let her hand linger in his just a minute too long. I know it sounds like nothing, but if you'd have seen it, you'd have thought it was something too."

It sounded like something. And if Deacon had seen it, he likely would have gotten very angry. Angry enough to kill.

Chapter Twenty-Three

"So, it's Deacon." Jane ground pepper over her omelet.

"I think there's a very good chance it's Deacon."

"Are you going to tell Xavier?"

"Not yet. I need a little more time. I want to see if I can talk to Grace again, get her to open up about her marriage and her relationship with Elliot."

"Wasn't Xavier planning to talk to her today?"

"Yes, but he and I have very different tactics."

"I was kind of hoping to do the origami class today. Will you come with me?"

"What about Quinton?" I fluffed his blonde hair, and he rewarded me by handing me a slobbered-on piece of cereal.

"Maybe Xavier will let us drop him off with Kyrie Dawn for a bit this morning."

"I'll bet he will if I ask realllly nicely."

"No."

"Come on."

"I know this is a cruise ship and not Rikers Island, but I'm still conducting a murder investigation, and she's still my prime suspect."

"They let babies be with their moms at Rikers Island."

He stopped pacing in his office to stare at me. "Is this true?"

"I don't know. I read it somewhere. It sounds true."

He ran his hand through his hair. "How long is this class?"

"Only one hour."

He exhaled. "Fine. One hour."

"Thank you! We'll be back as soon as it's over."

After passing a gleeful Quinton to his appreciative mom, Jane and I headed to Perseus—level four—for the origami class.

Jane was all about learning the Japanese art of paper folding, while I hoped to gather more intel that would lead us closer to the truth about Elliot's murder.

The theater where live performances took place was used in the daytime for various activities. Up on the stage was none other than Sensei Machigau holding a variety of square papers. On the table next to him was the classic swan, a crane, and lotus flowers.

"He's really taking this appropriation thing all the way, isn't he?" Jane snickered.

"I always wonder where the line is between cultural appreciation and appropriation. I think we're looking at it."

"Ladies," he greeted us. "Welcome. Take a seat anywhere."

Since it was made to be a theater, the seating consisted of rounded red velvet booths with bistro tables in front of them. We chose a booth in the center of the room. There were only about ten other people there when we arrived, but soon more trickled in.

Jane nudged me. "Look what the cat dragged in."

Willow, Grace, and Rhodie sauntered into the room, with Simon bringing up the rear. Fate had gifted me an unexpected opportunity to get information from Grace about Deacon.

"Hmm. I didn't take them for the arts-and-crafts types. Except maybe Willow. She looks like she could weave her own tablecloth and then top it with a bouquet of cut flowers and a ratatouille made with vegetables she grew in her garden. Oh, and freshly baked bread."

Jane laughed. "That's oddly specific."

"She also seems like the type to help her kids make Christmas ornaments but then put them on the back side of the tree so they don't mess up her décor."

"Oh, I definitely agree with that."

The foursome slid into the booth next to us.

"Fancy meeting you here," Jane said.

Simon held up his hands. "I'm only here so I don't get in trouble."

Willow gave him a playful swat. "You wouldn't get in trouble, silly. I just thought it would be fun to do something together."

"I've heard it can be peaceful." Grace shifted in her seat. "Lawd knows we could use some peace around here."

Rhodie snorted and then covered her mouth and nose. "Sorry. I just think you're delusional if you think trying to fold a piece of paper into the shape of an animal isn't going to make a couple of perfectionists like you to go completely bonkers."

She had a point. "Have you ever done this before?"

They all shook their heads.

"I did have a boy make one for me a long time ago," Grace volunteered. "I think it was a bird. We were on an airplane, and he wrote his phone number on it and then flew it to me a few rows back."

Rhodie blinked at her. "Are you sure it wasn't a paper airplane?"

Grace tilted her head. "Oh. Maybe. That does make more sense, doesn't it?"

Simon smacked his palm against his face. "Good grief, Grace."

She glared at Simon. "I need a drink. Anyone want anything from the bar?"

"Grace, honey, it's not even noon." Willow's disapproval hung from her words like wispy branches of the trees for which she'd been named.

"Willow, you had three mimosas with brunch yesterday," Grace snapped.

"Jane," I whispered under my breath. "I'm gonna go try to talk to Grace. Keep an ear out for anything any of the others might inadvertently let slip."

Grace leaned against the bar and exhaled.

Hawk placed a glass in front of her. "Vodka soda with

lime like usual?"

"Yep."

"Make that two." I sidled up next to her.

Hawk gave me a warning glance that I took to mean he didn't want me letting Grace know he was the one who spilled the beans about her friendly encounter with Elliot at the welcome reception. I gave him a slight nod. Message received.

"I pictured you for a light beer kind of gal." Grace's tone was wry.

No doubt she meant it as an insulting commentary of my breeding, but taking the bait wouldn't help me get information. "Sometimes. But I never go for anything sweet, like a mint julep or a French 75."

"Is that what you're calling him?" She gave me a sardonic smile.

"Who?"

"Xavier. Mr. French 75."

"Ha, no. I'm literally talking about the drink."

"Is that so? Because I could swear when you said *mint julep* you were referring to Willow." Her lip curled over the brim of her glass as she took a sip.

She was cleverer than I'd given her credit, so I needed to be cautious in my probing. "You seem to be handling the fact that you're solo on this cruise."

"What am I supposed to do? Wallow in my cabin because my dolt of a husband thought attempted murder was an appropriate way to cover for his other bad decisions?"

I hadn't expected her to be so blunt. I was about to ask

her about her relationship with Elliott when Sensei Machigau tapped a chopstick against the microphone stand.

I grabbed my drink and followed Grace back to our respective tables.

"Ladies and gentlemen." Sensei Machigau scanned the room. "Excuse me. Gentle*man*. I guess we have only the one."

Even in the club lighting of the theater, I could see Simon's cheeks flame pink. He tried to play it off, though, by standing and taking a dramatic bow.

"Very well," said Sensei Machigau. "Origami has been around for hundreds of years, and it is, as its name says—*ori* meaning to fold and *kami* meaning paper—the art of paper folding. Now, there are many types of folds but today, since I assume most of you are beginners, we will focus on pleats and sinks, book folds, the squash, the reverse, the valley, and the mountain. How appropriate is that? We are headed toward the majestic Fujiyama and learning about making mountain folds."

He demonstrated the various folds and then how to make a swan. As we each worked on our masterpieces, he strolled around the room observing our progress. Occasionally, he'd stop and redirect someone's efforts if they were struggling to turn the square piece of paper into something that resembled anything at all, much less a swan. He arrived at our table and made a pensive humming sound.

"What?" Jane asked. She was already annoyed with her swan, and his judgmental noises weren't helping.

"I just think you're too much in your head. You need to

be breathing." He clapped his hands twice and addressed the group. "Ladies. If you are trying too hard, you *will* fail. This is about creativity, and that comes from the soul, not from the mind. Your fingers are merely the tools your *seishin*—your spirit, the essence of you—is using to express itself. Breathe, silence those thoughts of perfectionism. When Michelangelo was carving David, he was not making a statue, he was allowing it to reveal itself with each chip of the marble. Allow your swan to emerge."

"Allow your swan to emerge," Jane mimicked under her breath.

Sensei Machigau, however, had already moved on to the next table. "Very nice, Mrs.—"

"Grace. Grace Beauchamp of the—oh, never mind."

He leaned over her shoulder. "Grace, your folds are so precise. Have you done this before?"

Color crept up Grace's neck. She fanned herself with the paper she'd been folding. "Why, no, I haven't. First time."

As he moved around the table, Grace gave a wistful sigh. I supposed some women might find him attractive, but I couldn't get past the inauthenticity.

To Simon he said, "You're in trouble."

Simon glowered. "What's that supposed to mean?"

"You've been sloppy. You think you can hide the messy part because it's inside, but it will show in the finished product. Your swan won't float."

Simon adjusted his glasses. "It's paper. It's not supposed to float."

"Oh, did I not tell you all? After we're done here, we're

going upstairs to Capri to float them in the hot tub."

A few excited murmurs were mixed with confused mutterings.

"Hey, Sensei." I waved at him.

"Yes?" He wandered back our direction.

"Can I ask you a question?"

"Of course."

I tamped down all the questions I'd been wanting to ask him since he'd first appeared on Ninja Night. *What's with the Japanese charade? Is that your real hair? Have you ever thought about taking your act to Vegas?* "Actually, I have two questions. First, how do you know Kyrie Dawn?"

He tilted his head and furrowed his brow. "Who?"

Genuine confusion. Interesting. "Petite blonde—"

"Those are a dime a dozen around here."

"Yes, well, this one didn't get it from the bottle." I snuck a quick glance to make sure none of the women at the next table had heard me. They were all concentrating on their swans. "She's the new yoga instructor. I saw you talking to her the other night." On security footage, but still.

"Do you mean Katie?"

I bit the inside of my lip. "Not Katie. Kyrie Dawn. Some people call her—" I swallowed. "K.D." I emphasized the D, so it didn't sound like a T.

He sucked in his cheeks and puckered his mouth like a fish caught on the line. "I don't really know her. I just met her that once. She came up to me and started flirting." He flicked invisible lint off his shoulder. "Of course, she wasn't the only one, but I'm used to it. Comes with the gig."

"Can you tell me exactly what she said?"

His blue eyes narrowed. "Why? She married or something?"

He scanned the room, possibly for a jealous husband lying in wait, but it was still ninety-nine percent estrogen. Well, maybe not ninety-nine, considering the only thing most of us were flirting with these days was menopause.

"No, not married. I guess you could say that she's kind of—" I swallowed. "Widowed."

"How can someone be kind of widowed? The guy in a coma or somethin'?"

Jane cleared her throat. She quirked an eyebrow at me.

"No," I said. "He's all the way dead. He just wasn't her husband. He was mine."

Sensei Machigau reared his head and bared his teeth. "Yikes."

Yikes indeed.

"The reason I'm asking is because I'm not sure if you're aware, but she's being detained in the security office as a likely suspect in Elliot Patenaude's murder."

"Oh, that's who's they fingered for Elliot's death? I just heard it was some chick he knocked up and then wouldn't take responsibility for the kid."

Jane clucked. "That rumor has been making the rounds. Any truth to it?"

"No clue. I didn't really know either of them."

The perfect segue. "That's funny, because I heard you were going to be Elliot's partner in his restaurant."

His demeanor shifted like the barometric pressure at the

onset of a typhoon. "Who told you that?"

"It's in the ether. Doesn't matter who said it."

"Sure, it does." He clenched his jaw.

We had a stare down until one of the ladies in the row behind us called him over for help with her wings.

"One sec," he called to the woman. He leaned forward until our noses were practically touching. "Elliot is dead. No amount of snooping into other people's business is going to bring him back." He stood and plastered a cheesy smile across his face. "Okay, Eleanor. Let's see if we can get that bird to float." And then he flashed me a look that said he wanted to drown mine.

Chapter Twenty-Four

J ANE AND I didn't bother joining the rest of the class to float our origami swans. It was obvious they'd sink straight to the bottom just by looking at them.

"I'm kicking myself."

We were headed back to the security office.

"How come?" Jane asked.

"I never got a straight answer from Sensei Machigau about what Kyrie Dawn said to him. He just said she was flirting."

"I'll bet Xavier has already had that conversation with her."

"Sure, but I had an advantage."

"What's that?" she asked.

"He didn't know why I was asking. He became defensive and shut down once I started asking about the restaurant, but before that he was Mr. Chatty Pants. I'd love to know what she was up to. I seriously doubt she was interested in him *or* his blow gun."

"Now that she's really under the magnifying glass, I'm guessing she won't feel like being too forthcoming."

"Believe it or not, she asked me for help finding a lawyer."

"Not easy, considering"—she waved her hand—"we're in the middle of the ocean. Thankfully, in Andy's case we had Clyde to step in. There's got to be one onboard. Maybe we should start asking around."

"Maybe. Or…"

She stopped in the middle of the hallway. "Or?"

"I'm not sure an attorney would help her situation."

"How do you figure?"

"An attorney would tell her to stay quiet, but that won't help us get the answers we need."

"Char."

"What?"

"Char, stop walking."

I stopped and turned to face her. "What?"

"You're not trying to sabotage her, are you? I thought we discussed that it's better for everyone that she doesn't go down for murder."

"I'm not sabotaging her. I'm trying to help her. *If* she didn't do it, then cooperation is her best tool. The more information we have, the more information Xavier has, the sooner we can solve this."

"Hmm."

"Don't *hmm* me. I've heard you, and I understand what you said about not being tied down with the responsibility of taking care of Quinton. I'm just starting to get my feet under me. I feel like I'm finally choosing my path rather than letting things happen to me. I, too, want to explore and eat new foods and meet interesting people who have more to talk about than their kid's soccer game or the politics of school PTA. I get it. I'm just not willing to let that little boy, my husband's child, get sent to some stranger's house where he knows no one and spends the rest of his childhood wondering what he did to be sent away and why no one stepped up to take care of him. I won't do it. I'll sign the suite over to you so you can still have the dream. No one is expecting you to give up your life."

"You really think I would let you take that on all by yourself while I'm bouncing between ports of call? Not gonna happen. Which is why I would really prefer that we keep the eye on the prize here: exoneration for Kyrie Dawn so that kid can be with his mother."

"We're on the same page. I swear." I held up my hands in surrender. "We good?"

"We're good. Now let's go get the little stinker and smother him with kisses."

"I MADE YOU a present." I set my attempt at an origami swan on Xavier's desk.

Jane had gone to see Quinton in the room where Kyrie Dawn was being held.

He eyed it like it carried malaria. "What is it?"

"What do you mean, what is it? It's a swan."

He picked it up and examined it from several angles. "Perhaps it needs just a little more time, but eventually it will grow into a swan."

"Are you calling my art an ugly duckling?"

The corner of his mouth twitched a smile. "Beauty is in the eye of the beholder."

I waved my hand. "Whatever. I tried. I have another gift for you."

"Rhinoceros? Unicorn? Ham sandwich?"

Funny. "Information."

He tented his fingertips. "Go on."

"Don't do that. It makes you look like an evil mastermind."

He leaned back. "Well, I am certainly not evil."

Or humble. "Remember when I told you that Sensei Machigau was financially involved with Elliot's restaurant?"

"Yes, and I have sent him a message to come speak with me, but he has yet to do so. Did you see him?"

"He was the one running the class," I said.

"Was he? A master of many skills."

"Truly. Anyway, I asked him about his interaction with Kyrie Dawn—"

Xavier folded his arms. "I have asked you not to interfere with my investigation, and I told you I would be interviewing him."

"I understand that, but I figured he'd respond differently to a curious passenger rather than the head of security."

His left brow arched. "And did he?"

"At first, he did. In fact, he didn't even know who I was talking about initially. The gist of it was he said she was flirting with him, but supposedly that happens all the time." I guffawed. "I find that hard to believe, but to each his own."

"Did he say what happened after they went off-camera? Did she keep the blow gun? Did she ask him to demonstrate it for her?"

I shrugged. "Well, that's where things kind of went off the rails."

"How so?"

"He said he didn't know Kyrie Dawn *or* Elliot, so I pressed him with what I heard from Margaret about him being Elliot's business partner." I shook my head. "He turned cold. Shut me down. And then he got in my face."

Xavier leaned forward, scowling. "Got in your face?"

"Yeah, right in my face. It felt like an unspoken threat."

"Where is he now?"

"He was leading the group to the hot tub to see if their swans floated. Jane and I decided not to join them."

He picked up my swan and examined it. "I am no physics expert, but I have studied Archimedes' Principle and I believe you made a good choice to come here instead."

I reached across the desk and attempted to swipe it from him, but he pulled it back, beyond my grasp.

"What are you doing?"

"If you don't like my swan, I'll take it back."

"I did not say I did not like it. I said it would not float. I appreciate the gesture." He swiveled his chair and set in on the bookcase behind him. "There. Now." He clasped his hands. "I have made a decision."

"What's that?"

"I will release Kyrie Dawn to your custody on a trial basis. Either you or Jane must be present in your suite at all times. I have a camera in the hallway that will be monitored, so if she leaves, or if I see you and Jane are both gone, I will remand her back into my custody."

Hadn't expected that. Hadn't emotionally prepared myself for it either. Logistically, it made sense. In reality, being locked in a cruise ship cabin with the woman who represented so much pain for me suddenly sounded like the worst idea I'd ever formulated.

Deep breath. "Okay."

He observed me so intensely, I had to look away.

"Are you sure?"

"Nope."

"I am uncertain what to do with that response. I can keep her here."

"No, we'll take her. It's best for Quinton. And hey, it's a growth opportunity, right?"

"I suppose…"

I slapped my hands on his desk. "Release the Kyrie Dawn!"

"Why are you yelling?"

"Never mind. It was a play on the *release the kraken* quote."

He shook his head. "Americans."

"Yeah, yeah."

We entered the room where he'd been holding her. Kyrie Dawn was sitting cross-legged on the floor with Jane opposite her and Quinton in between them. He was bouncing a small ball.

"What's going on?" I asked.

"Oh, we're just playing a game," Jane said.

Kyrie Dawn didn't tear her eyes away from her son for even a moment. "He's getting good at passing, but catching is still a challenge."

Xavier smiled. "That is always a more difficult skill to master."

"Not for me," I said. "Throwing has been way harder. Jane can vouch for me."

She laughed. "Char has a tendency to kick up her foot like a princess getting her first magical kiss whenever she throws a ball. Doesn't matter what kind. Baseball, shooting a basketball, serving a volleyball—that foot just pops up."

He only marginally suppressed a smile. "I would like to see that. In the meantime, I have some news."

This was enough to get Kyrie Dawn's attention. "For me?"

"*Oui.* I have decided to release you into the custody of Mesdames McLaughlin and Cobb—"

She jumped to her feet. "Oh, thank you!" She flung her arms around him.

He allowed a brief hug before pulling back. Good thing, because I was about to pry her off of him by her hair if necessary. I probably needed to talk to my therapist about these latent violent thoughts that kept creeping into my mind.

"Allow me to finish. This is a temporary arrangement. One or both of them must stay with you at all times. You are not to leave the suite unless I say you may."

"Of course. I'll behave."

"If at any point I deem the arrangement untenable, you will be brought back here until we reach our next port. Do you understand?"

"Absolutely. Thank you so much!"

"Do not thank me. Thank these two women who have agreed to bring you into their home."

She turned to face me. She'd aged just in the few days she'd been detained. Was it because she wasn't able to eat her perfectly organic diet and supplements, perform her daily exercises, or didn't have her expensive skincare regimen, which I'd discovered had been bought on Gabe's credit card when I looked at his statements? Or was it simply grief from being away from her baby?

"Charlotte, there are so many things I've wanted to say to you for so long. Now isn't the time for that conversation, but I do hope at some point we can have it. In the meantime, I want you to know how grateful I am to you—and to Jane—for taking such good care of Quinton and now allowing me to be with him. It's a lot, and I'm very aware that it can't be easy for you, for many reasons."

"I appreciate that. And I agree, we're long overdue for a conversation. But that can wait."

"You're a good woman, Charlotte. I'm sorry for all the hurt I've caused you. You didn't deserve it."

Her words hit me like a freight train. Air. I needed air. "I have to go."

"Charlotte—" Kyrie Dawn said as I lunged for the door.

"I'll meet you all back at the room!"

Once I was out of the security office, I headed for the

stairs. By the time I'd made it up the five flights to Kalispera, I couldn't catch my breath. I grabbed onto the railing as I gasped to fill my lungs with air. Had they collapsed completely? A wind picked up, and I braced myself against it.

What was wrong with me? I'd gotten the one thing I thought I needed and wanted—an apology—and now that I had it, it was like the fabric of my universe was ripping into shreds. Other than the affair having never happened—an impossibility—acknowledgment of its impact on me was the next best thing, and yet instead of feeling like a weight had been lifted from me, I was undone by it.

The sky above me began to darken as the clouds thickened, pregnant with rain. On the other side of the railing, a hundred feet or so below, the water began to churn. The normal lapping of the ocean against the hull became a frenzied pounding. In the distance swells grew and crested, moving ever closer to the ship.

No one else was around, understandably. A storm was coming and even before that, the temperatures were not warm.

I hadn't been up there since we'd boarded in Seattle. Intellectually, I knew we were in the middle of the Pacific, but it wasn't until I saw for myself that there wasn't a single boat or jot of land as far as the eye could see that the enormity of it hit me. It was humbling. A seemingly giant ship was really just a speck, and I was a tinier speck on that speck.

"You really should come inside. It is not safe up here with the storm approaching."

I whirled to face Xavier. "How did you know I was up

here?" Intuition? The universe conspiring? Cosmic destiny?

He jerked his thumb over his shoulder. "Security camera."

Ah. Of course. Why would I ever think the universe, or God, some master puppeteer, or whoever…*whatever* was yanking the strings of my life, wouldn't gift me a star-crossed romance to go along with all the rest of my disappointments? Destined to fail or never materialize in the first place.

As soon as the thoughts entered my mind, I had to laugh.

"What is amusing?"

"I haven't had a bad life, you know."

His forehead creased. "Do you believe I pity you?"

Did I? "I don't know. I mean, I've seen it in some of the looks you've given me. And everyone else I've encountered in the past several months." I turned away from him and rested my hands on the railing, peering out into the turbulent water. "You know that saying, ignorance is bliss?"

"I have heard it said. I do not know that I agree with the sentiment."

I turned around. "It's from the last stanza in a poem by Thomas Gray. 'Ode on a Distant Prospect of Eton College.' I memorized it in high school. It says, *To each his sufferings all are men, Condemned alike to groan, the tender for another's pain; the unfeeling for his own. Yet ah! Why should they know their fate? Since sorrow never comes too late, and happiness too swiftly flies. Thought would destroy their paradise. No more; where ignorance is bliss, 'Tis folly to be wise.*"

"Morose. What does this mean to you?"

196

"Several different things, really. Everyone will suffer, but who you suffer on behalf of is the question: the tenderhearted person who grieves for the pain that others experience, or the unfeeling person for their own struggles. That's the battle, right? Do we suffer for ourselves or for others? It's never a question of will we suffer. That's inevitable."

"Is it?"

"Isn't it?"

"Perhaps in difficult circumstances, but not all circumstances are difficult."

"Or maybe they are and we're just ignorant of their difficulties, lurking below the surface of our willful obtuseness."

"You speak of your husband's betrayal."

"Among other things."

"And now you wonder if you would be selfish to tend to your own wounds rather than attend to the needs of others, particularly those who played a part in that betrayal."

"Exactly."

"Has it occurred to you that tending to the wounds of others may result in a healing balm for you as well?"

A gust of wind knocked me sideways. Or was it his piercing words?

"We should go inside."

"You can. I still need to clear my head."

"Charlotte, I must insist. You do not have to go back to your room. Jane has escorted them there herself. But *s'il vous plait*, come back inside."

A violent rain began to pelt us. I stared at the hand he reached out. I wanted to take it. I wanted to trust him. To release the burden, I'd been carrying. Maybe even to forgive.

"I'm scared."

"I do not blame you. But you are not alone."

A loud crash behind us signaled the storm was at hand. It was no longer just a possibility, but a reality that had to be faced. Another wave, even larger, crested behind us and the ship swayed.

He didn't wait for me to offer my hand. He grabbed it and pulled me toward the stairwell entrance. The wind was blowing so hard, he struggled to get the door open. In just a few seconds, we were soaked.

Once inside, he held my cheeks in his hands. "You are not alone," he repeated.

I nodded. I believed him.

Chapter Twenty-Five

BEFORE ENTERING THE suite, I took two deep breaths.

"Hey." Jane was on the sofa.

Kyrie Dawn sat across from her in a chair, holding a pillow on her lap.

"Hey."

"You're soaked."

"Yeah, there's a storm raging out there. I think they're gonna cancel Manga/Anime night. Xavier says Captain Knutson should be making an announcement soon that they prefer everyone stay in their cabins."

Kyrie Dawn played with the fringe on the pillow, not making eye contact. "I like what you've done with the place."

"Don't."

She shifted her mouth, still running the tassels through her fingers.

"Where's Quinton?" I asked.

"Kyrie Dawn put him down for a nap."

"I told you, Jane, you can call me K.D."

"Not if I want my sister to keep speaking to me."

Kyrie Dawn reluctantly met my gaze. "Why are you so opposed to nicknames?"

I set my phone on the dining table. "I'm not opposed to nicknames as a general rule. I'm opposed to the familiarity it implies when it comes to people, I don't want to be familiar with."

"I'm not a bad person, Charlotte. I know I hurt you, but I generally live a life of kindness and compassion."

I sat on the sofa's armrest. If I needed to flee, it would be easier to make my escape if I wasn't sunken into the cushions. "I understand that in many parts of your life that's probably true. I also recognize that you didn't make a commitment to me, Gabe did. He's the one who broke my trust." I sighed. "I gotta ask, though. Did you know about me from the beginning?"

"I guess it depends on what you consider the beginning."

I let out an exasperated grunt. "Let me rephrase did you know he was married?"

Jane touched my hand. "Are you sure you want to do this? You've done so much healing, it would be a shame to rip off the scab and start poking at it."

"I think it's more like a broken bone that healed wrong. Sometimes it has to be rebroken in order for it to function properly. Go on, Kyrie Dawn. I'd like to hear it."

"Okay, well, he used to work out next to the yoga room. There were windows, so anyone could see into the studio from the free weights area. He'd be lifting and, on his breaks, he'd watch me teaching my classes. Sometimes he'd smile and wave, and I'd wave back. One day he came in while I was setting up and asked me if he could take me to coffee. I looked at his hand, but he wasn't wearing a wedding ring."

"That's because it didn't fit him anymore. He told me women were more likely to approach him with the ring on than without it. I was such a dummy."

"I wouldn't doubt it. I do know women that prefer married men. He wasn't the first guy to hit on me—he wasn't even the first married guy to hit on me—but there was something about him. I liked that he was kind of nerdy. Really good-looking guys make me nervous. I never felt nervous around Gabe."

Jane guffawed. "You liked him because he was a five instead of a nine?"

"Hey, that's my husband you're talking about. He wasn't a five. You think I would have married a five?"

Kyrie Dawn nodded. "No, he was definitely not a five. And he was smart. I'd never met anyone so smart. Anyway, I agreed to go to coffee with him."

"And at that point you still thought he was single?"

"I hoped so. We talked for an hour about ourselves, where we grew up, what he did for a living, our favorite music, favorite movies—"

"Favorite books?" Jane asked.

It was a dig. A librarian power move. I suspected she assumed Kyrie Dawn wasn't much of a reader.

"As I'm sure you know, Gabe wasn't a fiction reader. He kind of told me that up front. In fact, that's how he brought you up for the first time, Charlotte."

Gabe never read anything that wasn't about investing. One of our many incompatibilities.

"He said you were a librarian, and that you could spend

hours curled up with a book, but he just wasn't interested in what he called pretend stories."

"Yes, I'm well aware. So, he admitted he was married at that first meeting."

"Sort of. He said you were headed for divorce."

"Could he be any more prosaic?" Jane muttered under her breath.

"News to me," I said.

"He said you were incompatible—"

"True."

"And that you were as unhappy as he was."

Was that true? Was he able to see that I was becoming less and less of myself every day in that marriage? Or was it just a convenient excuse to justify his own actions?

"You were together for...how long?"

Her pitying expression made me want to scream.

She swallowed. "Nearly four years."

Dammit. The math alone had told me it had to be at least twenty-two months, since Quinton was one at the time of Gabe's death, but hearing that number—*four years*—really brought home to me the extent of their relationship. I knew people who met, married, and divorced in less time.

"So, for four years you believed he was on the verge of divorcing me. Did you ever stop and wonder what was taking so long?"

"Of course I did. We even broke up at one point."

"So how did he talk you into getting back together?"

"I found out I was pregnant."

Funny how even when you've already heard the bad

news over and over, it could still punch you in the gut like it was the first time. "How did he react?"

"He was freaked out. We both were. I mean, I'd called off the relationship and was trying to move on. He'd been trying to focus on improving his relationship with you. He told me he'd even thought about broaching the idea of a surrogate with you, thinking if he gave you what you'd always wanted, maybe the two of you could live happily ever after. I wanted that for him if that's what he really wanted. He said it was."

"Oof," Jane said.

It just kept getting worse. Gabe had considered surrogacy to have a baby with me? I tried to recall if I'd noticed any change in him around the time they were broken up. He had surprised me with a romantic Valentine's Day trip to New Orleans. We drank hurricane cocktails ladled out of a trashcan in an alley off of Bourbon Street, feasted at Commander's Palace, eaten our weight in beignets from Café Du Monde, and then stumbled back to our romantic suite in the heart of the French Quarter.

He'd been trying.

Shortly after we'd gotten home, things between us grew cold again. He was impatient and annoyed by everything I said or did. It hurt more than if we'd never shared that special time together. There were times when I found myself wanting to scream at him, *do you even like me?* He must have found out about the pregnancy around that time.

Kyrie Dawn cleared her throat. "I offered to keep him out of it entirely, but he didn't want that. He said he took care of his responsibilities."

A real knight in shining armor. Who said chivalry was dead? "So, what was the plan? He was just going to have a second family forever and hope I never found out?"

Her face clouded over. I watched as grief descended upon her like the Holy Spirit at Pentecost. "The day he—" She swallowed. "The day of the accident, he asked me to marry him."

It felt like the entire ship listed to the left and my stomach went with it. I fell off the armrest of the sofa and onto the ground. Had I fainted? I couldn't remember.

"Oh my gosh!" Kyrie Dawn shouted. "The boat feels like it's going to capsize!"

Wait. I wasn't the only one to feel that rolling motion?

Jane lunged for the lamp, which had begun to slide off the side table. "What is happening?"

Quinton cried out from Jane's room. "Mama!"

Kyrie Dawn made her way toward the bedroom, holding the wall to keep herself steady as the floor shifted.

Jane snapped her fingers. "Char. Charlotte. Can you hear me?"

"Of course I can hear you."

"Turn on the TV. There should be some sort of alert on the home screen."

The remote was no longer on the coffee table. I got on my hands and knees and crawled around until I found it under Kyrie Dawn's chair. Just as I pressed the button to turn on the TV, the overhead speaker squawked.

"Ladies and gentlemen." Captain Knutson's Scandinavian accent was easily recognizable. "As I am sure you have noticed, we are dealing with an unexpected issue."

"Ya think?" Jane glared at the ceiling speaker.

Kyrie Dawn stumbled back into the living room holding Quinton. His eyes were wide and filled with imminent tears. He was fervently sucking on a binky and holding his favorite stuffed animal.

"Hey, buddy," Jane cooed.

The speaker beeped once more. "I am being told the storm has knocked out our stabilizers. This is why the ship is rolling. Please use every precaution. Do not leave your quarters, and if you are outside your quarters, please return now. Our engineer is in contact with the team in Fort Lauderdale, and it sounds as though it may take a few hours to reboot the system and get it back online. In the meantime, secure any items that may cause injury. As you know, all of our cabinets and drawers are equipped with firm-close technology, so you should not have any issues with items that have been put away—"

"Captain."

The intercom went silent for what seemed like forever but was probably only a minute or so.

"Captain Bellucci has informed me we may possibly experience rolling blackouts while the system is rebooting. Do not be alarmed. Our crew is highly experienced and prepared. You are all in good hands. I will give you an update as soon as I have it."

"That's reassuring." Jane began clearing the surfaces of any objects that might become projectile weapons because of the ship's heeling.

Kyrie Dawn clutched Quinton to her like he was her life preserver. Maybe he was. Without him, she looked like she'd lost her purpose for living. With him, she was a fierce mama bear ready to take on anything for his sake.

"I'm glad you're here with him."

Relief washed across her face. "I'm so grateful. I can't even imagine what it would be like if I were stuck in that room wondering if he was okay."

Jane moved on from placing objects on the floor to opening and closing kitchen cupboards and drawers.

"What are you doing in there?"

"I'm auditioning for *Stomp*. What do you think I'm doing? I'm looking for a flashlight in case the lights go out."

Cue the darkness.

Each of us uttered a different curse word.

Chapter Twenty-Six

I'D BEEN READING an entry in my great-gramma Miriam's diary to Jane and Kyrie Dawn by the light of my phone. She'd described living through the 1923 Yokohama earthquake and its aftermath. The thump of the book as I set it on the coffee table was the only sound for several moments.

Someone sniffed in the dark. From the direction, I was pretty sure it was Kyrie Dawn.

"That's devastating," Jane said in hushed tones.

"All those people." Kyrie Dawn's voice cracked. Now I was positive she was my sniffer.

Something rolled across my foot. I shined the light on it. It was a bright green pen. I knew what it was before I even picked it up. On the side was the logo of the gym where Gabe had met Kyrie Dawn.

"What is it?" Jane asked.

"Just a pen."

"Do you think the ship will capsize?" The tremble in Kyrie Dawn's voice made her sound younger than her age, like a child hiding under the bed during a thunderstorm.

"I don't know much about stabilizers other than they sound pretty important for...you know...stabilizing the ship." As the words came out of my mouth, the lights flickered, and the rolling subsided.

"Oh, thank goodness." Jane gripped her throat. "I was really starting to worry we were going down."

"The unsinkable Jane Cobb." I set the pen on the table.

"What does that mean?" Kyrie Dawn picked up the pen. Her mouth formed an *O*.

"What does what mean?" I didn't want to talk about the pen, or the gym, or Gabe.

"The unsinkable Jane Cobb."

Jane and I exchanged glances.

"Oh, you sweet summer child." Jane laughed. "Don't you know about Molly Brown? *The Titanic*?"

She stared blankly at Jane. "I was only six or seven when that movie came out."

Jane dramatically grabbed the armrest of the sofa. "I have shoes older than you."

The loudspeaker squawked overhead. "Ladies and gentlemen, as I'm sure you have noticed, our stabilizers are back online. Thank you to our engineers who solved the problem quickly. We ask that you remain in your suites. Our crew will be attending to any damage done, any broken glass or messes that may have been created, so for your safety and for the sake of our employees, we ask that you continue to stay put. Again, we apologize for the situation. Please contact the main desk if you have any urgent questions or concerns such as damage. If anyone was injured in your party, contact the medical office. It appears we are through the storm, and all systems are working properly. I will notify you as soon as it is safe to leave your residence."

"Well, that's a relief. Anyone want wine?" Jane rose and headed for the kitchen. "I think we have a bottle of each that are already open."

"I'd love some white if that's okay," Kyrie Dawn said.

"Of course. Char?"

"Red please. Thanks."

I'll just bring both bottles." Jane handed Kyrie Dawn a glass. She set mine in front of me on the coffee table, along with the wine.

"Can I ask you both a question?" Kyrie Dawn asked.

I allowed myself a heavy pour. No clue where the conversation was going, and I wanted to be prepared. "Sure."

"Do you think I killed Elliot?"

Quinton was sleeping peacefully against her chest. He was her greatest character reference.

"Honestly? I don't know. I understand why Xavier believes you did it. All the evidence is pointing to you."

Jane chimed in. "I mean, you were literally standing over the body with the murder weapon in your hand. Hard not to think you had something to do with his death."

"I know it looks bad. Xavier hasn't really even told me all the evidence he has against me. How can I fight what I don't know?"

"Well, let's see. In addition to the scene that we found when we reached the yoga studio, there are the rumors about your relationship with Elliot—"

"Laughable."

"Maybe. I don't know. There are the fingerprints on the

murder weapon and the video of you schmoozing with Sensei Machigau where you actually took possession of it minutes before Elliot was murdered."

"Isn't all of that circumstantial?"

"As far as circumstantial goes, that's a pretty strong case. The motive is either spurned lover or scorned mother. The means is you acquired the weapon—on CCTV—and the opportunity is the dude was killed in your yoga studio. Obviously, you were there."

Jane tapped her lips. "Did she actually have the murder weapon?"

"What do you mean?"

"Well, she was definitely holding the blow gun. No doubt. But that's only a third of the weapon. There's also the dart, and the fugu."

Kyrie Dawn scrunched her face. "The hoogoo?"

Was she playing a part, or did she really not know? "Fugu. It's the poisonous Japanese puffer fish."

"Did someone hit him over the head with a fish?"

I blinked at her. Out of the corner of my eye I saw Jane blinking at her too.

"Welp," Jane said. "I find the defendant not guilty by reason of ignorance."

"Hey, that's not nice." Kyrie Dawn pouted. "I'm not ignorant, I've just never heard of a poisonous fish, and no one said anything to me about it being used as a weapon."

"You're right." Jane gave an apologetic smile. "The point I was making is, I believe you didn't kill Elliot because even though you have motive and opportunity, the question of means is up in the air if you don't even know how to use the weapon to accomplish the task."

"So, he wasn't hit with the fish? I used to watch Monty Python with my grandpa, and they had a sketch about slapping people with fish."

I laughed. "There was also the Muppet character that was constantly throwing fish at people."

Jane slapped her leg. "That's right! Did you see the fish slapping card game on *The Tonight Show*? That was hilarious."

"I did see that!" Kyrie Dawn bounced in her seat, jarring Quinton. "I was wheezing!"

"I had no idea fish slapping was such a phenomenon. I doubly apologize," Jane said.

As they explained the episode to me, Jane and Kyrie Dawn feeding off the other's recollection and then adding to it, we were howling.

So odd. For those few moments, with the three of us laughing and talking about something other than dead husbands, dead chefs, and looming murder charges, I forgot that I despised Kyrie Dawn. We were just three women enjoying each other's company. It was kind of nice.

"Oh geez, I needed that." She wiped tears of laughter from her face. Quinton squirmed in her arms, having been awoken by the noise. She patted his back and shimmied side to side. "Shhh. I'm sorry, I know you were trying to sleep."

"He's so precious," I said.

She smiled. "I think so. Tell me, if it wasn't death by fish slap, what was it?"

Jane pointed at me. "You wanna take this?"

"Sure. Elliot was killed by the dart in his neck. However, according to Dr. Fraser, it wasn't the dart that killed him, it was the poison on the tip of the dart."

"Poison? Where did someone get poison? How does that even work?"

"So fugu, which is the Japanese name for puffer fish, is a delicacy but it also has toxins in certain organs that make it deadly. Hidden in the corner of the walk-in fridge was a bucket of discarded fugu parts. Deacon Beauchamp had talked Elliot into a private meal where he and some of his friends could try fugu. You're not supposed to do that without extensive training, because wrong preparation could result in someone dying. Elliot had little to no experience."

"Except for some YouTube videos," Jane added.

"Right."

"Does that mean someone snuck into the walk-in and dipped a needle in the fish guts?"

"I'm not exactly sure. Jane, do you remember whether that was explained?"

"Not that I recall. All I remember is him saying dipped in that very long word that starts with *T*, the toxin that comes from that particular fish. We didn't even know where the bucket of gunk was until you and Xavier got locked in there."

"How was it? Being locked in there with him, I mean. I used to think he was hot before he arrested me for murder."

"Not romantic, if that's what you're asking. Pretty scary if you must know."

"Don't you think that whoever made the dart poisonous had to know the fish was here in the first place?" Kyrie Dawn asked.

"They had to have. I doubt anyone would randomly happen upon that bucket—Elliot hid it for a reason—and even if they did, would they know what it was when they saw it? I didn't get a close look because as soon as I found it, Deacon slammed the door shut and that took all our attention, but to me it just looked like slop."

"If Kyrie Dawn didn't kill Elliot—" Jane held up her hand to squelch Kyrie Dawn's imminent protest. "I already told you I believe you didn't do it."

She snapped her mouth shut and indicated for Jane to continue.

"I'm just saying we need to get a clearer picture of who might have done it."

If only it were that easy. "It's difficult to narrow it down. There are probably a hundred and fifty passengers plus however many crewmembers are onboard. The only other people that have stood out to me as having a possible motive are Deacon and Sensei Machigau. Possibly Margaret, although I doubt it. Oh, and the husbands of any of Elliot's special friends."

"We can rule out Deacon if Florence's death wasn't suicide. He was in custody." Jane's mouth tightened.

Kyrie Dawn's lashes fluttered. "Are we saying what I think we're saying?"

"I think we are." I glanced between them. "Are we all in agreement that Sensei Machigau likely murdered Elliot Patenaude?"

Chapter Twenty-Seven

THE NEXT MORNING Operation Suspicious Sensei went into full effect. Since one of us had to stay with Kyrie Dawn, Jane volunteered so that I could investigate. I had no idea what Sensei Machigau would be doing—the only scheduled activity was karaoke night at eight.

My first stop was the security office. Pike Taylor was behind the desk reading a bestselling police procedural.

"How is it?"

He set the book facedown. "Pretty good. Although I think I already know who did it and I'm only halfway done."

"Don't you hate it when that happens? I mean, how hard could it possibly be to throw in enough red herrings that it's not painfully obvious?"

"Exactly! So, Charlotte, Xavier hasn't come in yet this morning. Is there something I can help you with?"

"You know that Kyrie Dawn is staying with Jane and me, right?"

He grimaced. "Yeah. How's that going?"

"Better than going to the dentist, but only marginally."

"I hear ya."

"Jane and I would like to go to karaoke night tonight.

We already have our costumes picked out, and we think it will be a great opportunity to gather information about Elliot's murder."

To make the evening more entertaining, everyone was supposed to come dressed as their favorite singer.

Pike appraised me. "Lemme guess. Celine Dion?"

"Kelly Clarkson."

"Isn't she like twenty years younger than you?"

Ouch. That stung. "More like ten, I'll have you know."

"Hey, when you're aging like fine wine, does it matter?"

"Thank you, I guess?"

"What does karaoke night have to do with me?"

"Xavier's requirement for Kyrie Dawn being released was that she couldn't be left unsupervised in our suite. I was hoping maybe you or Lonnie could hang with her while Jane and I are out. Maybe watch a movie with her or something."

"Lonnie's on shift so he has to be able to leave on a moment's notice. I'm supposed to be off for the night, but I don't have any plans. I guess I could hang out with her for a couple hours."

"Oh, thank you so much! We'll be gone from like eight until ten-ish."

"Cool. 701, right?"

"Yep."

"I'll see you then."

I MADE MY way toward the solarium at the aft of the ship. A

ray of sunshine beamed through the glass ceiling of the solarium. A few dark clouds were still present, but it appeared we were through the worst of the storm.

There were a few people standing in line at the grab-and-go espresso stand, but the poolside area was empty, other than a striped towel and a pair of eyeglasses placed on top of a lounge chair.

No sign of Sensei Machigau.

Swimming laps, however, was Simon Strawbridge. He had just reached the opposite side, made a somersault turn, and was headed my way.

I stood at the pool's edge between the lane markers. His strokes were sure and swift. He seamlessly moved through the water, the muscles of his back contracting and releasing with each rhythmic movement of his sinewy arms and legs. He crossed the length of the pool, reaching me in no time at all he finished the lap, he wiped his face.

"Oh, hello, Charlotte. I didn't realize you were there."

"I just got here. I wanted to say hi. You're a strong swimmer. Did you compete?"

"I was on the swim and diving team in high school, but that was a long time ago. I prefer this type of workout to lifting weights." He pushed back from the edge and treaded water. "What are you up to this morning?"

"Oh, this and that. Have you seen Sensei Machigau?"

"That weirdo? I haven't seen him. Why?"

"I'm trying to find him."

"Charlotte, I think you can do better."

What did he mean by that? Did he want more of an explanation? Wait. He didn't mean… "Are you talking about romantic interest? No. *No*. I'm trying to find him to get information about his connection to Elliot, that's all."

Simon laughed. He swirled his hands on the surface of the water to stay afloat. "Good, 'cause I'm pretty sure he's gay, anyway. Wouldn't want you to get your hopes up."

"Really? Why do you think that?"

He shrugged. "Intuition, I guess."

There had to be more to it, but his expression gave nothing away. Oh, how nice it must be to have a face that couldn't be read as easily as a Denny's menu.

"Hey, Charlotte." Willow had appeared at my side from out of nowhere. It wasn't that she was quick or stealthy, but somehow, she managed to move from place to place without creating even a minute ripple in the atmosphere. Ghostlike. She looked down at Simon. "Honey, I went to see Teresa Corazon in the salon, and she gave me a sculpting pomade for your hair tonight."

She said the word *honey* like the substance was dripping from her tongue as she spoke.

"Perfect."

"You doing Elvis?" I asked him.

His laughter gurgled and bubbled beneath the surface. "Not even close."

"It's a surprise, Charlotte. You'll just have to wait and see."

"I'll be waiting with bated breath."

"By the way, what were y'all talking about?"

"I'm looking for Sensei Machigau."

K.B. JACKSON

Willow pursed her lips. "Oh, Charlotte. Bless your heart." Her words were heavy with disapproval, less like honey and more like that bitter barium liquid I had to drink prior to a CT scan to diagnose my reflux. "I know it can be difficult to be alone, but there are a lot of fish in the sea. You don't have to reel in the minnows."

Why did people keep assuming I was romantically interested in the sensei, a.k.a. Joe from Philly? The next time I was in front of a mirror I'd have to look for markings of desperation on my forehead.

"I promise you. I'm not interested in him. I need to ask him a few questions."

Willow fanned herself. "Thank goodness."

"What makes you think the ninja dude had a connection with the chef, anyway?" Simon asked. "He's new, right? I thought he was only onboard because they needed Japanese-themed entertainment. Although, whoever hired that guy should be ashamed. They couldn't find an actual Japanese person to do the demonstration?"

"Turns out he and Elliot knew each other. They were going to be business partners in Elliot's restaurant, so they must have known each other for a while. I haven't quite figured out the details."

"Why is that your business?" Willow asked. "It seems to me you should mind your own knitting."

"Mind my what?"

"No point in washing pigs, Willow." Simon splashed the water in front of him. "She's playing Jessica Fletcher. Charlotte, aren't you supposed to leave the investigating to

Mesnier? He seems like the type who wouldn't appreciate civilian interference."

I opened my mouth to protest being compared to a pig and an old woman but shut it when I remembered I was around the same age as Angela Lansbury when she originated the role. *Bugger.* "Is that your polite way of calling me a busybody?"

He grunted a laugh. "Maybe."

"Yeah, well, I'm gonna keep looking. If you guys see the sensei, let him know I'm headed down to Perseus and I'd really like to talk to him."

"Will do."

"And don't worry. I'll be sure to report anything I discover about the case to Xavier ASAP."

Simon sank a couple inches, covering his nose and mouth. Only his eyes and the top of his head were visible above the water he bobbed up again, he said, "Stay safe."

I waved at both of them and headed for the stairs to the lower level.

The theater was dark, Kuchi Sabishii had yet to open for lunch, the Italian restaurant was only open for dinner, and the cigar lounge was empty. That only left the casino.

I found Sensei Machigau hunkered down at the black-jack table with a half-empty highball glass and two small stacks of white and red chips. He was wearing white gloves. I'd never been a big gambler, and when I did go to Vegas, I preferred the slots, but even I knew that white chips were a dollar and red chips were five. My quick calculation came to about forty-seven dollars, give or take. Math wasn't my strong suit.

I slithered onto the stool next to him. "Hey." I nodded at the dealer.

The sensei slowly turned his head. His eyes were blood-shot, and his hair hadn't seen shampoo or a hairbrush in days. He muttered an expletive. "What do you want now?" He took a swig of his drink.

"Listen, Joe—can I call you Joe?"

"I'd prefer you didn't, but whatever." He sloshed the glass of liquor. "Just don't call me Joseph. That's reserved for my ma, and usually only when I'm in trouble."

"Are you in trouble?"

He set the glass onto the green felt and wiped the rim with his gloved fingers. "I dunno. Maybe." To the dealer he said, "We doin' this or what?" He placed five red chips in front of him. The table minimum was twenty-five dollars.

The man glanced at me.

"I'm just visiting."

He pulled four cards out of the deck sleeve one at a time. He placed Joe's cards face up—an eight of clubs and a six of diamonds—and gave himself two cards face down. He checked his cards, and then pointed at Joe's.

Joe stared at the cards. "Hit me."

The next card was a queen. Busted.

"Sorry, man." The dealer pulled Joe's stack of chips back and shoved the used cards into a slot.

Joe groaned. He was three dollars short of being able to play another hand. "Cash me out."

The dealer placed a twenty and two ones on the table.

Joe grabbed the bills and shoved them under the lapel of his gi. He grabbed his glass and threw back the remainder. He began to march off, but then he turned and pointed at me. "Come."

I followed him to the cigar lounge. I wasn't a huge fan of cigars. Gabe used to smoke them on occasion, and I detested the way the smell became embedded in his clothes, his skin, and his lips.

The good thing about the room, though, was it was quiet and private.

Joe grabbed two wrapped cigars from the free box. He unwrapped one and shoved it in his mouth and held one out for me.

"No thanks. I don't smoke."

"Suit yourself." He shrugged and picked up a cutter, which he meticulously wiped down with his gloves before removing them.

"I've never seen anyone clean a cutter."

"I'm a bit of a neat freak. I guess the clinical term is mysophobia. At least, that is, according to the psychiatrist who diagnosed me."

I thought back to all the times I'd seen him wiping things down and to the fact he'd been unwilling to shake my hand. Made so much sense in retrospect. "Can I ask you a question?"

He snipped the end of his cigar and lit it. After three puffs, he said, "I guess."

"What's with the sensei thing?"

"What do you mean? There's no sensei *thing*. I'm a

sensei."

"Well, like, yes, you may technically be a sensei, but don't you think the outfit and the, you know, theatrics, it's kind of disrespectful?"

"Disrespectful to who?"

"Whom." The librarian in me couldn't help it. "Culturally disrespectful."

His mouth fell open. "Culturally disrespectful! What are you talking about? I've devoted my life to learning about Japanese culture." He grabbed his left sleeve. "I'll have you know I received this gi as a gift from a top student of the great Nakayama in Tokyo in 1996. I'm not a poseur."

"I suppose there is a fine line between cultural appropriation and appreciation."

He scowled. "Not to mention that in Japan the idea of cultural appropriation doesn't really fly, as long as it's not done in a mocking or ignorant way or obsessively. I have found that Japanese people love that their culture is admired and respected globally."

"Okay, but you don't think wearing a gi 24/7 isn't a tad...obsessive? And the yin yang necklace? That's not even Japanese."

He touched the pendent. "First, while the yin yang may have come from China, it is global. Secondly, this is an *inyo* symbol. Similar meaning, but not the same." He blew a smoke ring. "I don't usually, but I've been hired to play a role on this cruise, and I intend to do it to the best of my ability."

"How did you get hired?"

"I applied."

"I understand that. I mean, what was your connection? How did you hear about the gig?"

His gaze narrowed. "Just come out with it."

"Did Elliot help you get the job?"

"Yes."

That was easy. "How well did you know Elliot?"

"Are you asking if we were lovers?"

"I wasn't, but since you brought it up…"

He fiddled with his pendant. "We were not. Not for lack of trying on my part."

"I didn't realize you were…or he was…"

Puff. "I am. For him it was all about how the encounter might serve his agenda. His sexuality wasn't labeled, but if it had been, it would have been opportunistic. He sure didn't love any of those biddies he was cavorting with." He flipped his blonde hair over his shoulder. "Honestly, I'm not sure he was capable of love. Probably the byproduct of his unpleasant childhood and mommy issues."

"He told you about that? About Florence?"

Puff. "Who's Florence?"

"The woman who died a few days ago."

"The suicide?"

"Maybe. Maybe not. Xavier isn't sure."

"Wait. Are you saying this Florence woman was Elliot's mother?"

"So it appears."

"Whoa." Puff. "That's wild. Did he know?"

"Yes, she told him. He wasn't happy about it. I guess

she'd offered to help fund the restaurant."

"Oh, that lady! Yeah. I remember him talking about her. I thought I just saw her yesterday. The one with all the wigs."

"No, that's Margaret. I guess she was also a possible investor. She's the one who told me about you being involved."

He screwed up his face. "Sorta."

"What do you mean, sorta?"

"I'm broke. I've got no money."

"How were you going to invest?"

He exhaled and a large plume of smoke filled the space between us. I waved my hand and coughed.

"Sorry. I just feel like a terrible person for what I'm about to say."

"No judgment."

He snorted. "Sure."

"I'm just trying to solve this case so that my husband's mistress and baby can move out of my suite."

"Huh. That's a new one." He inhaled. "Well, I may have given Elliot the impression I had resources to invest that I didn't."

"Why?"

He gave me a look that said, *come on now.*

"You lied to him about investing in his restaurant so that he'd get involved with you in other ways?"

"You could write greeting cards, you know? You're great with euphemisms. Just come out and say it. I was trying to con my way into his bed. Didn't work, though. Turned out it takes a con to know one."

"That must have been difficult, being rejected."

He jabbed his cigar toward me. "I didn't kill him if that's what you're suggesting. I cared about him, and I know he cared about me, as much as he was capable of caring about anyone other than himself. It just wasn't meant to be in this lifetime. Maybe in the next." His cheeks caved in as he took his next puff. There was a genuine sadness in his eyes. "What if his mom killed him? That Florence lady?"

"It's possible, I guess. And then she killed herself out of guilt and grief."

"It's a tough way to go, and kind of embarrassing, but hopefully she's at peace now."

"What do you mean, embarrassing?"

"Well, 'cause she was naked."

I tilted my head. "How did you know that?"

He furrowed his brow. "Not sure. I must have heard it somewhere."

That information hadn't been released. Very few people on the ship knew about Florence's open robe. Also, something about what he'd said had triggered a thought in my brain, but it had vanished as quickly as it had appeared.

Chapter Twenty-Eight

"FLORENCE WAS DEFINITELY murdered." I slapped my hands on Xavier's desk.

"And *bonjour* to you as well."

"I'm telling you; it wasn't suicide. How can you be so calm?"

He tented his fingers and leaned back in his leather chair. "I am calm because being in a frenzy never did anyone any good. Now. Tell me your theory."

"I just got done talking to Sensei Machigau, a.k.a. Joe from Philly—"

He raised his left brow. "You discovered his real name?"

I blinked at him. I jutted my chin. "I told you I'm good at solving puzzles and ferreting information."

"My apologies. I did not mean to offend."

"I'm indignant, not offended."

"These are the same things, *non*?"

"No, they are not. Indignant means you're being unfair. Offended means I'm being overly sensitive."

"I do not know this is true, but I will take your word for it. Continue, *s'il vous plait*."

I filled him in on everything I'd learned about Elliot.

"So then he says Elliot had mommy issues, and I brought up Florence. He acted like he didn't know who Florence was until I told him she's the one who died. So he says, *oh the suicide lady*. And I tell him maybe it wasn't suicide."

"I would prefer you do not share information pertaining to these cases, particularly with possible suspects."

"I didn't tell him anything, other than the fact it hadn't been determined."

"Which remains the status."

"Yeah. But get this. He starts saying how it was embarrassing that she was found naked."

"Did you tell him this?"

"I didn't! He claimed it was something he heard from someone else, but he couldn't remember who."

"Perhaps the employees have been talking."

"Maybe. Or maybe he heard it from her killer! Maybe he *is* her killer!"

"As I said, the status remains undetermined. It still may be suicide."

"Right. But it's not."

He sighed. "And how have you come to this conclusion?"

"She was naked."

"Only partially. She was wearing her robe. The only reason it was open was because she used the tie around her neck."

I vehemently shook my head.

"Why do you do this? This—" he mimicked me by jerking his head back and forth.

"Because that woman was vainer than Vanity Smurf and Narcissus combined."

Xavier suppressed a smile. "Vanity Smurf?"

"You know, the little blue guys." I la-la'ed a few bars of the theme song. "He was the one with the mirror."

"I know this. In France he is called *Schtroumpf Coquet.*"

"Interesting. But you're missing the point."

"Which is?"

"Florence was vain, but she was also self-conscious about aging. She'd already had multiple plastic surgeries. Someone like that could never be satisfied with their body enough to allow it to be on display, especially under those circumstances. That's why women are less likely to choose a violent method. Men hang or shoot themselves. Women try to go to sleep and never wake up."

"I am aware of the discrepancies in methods by gender, however, likelihood and certainty are two very different barometers."

"One more thing."

"Okay."

Judging by the intense way he listened to me—fully attentive and engaged—he was taking me seriously. Gabe would have derided my theories as fanciful. He always talked about my overactive imagination. Xavier appreciated my mind, even if he didn't appreciate my interference.

"Where's the note?"

"Not every person who takes their own life leaves a note. In fact, more than half do not."

"Sure, but in this case, wouldn't you think Florence

would want to explain? She'd spent more than four decades struggling with having given Elliot up, and when she finally found him and tried to connect with him, he rejected her. Maybe he didn't even give her an opportunity to tell her side of the story. If she killed him, wouldn't she want to explain that as well?"

"I do not know, Charlotte. Mental health and suicide are not my area of expertise, but I have always felt attempting to understand why someone does something irrational is an exercise in futility. You can make yourself mad."

"So you're leaning toward suicide."

"I did not say that. Your theory has merit, and I will consider it. There are forensic tests we are not equipped to do, so we must be patient and not jump to any conclusions before we have all the information."

I slumped in the seat. "I really believed I had figured this out."

"Let us follow your theory to its ultimate conclusion. Where do you see it leading?"

"Let's start with the presumption Kyrie Dawn didn't kill Elliot."

"Why?"

"Because that's the goal, to prove her innocent."

"That is your goal, not mine."

"Okay. But still, for the sake of this experiment, let's say Kyrie Dawn didn't do it, and we know Deacon couldn't have killed Florence, so we'll set him aside as a suspect in Elliot's death for the time being."

"I would not do that. These two things may be unrelated."

"I know you wouldn't do that, but this is my theory, so roll with it. We can pick it apart later."

"Fine."

"Okay. If Florence didn't kill Elliot and then herself out of guilt, and we believe she didn't kill herself from grief but that someone else killed her, we need to examine the motive. I also believe that the likelihood that there were two unrelated murders on this small ship of a mother and her estranged son is next to zilch. Zippo. Nada."

He smiled. "*Le rien.*"

"That too. So, we can assume the deaths are connected, probably that whoever killed Elliot also killed Florence. Not knowing the motive for Elliot's death makes it harder, but what if Florence knew something about whatever situation had gotten Elliot killed, and the person who killed him decided she had to die as well to silence her?"

The wheels turning in Xavier's head were so apparent in his expression I was surprised smoke didn't come out his ears. And then his eyelids flickered, like he'd had an epiphany.

"You bring up a good point."

I blinked. "And?"

"That is all."

"That is *not* all. You're holding out on me."

He crossed his arms, pursed his lips, and ran his tongue across his teeth. Then he exhaled.

He had a lot of nerve being exasperated with me, when I was trying to help him.

"What you said makes sense. Florence knew enough about Elliot to know what got him killed."

"Right."

"Someone would have to know that Florence knew those things."

"Okay?"

"Or…"

I wanted to jump across the desk and shake him. "Or what?"

"Or they just needed to *believe* Florence knew something that could point to the motive for Elliot's murder and ultimately to the perpetrator."

I thought back to that last dinner—Sakura Night—when Grace had revealed Florence's big secret. What had she said? Florence was quite proud of the fact she'd become Elliot's confidante.

Had she unknowingly made his mother another target for his murderer?

Chapter Twenty-Nine

"Now I remember why I don't have bangs." Jane brushed hair from her face. She'd secured her hair with clips in such a way so as to give the appearance of bangs without actually cutting it. She wore large gold hoops that swayed as she turned her head.

"You make a great Linda Ronstadt, though."

"Aww, thanks." She bloused her floral top. "It's already hot in here. I kind of wished I'd gone with the hot pants instead of bell bottoms."

"At least you look cute. I don't think anyone will understand who I'm supposed to be." I'd gone with a more obscure reference since Kelly Clarkson didn't have any iconic looks. My star-spangled dress and beaded necklace with a talisman charm—an American/idol—was bound to confuse most people. It was like the old adage: If you have to explain a joke, it's not funny. If you have to explain your lookalike costume, you're trying too hard.

"It was really nice of Pike to hang with Kyrie Dawn tonight so I didn't have to miss this," Jane said.

He'd arrived just before eight. I had expected Kyrie Dawn to be annoyed at having a babysitter, but she seemed thrilled with the company. I didn't blame her. He was an attractive, muscular guy. I'd thanked him for the favor, but he said it was his pleasure, and, judging by his cow-eyed mooning over Kyrie Dawn, I believed him.

Jane and I made our way through the lounge to an open booth. In front of us sat Rhodie, Grace, Willow, and Simon. From behind I couldn't determine who they were supposed to be dressed as. Rhodie had on a large blonde wig. Grace wasn't wearing a wig over her short hair, but she'd clipped in several strands of neon green. Willow wore a black hat, and Simon had clearly made use of the pomade she'd acquired for him from the salon. His brown hair was fluffed and coiffed into a pouf on the top of his head.

Jane leaned over and whispered, "Elvis?"

"You'd think, but he said no."

Margaret slid into the booth next to Jane. "Did I miss anything?"

Neither of us spoke for a moment, taking in the glorious sight before us.

Margaret wore a brown shag wig, a white cap, and a full yellow pantsuit.

"Big Bird?" Jane asked.

Margaret recoiled. "Big Bird! Rude. Big Bird doesn't even sing."

"Sure he does," Jane said. "'Wonderful Me.'"

If disdain were a weapon, Jane's face would have melted from Margaret's expression. "I'm Mick. Jagger."

She'd mentioned being a Rolling Stones groupie, so I should have figured she'd go for Mick Jagger, although Keith

Richards would have been an easier costume to identify. "You gonna sing 'Satisfaction?'"

"Of course not. Do you think I'm some sort of surface level fan? I'm doing 'Tumbling Dice,' and I'm going to win this competition."

I glanced at Jane to see if she was as confused by Margaret's statement as I was. "What competition? I think this is just for fun."

Margaret's expression soured. "You mean to tell me I'm getting up on stage to humiliate myself and there isn't even a prize?"

"If there is, I haven't heard it. And thank goodness, too, because I can't sing like Linda Ronstadt."

Margaret turned her attention from Jane to me. "So are you singing 'God Bless America' in the stylings of Kate Smith?"

"I'm not doing a patriotic song. It's a play on how my singer became famous." I held up the talisman.

She narrowed her gaze. "Is this like that conspiracy theory about celebrities doing some sort of voodoo or signing a contract in blood?"

"What? No! It's an idol. I'm dressed in American regalia, and I have an idol around my neck, you know, like the show. I'm the most famous singer from *American Idol.*"

"You sure don't look like Clay Aiken."

She was ridiculous. "Not Clay Aiken. Kelly Clarkson."

"The talk show host?"

My internal eyerolls threatened to emerge as external eyerolls. "Yes, but also the very first winner of the show. The woman has a song to fit every mood. If you're happy, if you're sad. If you're mad, if you want to dance. If you're breaking up or falling in love."

"Does your song fit your mood?" Margaret asked.

"It's called 'I Don't Think About You.'"

"Hmm."

Before Margaret could respond, Hawk appeared onstage.

"Hey, guys, so I was not scheduled to be your host tonight, but the person who was supposed to be here flaked, so you're stuck with me."

"But you're hot!" Grace yelled from the table in front of us. She already had two empty martini glasses in front of her.

"Why, thank you, ma'am. I guess how this is going to work is everyone has submitted their requested song, and we'll just go in that order. Unfortunately, some of you have selected songs that are too obscure for our catalog. Uh, Alexis Conner?"

A woman in the far corner of the lounge with her hair sculpted into waves on each side, flat in the middle, shouted, "Yes?"

"Unfortunately, our DJ has informed me that he does not have 'The More You Live, the More You Love.' The only Flock of Seagulls song he has is 'I Ran (So Far Away).' Are you okay with switching?"

"Ugh. Fine."

"Great. Also, Simon Strawbridge?"

Simon raised his hand. "Don't tell me."

"Yeah, man, sorry. Morrissey tends to be a bit of a downer at karaoke parties, so he doesn't have any. How about

R.E.M.?"

"I'd rather sing Barry Manilow."

"That's good because we have about fifty of his songs. 'Copacabana' always hits, I'm told."

Simon threw a dismissive hand.

Hawk jotted something on his notepad. "That's a no on R.E.M. and Manilow, I take it. Okay. First up is Margaret King singing 'Tumbling Dice' by the Rolling Stones. Let's give her a hand. It's not easy going first."

The crowd applauded, and Margaret preened.

"Break a leg," Jane told her.

"I was born to perform."

She wasn't lying. Margaret owned the stage. Her Jagger chicken strut was epic. Her vocals weren't great, but she made up for it with the performance aspect. By the time she'd sung the final repeated line of the chorus, the audience was on their feet.

Jane was mortified when Hawk called her name next. "How am I supposed to compete with that? The woman's a triple threat."

Margaret returned to our booth. "Knock 'em dead, kiddo."

My sister grabbed her throat. "I think I've developed sudden onset laryngitis."

"That's not a thing," I said. "You can do this. Just have fun."

She gave a passible performance of "When Will I Be Loved," and she even got catcalled by a gentleman in his seventies who was dressed like David Bowie in his Starman era.

"I'll love ya tonight, baby!"

His female companion—mid-eighties Madonna—whacked him on the arm.

Rhodie was up next, in full Dolly Parton. How she managed to enhance a small C cup into overflowing DD cleavage was a feat in itself. Her version of "Here You Come Again" wasn't half bad. Was she singing from personal experience about a man who came and went in her life, or was it just a song she liked? Was she singing about her husband, Bubba? Hard to imagine she felt so poetic about Bubba, but anything was possible.

Grace's green hair was an ode to Billie Eilish—a surprising choice for a woman in her forties—and her song selection "Everything I Wanted" was a poignant reminder that what we see on the surface rarely shows who a person is behind the mask. I made a mental note to look up the lyrics, because it seemed like there was a message in there.

I wondered the same about Willow's song. Her outfit—black hat, black sunglasses, red lipstick, and a T-shirt that said NOT A LOT GOING ON AT THE MOMENT—was familiar to me as iconic Taylor Swift, even before she began singing "Look What You Made Me Do."

Could it be that this was a confession of sorts?

I was relieved to have my name selected last. The lounge crowd had begun to shrink thirty minutes prior, so I had fewer people to view me embarrassing myself.

It was important to me that I select a song with meaning. I guess that's why I was reading into the choices of Grace and

Willow, assuming they might have done the same.

I closed my eyes as the first piano notes played, I opened my eyes, I looked into the darkness at the back of the lounge, focused on what I couldn't see, and allowed my heart to speak.

"I Don't Think About You," told the story about what happens in the aftermath of a relationship where you've put your hopes and dreams into another person and then realize they were unworthy of your trust or your faith. How lost that can leave you, adrift at sea. But then you learn about yourself, who you are, and what you're capable of becoming, what you're capable of overcoming. And that's when you're free to move on, to take risks, to remake yourself into someone you can feel proud to have looking back at you in the mirror.

It felt like an anthem for me.

I thought about the things I read in Miriam's diary, and wondered how many of her regrets were directly correlated to trusting the wrong men. Why was that habit so difficult to break? Was it even possible? Was there someone out there for me who wouldn't abuse my trust and would I know him if I met him?

I couldn't say whether my pitch was on key, if I hit the notes, or got all the words right. I just knew I felt the lyrics to the depths of my soul.

I hadn't allowed myself that kind of public vulnerability since Gabe's funeral. I was exposed. It should have been terrifying, and yet somehow it was the most exhilarating moment I'd experienced in a very long time.

When I finished, the room was deadly silent. Immediate self-consciousness rose within me. What had I done? Had I made a fool of myself? Why did I let myself be seen that way?

And then there were cheers. Whoops. Applause.

In the front row light reflected off Willow's cheeks, her tears glistening. Jane was on her feet, stomping and shouting my name.

I'd put my heart on display, and it had resonated with the audience. It didn't matter whether it was vocally great. It was authentic.

In the corner Xavier was standing with his arms folded. He stared at me like a museum curiosity. His gaze was so intense I had to look down at my feet.

"What a way to end the night!" Hawk joined me on-stage. "As you make your way out, don't forget to tip your fantastic bartender Cortes in the back. If you enjoyed having me as your host tonight, feel free to show it monetarily as well."

The remainder of the audience streamed out of the theater. Jane waited for me to climb down from the stage, and Xavier stayed by the back door.

"Char, I knew you could sing from when you were in choir back in high school, but that was something else. I felt every word of that down into my soul."

"Thanks. I haven't sung in public since the talent show senior year. I thought I'd hate it, but I enjoyed it."

"You should do it more often." Xavier walked down the steps toward us.

My body buzzed, and I battled between wanting to run

away and hide, burst into tears, or hug him. I tamped down the urge to reject or diminish his compliment, settling on a modest *thank you.*

The three of us left the theater and headed toward the elevator.

As we passed the cigar room, Jane grabbed her right ear. "Oh, shoot, I must have dropped one of my hoops. Wait here. I'll be right back."

"I would try to guess who she is costumed to impersonate, but my knowledge of American pop music is limited."

"Linda Ronstadt. Was she known at all in France?"

"Of course. I was about eight years old; my mother bought a retrospective album of hers that she played often. Instead of black, the vinyl was a brilliant indigo color."

"That's cool." I attempted to lean casually against the cigar room door, but it was not fully shut, so it opened, thrusting me backward into the room.

Xavier reached out to grab my hand to keep me from falling, but he was too slow. I landed on my bum and squawked.

"Charlotte, are you alright?"

I rubbed my palms, which stung from impact. "Yeah, that just hurt."

He offered his hand, and I took it. As he pulled me to standing, I caught sight of something in the dim corner of the room where I'd been visiting with Sensei Machigau earlier.

"Oh no." I closed my eyes, willing them to see something different when they reopened. No luck.

"What is it?" He squinted to look in the direction I was pointing. "*Mon Dieu.* Not again."

Slumped in the very chair where I'd left him several hours earlier was Sensei Machigau, a.k.a. Joe from Philly. A cigar still hung from his flaccid lips. His eyes were wide open, and his arms hung limp at his side. His flaxen hair was disheveled, and his orange-tinted skin had paled to apricot.

"My mom always said smoking could kill you," I said. "But I don't think this is what she meant."

Chapter Thirty

JANE AND I stumbled into our suite, shell-shocked. Kyrie Dawn and Pike quickly moved away from each other on the sofa. I didn't have it in me to contemplate what we'd just walked in on.

"How was karaoke?" Kyrie's voice was strained and two octaves higher than normal.

Pike wiped his forehead.

Jane clucked. "Char killed it, but someone killed the sensei."

Pike jumped from the sofa. "What?" His eyes darted around the room. "I gotta go. Where's my phone?"

Kyrie Dawn pulled her mouth. "Uhhh, it might be in Jane's room."

His gaze widened, and he hustled into the other room.

"Really, Kyrie Dawn? In my bed? I have to sleep in there."

"What do you mean?"

Her faux doe-eyed innocence fooled no one, especially not Jane. "Save it. Where's Quinton?"

"He's sleeping in the portable crib in Char's…uh…Charlotte's room."

Pike emerged holding up his phone. "Found it. I missed three calls. I gotta get down to—wait. Where am I going?"

"The cigar room. Xavier's down there, and he'd already gotten ahold of Lonnie by the time we left."

Pike turned to Kyrie Dawn. "I'll, uh, catch you later, okay?"

"Sure." Her smile was strained. "You know where to find me." She held up her hands in a *whatever* gesture.

I slipped off my shoes and dropped onto a chair. "What the hell is going on around here? Is this ship cursed? Haunted? There are less per capita murders in downtown Seattle."

Jane sat next to Kyrie Dawn on the sofa. "It's the money. It's got to be. The three major motives for murder are money, love, and revenge. It's more likely for money to be a motive when people have a whole lot they're trying to hoard or very little and they're trying to survive. There's a lot of money on this boat."

Kyrie Dawn scrunched her nose. It was annoyingly adorable. "I dunno. I think I'd stick with the love motive. Elliot was a playboy, and he either slept with the wrong chick and she killed him or her jealous husband did."

"I'd lean that direction, too, if it weren't for the fact that we now have *three* victims."

"Wait, I thought Florence killed herself."

"I don't think so. I was talking to Joe—Sensei Machigau—earlier today, I realized she would have never allowed for her body to be on display in such an unflattering way." I paused. "Hard to believe I was the last person to see him. Dr. Fraser said it looked like he'd been dead for hours. I guess people don't use the cigar room that often. Something about the scene felt wrong, but I can't put my finger on it."

"How did it happen?"

"They're not sure yet. There was no obvious wound."

Jane sat up. "The cigar!"

"What about it?" I asked.

"I thought it was a whole roomful of cigars," Kyrie Dawn said.

"The cigar in his mouth that had barely been smoked, the way he looked...I'll bet that cigar was dipped in the same poison that killed Elliot."

Kyrie Dawn gasped and covered her mouth.

"If that's true, it bodes quite well for your defense," I pointed out.

"I didn't want someone else to die to prove my innocence." Her voice was timid, cracking with emotion.

Her statement caught me off-guard. For so long I'd painted her as this one-dimensional villainess, the homewrecker, cavalierly creating devastation wherever she went. Selfish. Amoral. But if she were those things, she probably wouldn't be grieving since this death exonerated her. On the contrary, she exhibited empathy and survivor's guilt over how her redemption was at the expense of someone else's life.

Dammit. It was so much easier to despise her.

"So, Pike, huh?" I raised my left eyebrow. "Can't say I blame you."

Her cheeks flushed. "I swear I didn't mess around in your bed, Jane. We were only in there briefly, just a little making out. Nothing major."

Jane dismissed her with the wave of a hand. "It's fine. Just try to keep it PG. I have to sleep on those sheets."

"How long has it been going on?"

"It hasn't. I mean, we flirted a bit when I'd come aboard with Gabe, but I flirt with pretty much everyone. It's part of my personality. It never went anywhere, and I never cheated on Gabe. We were devoted to each other."

The implications of her statement in terms of what it said about my relationship with Gabe seemed to be lost on her. It was a twisted version of fidelity. Within their affair, they were faithful to each other. It was like when they were on the ship, the outside world—including me—didn't exist.

"Why do you think so many of the crew believed something was going on between you and Elliot?"

"Well, for starters, if you threw a quarter, it would be easier to hit a woman who had a thing with Elliot than one who hadn't. People assumed since he'd make passes at anything with boobs and his success rate was quite high, I was one of them. Truth is, I was immune to his so-called charms. I've spent my entire adult life—"

"All thirty minutes of it."

"Jane, don't be snarky." How did I get to the place where I was defending my husband's mistress against my own sister?

Kyrie Dawn gave a sad smile. "We could be friends, Jane. Despite what I did, I'm a loyal friend, and I can be lots of fun."

Jane shifted on the sofa. "I can't be friends with you as

long as Charlotte can't be friends with you."

Kyrie Dawn looked down at her hands in her lap. "Understood. Anyway, like I was saying, I've spent my entire life—"

"I might."

She jerked her head to look at me. "What?"

"I might be able to be friends with you. Just not yet. Not now."

"Of course not." She tried to suppress a smile. Her eyes welled with tears. "It doesn't have to be now. But maybe someday…"

"Maybe someday," I repeated. "So, what were you saying?"

"Huh? Oh, uh, just that I've met a lot of guys like Elliot. Everybody always said how charming he was. I didn't think so. I saw right through him, and he knew it. Charm doesn't ooze. Real charm glows from within. It seeps through the cracks like a ray of light, not like toxic waste. And frankly, I've always been a sucker for the nerds. I can't explain it."

"Nerd whisperer," Jane said.

Kyrie Dawn laughed. "Exactly. I don't want to be with a man who's prettier than me. That's too stressful. It's okay if he's smarter, though. I can learn stuff from him. I learned a lot from Gabe. Charlotte, you're super smart. You guys must have had lots of great conversations."

Did we? I had to think about it. "When we were first dating, absolutely. Over time, though, it felt like we ran out of things to talk about." I debated whether to share a piece of information that might ease her burden a bit. Part of me wanted her to understand more, another part was disinclined to set her free from all the guilt I could heap on her. Maybe saying the words out loud would set us both free.

"We weren't compatible. Gabe and me. I've no doubt eventually our marriage would have ended on its own. In many ways, it already had, I just didn't realize it."

Her mouth formed an *O* of surprise, followed by a reticent smile that morphed into a broader one. Unburdened. Relief. Freedom. A gift for both of us.

"He said something similar, but I chalked it up to him justifying what we were doing. I wish I could say I was so naïve I believed it, but I didn't really think of you at all. It was easier to compartmentalize it. Like a box up on a high shelf that I didn't want to have to consider. Sometimes he tried to bring the box down off the shelf and set it on the table in front of me, but I stopped him. Eventually, we stopped even mentioning the box, pretending it wasn't there."

"I take it I'm the box in this metaphor?"

"Well, you were *in* the box."

"I see. I guess both of us dehumanized the other to a certain extent. If I could keep you one-dimensional, it would be easier to make you the villain, and I could continue to play the role of victim."

"In my scenario, you were the villain who kept Gabe, Quinton, and me from being a family. It was the only way I could live with what we were doing to you."

"It takes more than one person to make a marriage work, and it takes more than one person to ruin it. I own my part, and I know you've done enough penance for your part. As for Gabe, well, he'll never get the chance to apologize to either of us for his part."

"Sometimes I wish you weren't so nice to m—" She was interrupted by an insistent knock.

"Geez, chill out." Jane walked over to the door.

Xavier marched into the living room with a pale Pike on his heels.

"What's with the charge of the light brigade?" I asked.

Xavier's expression told me it wasn't the time for jokes.

"Kyrie Dawn, you're coming with me."

"Why? What's going on?"

Pike was near tears, but his jaw clenched angrily as well. "How could you?"

"How could I what?"

Something about her tone rang false. Nervous. Oh no.

"What did you do?" I turned to Xavier. "What did she do?"

"She left."

"What do you mean, she left?"

"We have CCTV footage of her sneaking into the stairwell while you were at karaoke."

"That can't be. Pike was here."

Pike's mouth tightened. "I briefly fell asleep. She probably drugged me!"

"I did not!"

"And then she seduced me. Probably just another distraction."

Kyrie Dawn stood and reached out to him, but he recoiled. "Pike, you can't believe that I would—"

"Please," I begged her. "Please tell me this isn't true. You couldn't possibly be that dumb."

She gave a hard swallow. "I'm not dumb. I just needed to get something from my room."

"You don't think it's dumb—not to mention reckless— to risk your ability to be with your son instead of that tiny room in the security office. For what? What could you possibly have needed so badly you would jeopardize everything to get it?"

She chewed on her bottom lip. "It's personal."

I wanted to shake her, and, from his posture I could tell Xavier did too. "I've set aside all my own issues with you to help, and this is how you repay me? By sneaking around and then stonewalling? I can't help someone who refuses to help themselves. You know what you've done, right? You've robbed yourself of an alibi for Sensei Machigau's death."

"I didn't know anyone would kill him, so how could I know I needed an alibi?"

Jane gave a haughty laugh. "The whole point of you staying with us was to give you access to Quinton *and* to make sure your whereabouts were accounted for at all times!"

Her mouth trembled. "I didn't think anyone would notice."

"If you needed something, Jane or I would have gotten it for you."

"I just…I couldn't have you do that."

My scalp tingled. A hot flash flared within me. Damn. "It was something to do with Gabe, wasn't it?" She refused to make eye contact with me. There was my answer. Or was it? Maybe it was a ruse to distract me from what she'd really been doing. "The dumb blonde thing never played with me. You're smarter than you let on. Conniving might be a better term. Maybe you've been playing me the whole time, using Quinton to tug at my"—I glanced at Jane—"*our* heart-strings, when in actuality you're a cold-blooded murderer. Maybe all those rumors about you and Elliot were true."

"They weren't! I swear they weren't!"

"Xavier, please get her out of here. I can't stomach the sight of her."

Grim-faced, he took Kyrie Dawn by the arm. "It did not have to be this way."

"Char, please!"

"Don't call me that," I said through gritted teeth. "I defended you. I tried to exonerate you. You manipulated me. Never again."

As she was escorted out of the suite with Xavier on one side and a fuming Pike on the other, she called out, "It's in the diaper bag. I'm sorry."

Jane placed a hand on my shoulder. "Are you okay?"

"No." I rose from the chair and walked into my room where Quinton's breathy sleeping sounds filled the air with calm. He had no idea what had just transpired or that when he awoke his mother would be gone. Heartbreaking. The diaper bag was unzipped and sitting on the bed. I pushed aside the diapers, formula canister, cloths, wipes, and toys. Digging around in the bag, I tried not to think about what it was used for and what might be lurking. After a minute, my hand touched something cold. Round. Metallic. I pulled out the item and stared at it.

Resting in my hand was a locket on a chain. The locket was gold and about the size of a half dollar, maybe even larger.

I recognized it. Gabe's grandmother had gifted it to him just before she'd passed away. It had been given to her by his grandfather on the night of their wedding. I'd overheard her telling him he should pass it on to me. He never did.

I wedged my fingernail between the two parts to pry it open. Gone were the photos of Gabe's grandparents.

Inside on the left was a tiny photo of Gabe, Kyrie Dawn, and newborn Quinton. I drew it close to my face. Gabe had never looked so happy in all the years I'd known him. He hadn't even smiled that big at our wedding.

On the other side was an inscription.

To KD, the mother of my son and the love of my life. G

Ouch.

Chapter Thirty-One

"SHE WASN'T LYING." I kept my voice low to not wake Quinton sleeping peacefully in the portable crib.

Jane stood in the doorway. "What was it she went to get from her room?"

"A locket. A gift from Gabe. It's engraved. He called her the love of his life."

Jane muttered an expletive under her breath. "That's why she didn't want to ask you to get it for her."

"That, and the fact it was his grandmother's."

"Geez, Gabe. Twist the knife, why dontcha?"

"She was trying to protect my feelings, and it got her into trouble."

"She got into trouble because she was too impatient to be exonerated. We'll be stopping in Kushiro on Thursday. Tonight, we cross the International Date Line, so we skip a whole day. If she'd waited a few more days, she'd have been able to get it."

"Maybe."

"So, what now?"

"Now, we go to sleep. Tomorrow, we regroup and figure out how to solve these murders without getting ourselves killed in the process."

⚓

"GAH!" QUINTON CLAPPED his hands and then flung them in the air.

Gah was right. Spotlights shone onto the stage of the theater. A large circle about ten feet in diameter, demarcated by bags of rice. In the center of the circle stood a large man—about six foot two and upward of three hundred and fifty pounds—wearing nothing but a black canvas loin cloth and a manbun.

"I think I'm in love," Jane said.

"Really? I never figured you for the beefy type."

"Think about it. For the first time in my life, I'd feel petite. It wouldn't matter how much I ate; I'd always be the one with the small appetite."

She had a point, but I had no desire to encourage her line of thinking. "You know they don't wash their gear, right?"

"Yeah, I think it's considered unlucky. The last thing you want is an unlucky sumo wrestler roaming through the house."

Jane pushed the stroller to an open table. Next to us, the fair-haired federation—Rhodie, Grace, and Willow—were already several drinks in, judging by the many empty glasses on the table. None of them seemed like jolly drunks, and the tension was so thick it was palpable. Simon had the appearance of someone who'd been brought against his will.

Between bouts of forlorn stares, he'd occasionally dart longing eyes toward the exit.

Margaret wore a royal blue silk long-sleeved kimono, a full face of white geisha makeup, and a black *katsura* wig.

I leaned closer to her. "You look fancy."

Beneath the powder on her face, her cheeks reddened. "I got my nights mixed up."

"Ah." Kimono Night was scheduled for the following evening.

Hawk handed the man in the center of the circle a microphone.

"Ladies and gentlemen, my name is Kohaku Sashi," he said with a thick Japanese accent. He slid into the splits and the crowd oohed. He popped upright with the deftness of a man half his size. "I am retired sumo, and tonight I will share with you the many beautiful things of this sport. But first"—he removed the topknot from his head, revealing his fuzzy scalp—"because I am no longer competing, my head is shaved. This was done in a ceremony at my retirement."

Margaret scratched under her own wig.

"This cloth I wear is a *mawashi*. Depending on many factors, the mawashi could be canvas or silk, it could be white or black. The most important thing is that it be wrapped correctly, because in a match, the *mawashi* will likely become ma-wedgie."

Hoots of laughter and applause erupted from the audience.

"The circle I am standing inside is called a *dohyo*. Standard size is 4.55 meters, or just under fifteen feet. Because space is limited here, we have shrunken the *dohyo* by a third. Typically, it would be mounded and not flat. Now, a sumo warrior's lifestyle is highly regulated. I will not go into the details here, but you can do the google."

More laughter.

"Sumo has been in existence for two thousand years. Originally it was a ceremony for the emperor."

Kohaku continued to talk about how sumo had evolved over time. I glanced at the table next to us and caught Willow staring at me. Her eyes were cold, and in the dimness of the theater, appeared nearly black. I felt her animosity linger long after she turned away.

What could possibly have caused her attitude toward me to shift so severely? I'd done nothing to her, and her demeanor was completely out of character. Where had Mint Julep Willow gone, and who was this scowling, bitter Negroni in her place?

"Before we begin this evening's festivities, the staff will be serving traditional sumo hot pot. The dish is called *Chanko Nabe*, and it is a stew made of chicken, vegetables, and tofu."

Servers brought out trays of soup in blue-and-white porcelain bowls and handed them out to all the guests.

"Wow, this is delicious. I could live on this," Jane said.

"You'd have to if you lived with a sumo."

"Can they even get married?'

"It depends." Kohaku had appeared at our table. "In the lower four divisions, for the *rikishi*, life is much more difficult than for the higher two divisions. *Sekitori* can get married and receive a generous salary. One is like heaven and the other is hell."

"Which were you?" Jane asked.

"What is the number one rule of sumo?" He gave her a wry smile.

She laughed. "Never talk about sumo."

He touched the tip of his nose. "*Sonotori*. Exactly."

After the meal was finished and the dishes had mostly been cleared, Kohaku returned to the stage.

"Who is ready for a demonstration?"

The crowd whooped and cheered.

"I need a volunteer."

Several hands went up, including Grace and Rhodie. Simon and Willow's hands were firmly in their laps, but still Kohaku called on Willow.

"You, ma'am."

She touched her chest. "Me? Oh, no, no thank you. I didn't raise my hand. My friends did."

"Do you not want to try? Your face tells me you would like to let off a little steam."

"No thank you, I'm fine."

He narrowed his gaze but didn't press the issue. Instead, he selected a man sitting in the front row with his wife. He took the man backstage, and when they reemerged, the man was wearing an inflatable sumo costume. It even included some sort of cap designed to look like a topknot. The audience roared with laughter as the man bumbled around onstage. He reminded me of the Weeble toys from the seventies. They were egg-shaped figures, and the commercials featured the catchy slogan WEEBLES WOBBLE, BUT THEY DON'T FALL DOWN! Although, I gave this guy a 90 percent chance of going ass over teakettle and not being able to right himself.

Kohaku demonstrated several sumo maneuvers before bringing the man's wife onstage. He got her suited in another costume, and the two of them rolled around like hamsters in balls. They were both laughing so hard I worried one of them might have a coronary. Considering the median age of residents was around sixty, it wasn't an unfounded concern.

Quinton didn't like the noise, so Jane offered to take him back to the suite and put him down for the night. I told her I'd go with them, but she said she could see how much I was enjoying the show and practically ordered me to stay.

When the show finished about twenty minutes later, I felt light from such a fun evening. For that brief moment, everything else drifted into the background.

I approached Kohaku and told him how much I had enjoyed the show. He told me I should visit his kyogen theater in Kyoko where he performed comedy sketches. And then he winked.

Jane would be so jealous.

I practically floated to the elevator but came back to earth when I caught sight of the horde waiting to ride it.

It didn't hurt to take the stairs. After all, the stew we'd eaten was designed to help sumo warriors keep their figure, so the extra cardio was probably a good idea anyway.

I took the aft stairs, since there was a streaming crowd

heading for the other staircase. It was funny. People often traveled in droves, even when there was another way with less congestion. No one seemed to have considered using the alternative staircase.

About one and a half flights up, I was already getting winded. Below me, a door screeched open and slammed shut. I wasn't the only one with the bright idea to use the back stairs after all. The footfall was loud but not excessively heavy. It was faster than the pace I was going, and I was losing steam with every step.

The pounding became more insistent and was accompanied by a swishing sound. It reminded me of all the windbreaker sweatsuits I wore in the early nineties.

I paused to catch my breath and peeked over the railing.

"What the—"

The figure below me looked up. They wore one of the inflatable sumo suits, along with the topknot cap. In addition, their entire face was covered by a black cloth. The only part of them that was visible was their eyes, which looked dark in the dimly lit corridor.

As we made eye contact, we both froze in place. Their intentions toward me weren't clear, but I had no doubt they weren't good. My chest constricted, my heart raced, and I took off like I'd been shot out of a cannon. Below me, the swish-swishing grew louder, closer, and the footsteps more rapid. If I thought I could move quick enough, I would have pulled out my phone to call Jane. I'd also noticed previously that phone reception was spotty in the stairwell.

I had no idea what the sumo stalker might do to me once

they reached me, and I didn't want to find out. I got to the seventh floor and grabbed the handle, but the door was jammed. I yanked again, but nothing happened.

I ran up to the eighth floor, but that door wouldn't budge either. If I survived the encounter, my next order of business would be to yell at whoever was in charge of maintenance.

Thankfully, the ninth-floor door opened after only a couple pulls. The aft stairwell opened onto the helipad, less desirable than a residential floor where someone might hear me scream.

I needed to get to the other side of the ship as quickly as possible. The door to the Azure lounge was at least thirty feet away, and my legs were starting to cramp from running up three flights of stairs. I couldn't imagine how difficult it would have been in a full sumo costume, even if it was inflated with air. They had to be in pretty good shape to do it.

I was just a few feet from the entrance when the door slammed open behind me. I glanced back, and the sight of a winded sumo ninja (or was it ninja sumo?) sent a spark of hope and a bolt of terror through me. I inhaled all the oxygen my lungs could carry and willed my wobbly legs to move. My quads ached and my calves cramped, but I forced myself to keep going.

Relief washed over me as I flung myself through the doorway and into the hallway outside the lounge. A couple passing by gave me a strange look, but I didn't care. The menacing parade float chasing me would never follow me inside.

I made it to the elevator and pushed the button, keeping an eye out for anyone—or anything—that might come through the door.

When the elevator opened, Willow was inside smoothing her hair. She reared her head back in surprise. "Oh, Charlotte. I didn't expect to see you. How did you get up here so quickly? I thought you were still down in the theater." She smiled.

Her Negroni persona was inexplicably gone as quickly as it had come. Not only was she not scowling at me, she was downright friendly.

"Long story. Are you going up or down?"

"Out. I need a drink."

A drink sounded great after what I'd just endured. "Me too."

"Bless your heart. Care to join me?"

"I would, but I need to do something. Maybe I'll come back in a bit, and if you're still here, we'll have that drink."

"Sounds good."

I held the door for her, and once she was out, I stepped into the elevator. The fourth-floor button was illuminated. Was she going back down to the theater and changed her mind when she saw me?

I pressed the third-floor button. As the doors closed, I glimpsed Willow watching me.

Chapter Thirty-Two

"WHAT DO WE know about Willow Strawbridge's relationship with Elliot?" I stood in the hallway outside Xavier's berth.

"And good evening to you as well."

"Can I come in?" I looked each way to make sure none of the crew saw me lurking in the hallway outside his room like a creep. Or a groupie.

He widened the door opening for me to pass through. "As far as I am aware, we have heard nothing about a relationship between Willow and Elliot. Why?"

I indicated the sofa. "Is it okay if I sit?"

"By all means." He sat in a chair across from me.

"Someone just tried to…well, frankly, I don't know what they were trying to do. I was chased in the stairwell by a ninja sumo."

He blinked at me three times. "Ninja…sumo?"

"Or sumo ninja. Either way, they were after me."

"Tell me what happened."

I relayed the story, and to his credit, Xavier only laughed once, and he tried to suppress it. The further into the story, the less amused he became. By the end, he was visibly upset.

He rose and walked over to pick up his cell phone. "This is Xavier Mesnier. I am going to need someone working on the aft stairwell doors on floors seven and eight tonight. They are jammed or something, and it is a safety hazard." He rubbed the back of his neck. "No, it must be tonight. *Oui.* Thank you."

He paced for a minute and then stopped with a curious expression.

"What?"

"So, you believe that Willow Strawbridge may have been the one chasing you?"

"I don't know. Maybe. I mean, it seemed like she was coming down in the elevator, which could have happened if she ran from the helipad up to the tenth floor and got on there. The button for the fourth floor was pushed, so maybe she was putting the suit back where it belonged."

"Did she have the suit with her?"

"I mean, I didn't see it. How compact can those suits be folded?"

"How would I know this?"

"True."

"Help me understand why you believe Willow would come after you."

"It's strange. I guess it never occurred to me that she might have been romantically involved with Elliot. I was more focused on the other ladies. Maybe it's because she and Simon seem joined at the hip. Maybe it's because she's so sickly sweet." I paused. "Except tonight. I caught her giving me the stink eye. I can't imagine what I could have done to have her upset with me. Then, when she saw me in the elevator, she was back to her syrupy self."

"That is not the most compelling argument."

"Well, how about this...her song choice for karaoke was 'Look What You Made Me Do' by Taylor Swift."

"I do not know this song."

"Well, the gist of it is a woman who's been treated badly, but she's grown stronger and wiser, and karma is working in her favor, but against those who have wronged her."

"It sounds like there is more to Willow than it appears."

"That's what I'm saying."

"We should go upstairs and look around the theater and stage. See if we can find the suit that was taken."

"You mean you and me, not you and one of your officers, right?"

"*Oui.* They have their hands full with Deacon and Kyrie Dawn."

I tried to play it cool, but there was an extra spring in my step as we made our way up to the fourth floor. It was nice to feel useful and trusted. Gabe only trusted me to do the grocery shopping. He didn't even let me see the bills, much less pay them. One of the many ways he was able to hide both our financial status and the money he spent on his double life.

We took the stairs and had no trouble getting the door to open. Could it have been that my fear made me weak or panic kept me from being able to push through to the other side?

There was still a barrier and posted sign on the cigar

room letting residents know it was off-limits for the duration of the sailing. I said a quick prayer for Joe from Philly, aka Sensei Machigau, as we passed.

The theater was completely dark, but Xavier had thought to bring a flashlight. I hit the button for the light on my phone. The button was sensitive and conveniently located in the lower left part of the screen. I had a tendency to accidentally turn it on without realizing why people were staring at me. I walked through an entire shopping mall once with my phone light shining in the faces of everyone I came near. I only realized it when a child in a stroller covered their eyes and squawked, "Ow! It's so bright!"

In the dimness of the theater, the phone light was less effective.

"You take the tables. I will look on stage."

"Okay." I angled the phone toward the ground. "What exactly are we looking for?"

"Anything that seems out of place."

"Helpful." As I scanned the back row, my phone buzzed with a text from Jane.

"Isn't the show over?"

Whoops. I'd forgotten to update her.

"It is. I'm helping Xavier do a search of the theater. I'll explain everything when I get back. Shouldn't be too long."

"I should have clued into the possibility Willow was another one of Elliot's paramours. The woman is the embodiment of shoofly pie. No one's really that sweet."

Xavier stopped in center stage and squinted at me. "Did you say fly pie? A pie filled with flies?"

"Shoofly pie. It's a sticky sweet molasses pie. Although, come to think of it, that's Pennsylvania Dutch, not Southern."

"Americans are weird."

"You have no idea. Anyway, if I'd have been paying attention, I would have noticed the saccharine baby voice is a ruse to cover what she's really thinking. *Bless your heart.* Every time she said it, she was cursing someone out in her mind."

"You are jumping to many conclusions."

"Am I, though? Think about it. She's been flying under the radar this whole time. No one even intimated she might have been messing around with Elliot, probably because Simon was there, and that would have been tacky. Have you even checked her alibi for any of these deaths?"

"I have spoken with her, and she claimed she was with her husband."

"Convenient. Of course he'd cover for her."

"Would he?"

"What do you mean? Of course he would. Husbands and wives cover for each other."

"Think about it, Charlotte. Would he cover for his wife once he realized her possible motive for murder was that she was having an affair?"

I didn't know what to say to that. Our conversation had jarred something in my brain, but the thought evaporated as quickly as it had surfaced.

"I am going to check backstage," said Xavier. "They must be storing the costumes back there."

"Okay, I'll keep looking under these booths. You know, for a bunch of rich people, they're slobs."

"Money does not ensure good breeding, nor does it replace it. Also, you can have everything handed to you and still make terrible choices. Financial means and morality have nothing to do with each other."

He had a point. Privilege bias was a real thing, and I was often guilty of it. I hadn't grown up with a lot of money, but we'd been comfortable. Bernard, Jane, and I had new clothes and shoes every school year. We went out to dinner once a week—even if it was just to the local Mexican restaurant—and we'd usually get at least one of the hottest toys every Christmas. I knew the wealthy kids in my school, and while I never thought they were better than me, I was more likely to ignore their bad behavior than the kids I knew who came from the rougher parts of town. The ones whose moms worked two jobs and had a different boyfriend every week. The ones with older brothers labeled bad influences by parents and teachers. Unfair, but biases by nature were unfair.

"You wanna know what I think?"

My question was met with silence.

"Xavier?"

Still nothing.

"I guess you don't wanna know what I think."

Had he been offended by my comments? I couldn't think why, but then again, I knew very little about him, so it was tough to know what might bother him.

"Good chat."

I got down on my hands and knees and scoured the area under the table where Willow had been sitting with the other members of the blondie bunch, plus Margaret and Simon. My light glinted off something on the floor, but it was deeper under the bench. I wriggled my way farther under the table, willing away any sense of claustrophobia and trying not to think about what might have been ground into the carpet. The more I wedged myself under, the dustier it became.

I reached for the object, feeling around with my fingertips. "Got it!" I grabbed it, and it crumbled. I yanked my hand back. "Oh, gross! What was that, a crouton?" My whole body shivered in disgust. I took a deep breath and jabbed my arm under the booth once again. This time I managed to locate the item. It felt smooth on one side, rough on the other. I pulled it out and shined the light on it.

I gasped. "Oh. Oh, wow."

It was Sensei Machigau's *inyo* pendant.

That's what was wrong with the crime scene. Some part of me had noticed it was missing, but it was easier to see something that shouldn't be there than something that should.

"Oh fuuu—"

"My thoughts exactly."

I bonked my head on the underside of the table.

"Xavier?" It hadn't sounded like Xavier, but the alternative was unthinkable.

"I'll take that." The whispered voice could have been a woman or a man.

An arm reached under the table, but it wasn't any arm. It was the puffed-up arm of an inflatable sumo costume.

"Xavier!"

"He's preoccupied."

A large kitchen knife banged against the edge of the table, the tip of the blade inches from my face.

My mouth dried and it became difficult to swallow. "Is he okay?"

"For now. As are you, as long as you give me the rock."

What were my options? None of them seemed great. I could grab them around the leg, but the chances of getting stabbed in the process seemed high. Cooperation might get me out unscathed, but if this person had killed two—or possibly three—already, what was one more?

I decided to go with option three.

I tossed the pendant across the floor toward the stage.

"Argh!" the sumo ninja yelled.

As soon as they lunged for the pendant, I scrambled out from under the table. They turned and started chasing me, knife out.

"Help!" I yelled. "Anybody!"

I was halfway to the door when the sumo ninja caught me from behind, yanking my hair and pulling me back. I felt the blunt edge of the knife at my throat. Their breath was heavy in my ear, and their scent was familiar.

Sweet tobacco.

Chapter Thirty-Three

"SIMON. LET ME go. Please."

He grunted. "Not Simon."

"Whatever you say." I struggled against his grip, but he held me tight against him. Perhaps if I got him talking, Xavier would have enough time to break free from whatever was keeping him backstage. I said a quick prayer that he was still alive and he could rescue me before I got bonsaied. "I thought for sure it was Willow, but it makes sense now that it was you. You found out that she was having an affair with Elliot, so you killed him."

His laugh was harsh. "If only that were the worst of it."

He'd given up the ruse that he was anyone other than Simon Strawbridge. He wanted to talk about it. It must have been eating away at him, and he had no one to talk to about it. I could be that person.

"What do you mean?"

"It's bad enough she cheated on me. But with that grifter? She's a fool. Any woman who thought he loved them was a fool. She was the worst kind of fool, though. She was a fool with her heart *and* her head."

"How?" I grunted the word since his thumb was digging

into my Adam's apple. Wait. I didn't have an Adam's apple, right? Would I ever get a chance to google what women called their non-Adam's apple?

"She let him con her out of *my* money. Like it wasn't bad enough she was running around on me, but then to give him money from our bank account to fund his stupid restaurant."

I wriggled enough to swallow and speak. My back swished against the sumo costume. "She wasn't the only one. I think he was getting money from several women, none of whom knew about the others."

"So what? Does that make it better? All these dumb women thinking that scoundrel cared one whit about them, throwing their husbands' cash at him in hopes of ...what? That he'd run away with them? To where? With what? He had not a single penny of his own to his name. Everything he had he scammed other people to gain. And the cherry on top? The money she gave him wasn't even ours to give!"

His knuckle dug deeper into my throat.

"Whose. Was. It?"

"I have these clients, right? They're investors, but they're not your average investor. They're not like my dad, who put a hundred dollars a week into IBM and Microsoft for thirty years and kept it there until the day he died. No, these guys are risk takers. Gamblers. They make big wagers, and they ride those waves until they crash or cash out. There's so much money moving around, and I'm good at what I do. I make the rich richer. So, every once in a while, I paid myself a little bonus."

I shifted to give myself some breathing room. "Lemme

guess. An off-book bonus?"

"My company is a little loose with the auditing. I was getting away with it. Until I wasn't. One of my clients caught on, and he was not happy. He isn't the kind you wanna mess with if you know what I mean. He's *connected*."

I did know what he meant, which begged the question: if it was the kind of client he shouldn't have messed with, why did he? He talked about Willow doing dumb things with money, but what was dumber than stealing from people that broke kneecaps as a warning and did worse if they didn't get their way?

"He wanted it all back plus interest. It was gonna wipe out my nest egg, but that was preferable to having my fingers broken or my tongue cut out of my mouth. I told him I had the money. I promised him I'd wire it later that day. That's when I discovered my tramp of a wife had ordered a cashier's check amounting to a quarter million dollars made out to Elliot Patenaude. I could have killed her with my bare hands."

Ironic. "And why didn't you? You're obviously capable of murder."

"Well, first, she didn't know I knew. Still doesn't, as a matter of fact. Second, it was the morning we were leaving for this cruise. I knew my client couldn't murder me while I was onboard the ship, and I also knew Elliot would be here. I figured I could get the money back and order the wire as soon as we landed in Yokohama."

"Did you confront him?"

"Of course I did. After the welcome reception. He said

the money was a gift and he didn't have to give it back even if he still had it, which he claimed he didn't. He said the money had already been invested in the restaurant."

"So you stabbed him with the poison dart?"

"Pretty clever, don'tcha think? Deacon had invited me to his secret fugu dinner, so I knew Elliot would be preparing it. There was no way in hell I was going to eat that fish. I've heard enough stories to know there's a reason chefs go through extensive training to learn how to prepare it properly. I snuck into the kitchen and cut off a small chunk of liver. They say that's one of the most poisonous parts. I thought about putting it in his food, but that ninja demonstration convinced me the dart was the way to go. Plus, I could kill two birds with one stone. Well, technically one bird was killed and the other would be framed for his murder."

"Your plan was to frame Sensei Machigau?"

"It was the perfect setup. I knew he was also investing in the restaurant, because Elliot had mentioned it the night before, and it was also painfully obvious the sensei had an unrequited crush on Elliot. All I needed to do was get the blow gun and a dart, which was easy enough. I figured his DNA would be all over the mouthpiece, so I planted the blow gun, but I never actually used it. I didn't want my own spit on there." He chuckled.

"One problem. Actually, two."

"Oh yeah?"

"Sensei Machigau never invested. He'd promised it to Elliot, but he didn't actually have the money. He was trying to con his way into a tryst."

"Clever. And what is the other problem?"

"There was no spit residue on the blow gun. You must have grabbed one he'd already sanitized. Turns out Machigau was a major germaphobe. Mysophobia, he called it. He was actually under psychiatric treatment for it. He was constantly cleaning everything, including his equipment."

"Huh. Well, good thing I got a bonus suspect."

"Kyrie Dawn."

"Don't act like you're not ecstatic your husband's mistress is getting sent up the river."

"I'm not, actually. She has a baby."

"Yeah, that's too bad. Oh, and Deacon got himself in trouble. I had nothing to do with that." His shrug released the pressure off my throat momentarily.

"But wait. What about the blonde hair that was found?"

"Oh, that was part of the genius of my plan to frame the sensei. I knew Margaret always brought a ton of wigs with her, so I grabbed the one that looked the most like his hair. Long, straight, and blonde."

"She said she was missing other wigs too."

"Yeah, I grabbed a purple one and a short brown one just so it wouldn't be obvious why they'd been stolen." He tapped my temple. "Smart, huh?"

"Mm-hmm."

"You never know where the cameras are, so I kept my head down and tried to look like every other blonde woman on this ship."

"How did you get him into the yoga studio?"

"Easy. I grabbed Willow's cell phone and texted him that

I—she—had a surprise for him. He was surprised, alright."

"Did you kill Florence too?"

"When I heard mention of the fact she'd become Elliot's confidante, I had no choice. Feel like I did that woman a favor, anyway. She was so miserable she would have done it herself eventually. I just pushed along the process."

The cold way he spoke about taking her life, and the value of it, sent a shiver down my back. Out of the corner of my eye, Jane appeared at the entrance to the theater. So far, Simon hadn't noticed her or the stroller she was pushing. Her eyes grew large, and she ducked into the shadows.

"And why Sensei Machigau, *Simon*?" I emphasized his name so that if I didn't make it out of the situation, at least Jane would be able to tell someone who'd done it.

"As I snuck out of the area where he'd prepared his performance and had stored all his supplies, he saw me. He was drunk, so I didn't know if he'd remembered until I ran into him last night. It seemed to be coming back to him, but he wasn't sure what was real and what was a liquor-induced hallucination. I brought a box of Arturo Fuente cigars on this trip, and I knew he was a connoisseur. It was painful dipping a three-hundred-dollar cigar in poison, but it was necessary. I couldn't have him connecting me to the blow gun."

I glanced at Jane, who had stepped forward just enough to be visible. She was ducking down over and over like she wanted me to copy her. Quinton let out a squeal of delight, and Simon jerked us both to face the direction of the sound. I dropped like a lead weight to the ground, and out of

Simon's grasp. A stinging sensation on my cheek was followed by warm liquid. I touched it with my fingers and pulled them away when I felt wetness. I looked at my fingertips and saw something dark.

I was bleeding.

An object came whizzing through the air, nailing Simon smack in the head. As it did so, an obnoxious alphabet rap echoed through the theater, along with the sound of tapping feet and the clatter of the knife hitting the ground. Pandy to the rescue.

"What the—"

The attack of Quinton's hip-hop red panda toy distracted Simon enough for me to scramble away.

I jumped onto the stage and ran behind it. A thumping sound in a storage closet was followed by Xavier calling my name. A chair had been wedged underneath the doorknob. I pulled it away, just as Simon bounded toward me, knife in hand.

Xavier thrust open the door, spotted the inflated sumo ninja, and lunged for him. In their scuffle, the knife must have penetrated the suit because it began to deflate with a whining noise. Xavier managed to get Simon in prone position, with his hands behind him. He forced his knee into Simon's back. He scanned the area.

"Hand me that rope."

I grabbed the gold rope holding back the burgundy velvet stage curtain. He tied the rope around Simon's hands.

"Do you have your cell phone?"

"I don't. I think I lost it somewhere in the theater. Probably under the table where I found Sensei Machigau's pendant. Apparently, Simon wanted a souvenir for his latest murder, but then he accidentally dropped it during karaoke night."

If Simon had muttered, "and I would have gotten away with it too if it weren't for these meddling sisters and the baby," I wouldn't have been surprised.

He didn't. He said, "I want my lawyer."

Jane and Quinton appeared backstage. Quinton had a tight grip on Pandy, who was thankfully silent.

"Is everyone okay?" Jane asked. "Oh my gosh, Charlotte! Your face!"

I'd forgotten momentarily about the gash on my cheek. The blood had begun to congeal.

"I will take Monsieur Strawbridge to the security office, and you will go find Dr. Fraser. Jane, accompany her, please. Charlotte, I will debrief you later."

"Are you sure you don't want us to go with you to make sure he doesn't get away from you?"

Xavier narrowed his gaze at me. "I think I can manage. Go, take care of yourself."

I suppressed the urge to hug him. There were witnesses, and he already had his hands full with Simon.

I watched them walk away, Simon looking shriveled in the deflated sumo costume and Xavier looking strong and in control. I exhaled my relief.

"Gah!" Quinton thrust Pandy at me. "Gah!"

I knelt down and looked him in the eye. "Are you offering Pandy to comfort me?"

Quinton pushed Pandy's nose, and the creature began to tap his feet and scream, "A is for awesome, auntie, and ace. B is for brave, beautiful, and bass. C is for cuddles, cupcakes, and cool. D is for daddy, doggies, and drool."

I hated the toy, but it had also saved my life.

I pushed the nose and the singing and dancing stopped. "Come on, kiddo, let's go get your mama."

"Mamamamamama."

"Yes, Mama," Jane said. "But first, Auntie Char needs her boo-boo fixed."

"Boobooboobooo."

I got to my feet. "You've still got it."

Jane flexed her biceps. "Right? Washington State softball pitcher of the year, 1985."

"Maybe you can teach Quinton to throw a ball, since his dad isn't here to show him."

She gave me a wistful smile. "I can't think of anything I'd enjoy more."

Surprisingly, neither could I.

Chapter Thirty-Four

A FTER A VISIT to Dr. Fraser, Jane and I entered the security office. Irving and Pike were behind their desks, Xavier was leaning against Pike's, and Kyrie Dawn was sitting in a chair.

"Oh baby!" Kyrie Dawn squealed. "It's over. The nightmare is finally over!" She ran over to Quinton, who looked a bit startled at the greeting.

She swooped him up in her arms and whirled him around. His belly laugh was contagious, and the rest of us joined in.

"You know," Jane said, "something happened that should have clued me in that there was more going on with Simon than meets the eye."

"Really? You never mentioned it." I said.

"It was the other night at dinner. Quinton dropped something on the ground, and when I bent over to pick it up from under the table, I saw that Simon was bouncing both his legs, like he was really worked up. The strange thing was, you'd have never known it from the way he was acting. He seemed cool, calm, and collected at the table, but underneath, he was a jittery mess."

"I remember that!" I said. "I remember you had an odd expression on your face, but then something happened, and I never got a chance to ask you about it. Just goes to show, what you see on the surface isn't always reflective of what's really going on."

"So, from what I've been told from these guys, the motive wasn't love, it wasn't money, and it wasn't revenge. It was all three!" Kyrie Dawn said.

"It was indeed. Cheating spouse, stolen money, and a remorseless lothario who laughed in his face when he demanded he give the money back."

It sounded so simple when I described it, but none of it was simple. Women unfulfilled in their marriages or worse, like Grace, actually being abused. Shady business practices, outright theft, and unscrupulous investors. And a complicated man who lived a complicated life, choosing to be opportunistic over real connection.

"So Simon snapped." Kyrie Dawn shook her head.

"Sort of. In a general sense, but he also planned these deaths out pretty meticulously once he'd decided to go through with them. And the way he held that knife to my throat while he talked about it, I got the feeling he wasn't just desperate. He was getting a kick out of it."

"Sick," Pike muttered.

Quinton started fussing.

"Me too, Q," Jane said. "Me too."

"Do y'all mind if I go put him down?" Kyrie Dawn asked. "It's way past his bedtime."

Jane shifted foot to foot. "You're going back to our

room, right? I mean, all his stuff is there, and it's late, sooo…"

Kyrie Dawn turned to me. "Charlotte? Is it okay if we stay one more night?"

I thought about Miriam's diary and the insight I'd gained into who she was beyond the choices she'd made. The desperation she'd experienced in her quest to feel love and acceptance. The regrets. She needed someone to set her free from her shame. If she were here now, what would she advise me to do with Kyrie Dawn?

I suspected I knew the answer. Grace. Not the woman whose husband tried to turn me into an ice cube. The concept. The idea that love, compassion, empathy, and forgiveness were the only way forward. For her. For me. For Quinton.

"Of course. What Jane said. Also, what Quinton needs most right now is familiarity, stability. Things have been so chaotic these past few days. We've developed a bit of a routine, and…" My voice cracked.

Tears welled in her eyes. She gave me an impulsive hug. I froze. It was strange. I waited for my body to reject her, but instead, I felt my stiffness dissipate, and I actually found myself hugging her back.

"I'll see you all in the morning!" She gleefully wheeled Quinton out the door.

Jane exhaled. "This hasn't exactly been the most relaxing cruise I've ever been on, but then again, I can't say it's the least relaxing either. Last fall's sailing to Alaska wasn't exactly tranquil."

I rubbed my neck. "I'm signing myself up for a massage in the morning."

"I think I'm gonna follow them back to the room. Char, are you coming?"

I glanced at Xavier. "I'll come soon. I promise."

I SAT IN an overstuffed leather chair across from Xavier's desk as he closed the door to his office.

He sat and stared at me for several moments. "This is difficult for me."

"Why do I feel like I'm about to get bad news?"

"No, no, nothing like that. I mean this is difficult for me knowing that once again I have failed to protect you."

"This isn't your fault."

He bunched his lips and gave his head a half shake. "I have devoted my life to serve and to protect. I have always been very good at my job. My reputation is what got me hired for this position. So, why is it that I have known you for half a year and you have been in grave danger two times already?"

"In your defense, I do tend to get myself into predicaments."

He allowed himself a partial smile. "This is true."

"You're good at your job. You have hundreds of people you're responsible for. You can't be everywhere. Things will happen."

His gaze bore into me. "I cannot be everywhere for everyone." His voice softened. "You are not everyone." He cleared his throat. "That is to say, you live here year-round. I should at least be able to keep attempts on your life to less than one per quarter."

I shrugged and smiled. "It would be nice."

We exchanged grins.

"By the way, Dr. Fraser did a great job on your wound." He touched his cheek.

"He glued it with superglue." I laughed. "He says he doesn't think the scar will be permanent, but it may take a year or so to fade. I'm going to look like I'm in a biker gang."

"I was thinking more like Edward Scissorhands."

"Hah. Very funny." I slapped my thighs. "Okay, well, I'm going to go spend one last night with Kyrie Dawn and Quinton."

He tilted his head and observed me. "You seem a bit sad about that."

Was I? I recognized a lot of different emotions inside me. I imagined Quinton being gone from my life and my chest tightened. It felt a lot like sadness. Longing. Grief. Crap.

FOUR DAYS LATER Jane, Kyrie Dawn, Quinton, and I sat at the dining table in our suite. We'd shared breakfast every morning since they'd moved back to her room. This time, Windsor had brought coffee service, muffins, and a fruit tray. Quinton had managed to crumble his poppy seed muffin into a fine dust. Kyrie Dawn was picking at the fruit.

"Did you guys get off the boat yesterday?" she asked.

The ship had docked for a few hours in Kushiro. Xavier and Irving had escorted Deacon and Simon to the U.S. Consulate, where they were being detained pending extradition back to the States.

Willow and Grace decided not to accompany their husbands, and both had made a pact to file for divorce as soon as they got ahold of their attorneys. They told me they were inspired by Jane and me, and they were going to be traveling buddies for the foreseeable future.

Meanwhile, Jane and I had explored the nearby Kushiro Shitsugen, a marshland home to deer, sea eagles, and Japanese red-crown cranes. The trail wound through the marsh, and we ended up at the observatory, an architecturally stunning building from which we had unobstructed views of the wetlands, Kushiro, and the Mountain of Akan. We also checked out the Fisherman's Wharf and the Nusamai Bridge.

"We did. It was fun, although Jane was a little grumpy that we were too late in the season to see the red-crowned cranes."

"Who knows when we'll be back there again?"

Kyrie Dawn popped a grape into her mouth. "Probably not for a bit. I heard we're headed south to Australia and New Zealand and then over to South America. I'm excited to see the Sydney Opera House and the place where they filmed *The Lord of the Rings* movies."

"I'd love to see Peru. I've heard Machu Picchu is amazing."

"Jane, you can't stand heights."

"Is it high?"

"It's like almost 8,000 feet above sea level."

"That's high."

"Hi!" Quinton waved at her.

"Hi, Q! How's that muffin? Is it yummy? Have you eaten any of it, or are you just smashing it into the table?"

"Yummy!" He grabbed a fistful of crumbs and shoved them into his mouth.

"He gets his manners from his father," I quipped.

Kyrie Dawn covered her mouth. "I shouldn't laugh, but it's so true!"

"One time we had corn on the cob..."

"Oh no! That must have been a nightmare." She grimaced. "Charlotte, I have a confession."

"You can call me Char."

She opened her mouth and snapped it shut. Her chin quivered.

"Oh, please don't cry."

"Yeah," Jane echoed. "If you start crying, Char will start crying, and then pretty soon we'll all be crying."

Kyrie Dawn composed herself. "Does this mean you'll call me K.D.?"

"Don't push your luck."

She laughed. "Okay, okay."

"What's your confession?"

"I told Gabe I developed an allergy to popcorn so he'd stop getting it when we went to the movies. I couldn't take it anymore." She was now crying with laughter. "Am I a terrible person? Wait. Don't answer that!"

"You're not a terrible person. You wanna know how I know that?"

"How?"

I nudged my chin toward Quinton. "That little punkin is a beautiful human. You're a great mom."

"Thank you for saying that. It means the world to me."

"You're welcome. And I'm glad you've decided to stay onboard."

"Me too. It will be good to make this fresh start, and Quinton will get to experience so many cultures."

"Ooh!" Jane bounced in her seat. "He's going to love seeing kangaroos."

"Totally. And maybe one day he'll get to see real life Pandys." Kyrie Dawn tickled him. "Do you want to see real Pandys?"

"Pandy!"

"That's right, baby, Pandy. What are you guys wearing to the gala tonight? Char, you've got to wear something super sleek for Xavier."

I felt heat creep up my neck. "What are you talking about?"

"Oh, come on, anyone with eyes can see there's chemistry there."

Jane smirked. "She's still in denial."

"I'm not in denial. We're just friends."

Jane and Kyrie Dawn exchanged knowing glances.

"We are. I swear." I paused and gave a sheepish grin. "That doesn't mean I wouldn't mind a dance or two tonight."

They burst into gleeful laughter and clapping, both Kyrie Dawn and Jane talking over each other about how I should do my hair and makeup.

In that moment I felt content. Hopeful. And at peace for the first time in a very long time.

If someone would have told me several months earlier that I could get to this place, where I genuinely cared about Kyrie Dawn and Quinton, where I could forgive and let go, I would have said they were bonkers.

And yet here I was.

In many ways, I felt like I'd already scaled the summit of the mountain, and the view was spectacular.

JANE AND I stood at the base of Mount Fuji and looked up at its peak.

"You'd think somewhere in the description of this itinerary, someone would have mentioned the hiking trails are closed October through June."

I sighed. "Yeah. I mean, the cherry blossoms are beautiful, and I'm glad we got to see them, but this feels a bit anticlimactic, don't you think?"

"It does."

"I really wanted to take a picture in the same spot as great-gramma Miriam."

"We can come back in the summer some time. It will happen."

A brisk wind blew, and I tightened my coat against my body to fend off the cold. "It's fine. We'll take the picture here."

I waved at another tourist and asked them to take a photo of us.

Jane and I stood tall, with the mountain looming behind. It hadn't been what we'd expected, but that was okay.

"Kyrie Dawn, bring Quinton over here for a picture."

Her eyes widened, as did her smile. "Are you sure? I know this was important to you."

"We got our picture, now we want one with all of us. We're family."

She pushed Quinton's stroller over to where we were standing. I heard her sniffle. She picked him up, and he squealed with delight.

The four of us—Jane, Quinton, Kyrie Dawn, and I—posed in front of the mountain.

Excerpts from Miriam's Diary

August 18, 1922

You know that saying "be careful what you wish for, you might just get it?" I understand that phrase more than I ever have. I always thought I wanted adventure, but now that I'm at the precipice of the greatest adventure of my life, I find myself wanting to back out. Call it off. Wave the white flag.

Today we boarded a train for the three-hour ride to Mt. Fuji. It was a long trip to reach something that looked so near to our home I could reach out and touch it with my fingertips.

The plan is to scale the mountain with Dewey and Louise, a hike that will take two days. It's more than 3500 meters up to the summit!

I know it's been quite a while since I've written to you. There hasn't been much time.

Hard to believe, but Clive and I have been married just over six months, and I've been in Japan for nearly a year and a half. Time has moved quickly as I've acclimated to my new life. We took a long weekend to Tokyo for our honeymoon. Tokyo is a vibrant city, an eclectic juxtaposition between ancient history and modern pro-

gression. *Enlightenment meets tradition. We stayed at the Imperial hotel. A serendipitous thing, as it was tragically destroyed by fire just four months later.*

When Clive isn't working, we explore Yokohama. It seems like every other week there is a festival of some sort to attend. Local shrines and temples are my favorite places to seek solace. I spent an entire day at the Daijingu Shinto Shrine just taking in the glorious cherry trees in full bloom. The blossoms rained upon me, it reminded me of the plumeria trees as they shed their flowers back home.

Home.

I still consider Hawaii to be my home.

Clive has renewed his contract and plans to stay here for a few more years. I'm starting to get restless, though, and he can sense it. That's why he planned this expedition to Fujiyama.

One night back in March he met a man—a professor of anthropology from Chicago—at a bar. The man painted an exciting picture of scaling the heights of Japan's most iconic feature and having the story to tell. He'd made the ascent himself twice prior and was preparing for another attempt. Clive came home smelling strongly of liquor, feeling inspired and amorous. I agreed to make the trek, partly to satisfy Clive, and partly because it was Karl's fourth birthday, and I was feeling down. An adventure seemed just the thing to lift my spirits.

That was in theory. Reality is another story.

When we arrived at the base this afternoon, there

were a least three other groups of varying sizes who had already set up camp. The plan is we will rise early in the morning and start out together.

After assessing the shape and fitness of the gathered hikers, I suspect the pace for some will be faster than the others. Some of the climbers are muscular, some quite lean. Other than Louise and me, however, none of them are women.

Have I made a grave error in judgment agreeing to do this?

Clive says women were banned from climbing until the late 1860s, when an Englishwoman named Lady Parkes defied the rules and ascended without permission. If Lady Parkes could do it, so can I, right?

I want to prove my mettle. I'm just scared. What if I fail? Am I up to this challenge? Am I up to the task at hand?

I suppose the only way I'll know for sure is if I try.

August 19, 1922

We did it.

I did it.

I faced my fears, and I overcame the biggest obstacle I've ever encountered. I didn't think I could do it. I wanted to run away. But I didn't.

Just after sunrise yesterday morning we gathered our belongings and began our journey up the mountain. Louise brought along her small Kodak to take photographs. No use doing something extraordinary without something to show for it. The weather was cool, mostly *because of strong winds. Despite it being the heart of summer, we dressed in wool pants, jackets, and hats.*

There were multiple stations along the trail to indicate our progress. With each step it felt like my lungs were shrinking. I was afraid to turn around, for fear I might fall off the surface of the earth. Ridiculous, I know, but fear doesn't always correlate to reality.

We stopped for the night at station six. The summit was in view, but after the arduous hike, our guides insisted the wisest thing to do was rest. There was still plenty of climbing to do, plus a four-hour descent.

The best part was the silence. Everyone was so focused on their next breath and their next step that most conversation was considered a waste of resources. Clive patted my rear a time or two in playful encouragement, but for the most part I was left alone with my thoughts.

The winds began to pick up as the sun vanished below the horizon. While there was still enough light to see, I took in the magnificent sight below.

If they could see me now, I thought.

But then I wondered who I was wishing could see me. Not Karl. I doubt a four-year-old would be proud of his mother for climbing a mountain in a foreign land when that meant she wasn't with him.

He probably wouldn't even recognize me if I arrived on father's doorstep tomorrow. Why would he care about what I'd achieved?

Would my father be proud of me? Would he be impressed? He's never indicated I have much about me to find impressive. Perhaps this would be one of those mo-

ments. Perhaps not.

I thought of my mother. I have hazy memories of her telling me I'm beautiful and smart and brave. She would be proud, wouldn't she?

Even at this moment my heart feels the clench of loss. I used to experience it much more often, but I rarely do anymore. I usually don't allow myself to think about the things or people I've lost. It's too painful.

After what felt like a short sleep, we were back on the path to the summit. The clouds of yesterday had cleared, leaving us to walk in full sun. Kengamine, the highest portion of the summit beyond the crater, towered above us to the right. We circled the crater until we reached the steep slope of the true summit, using our picks to scale the remainder of the way to the very top.

My eyes could barely comprehend what they were taking in. Blue sky spread out as far as I could see, and I felt like I was standing on the top of the world. I nearly was.

I imagined myself a sparrow—no, a red-crowned crane. I've lived much of my life as a sparrow: small and insignificant, uninteresting, and common. In my mind I was transformed into a graceful crane, imposing in stature, and at my feet lay the whole world, ready to explore.

The End

If you enjoyed *A Matter of Life and Depths*,
you'll love the next book in...

The Cruising Sisters Mystery

Book 1: *Until Depths Do Us Part*

Book 2: *A Matter of Life and Depths*

Available now at your favorite online retailer!

About the Author

Kate B Jackson (KB Jackson) is an author of mystery novels for grownups and mystery/adventure novels for kids. She lives in the Pacific NE with her husband and at least one of her four grown children at any given time. Her debut middle grade release is "The Sasquatch of Hawthorne Elementary" (Reycraft Books) about a twelve-year-old boy hired by the most popular girl at his new school to investigate what she saw in the nearby woods. Book one in the Chattertowne Mysteries series, "Secrets Don't Sink," (Level Best Books July 2023) introduces Audrey O'Connell, a small town feature reporter who, when her former boyfriend's body is found floating in the local marina, uncovers the depths to which some will go to keep secrets submerged.

Her debut novel in the Cruising Sisters mystery series, Until Depths Do Us Part (Tule Publishing) will be released Spring 2024.

Thank you for reading

A Matter of Life and Depths

If you enjoyed this book, you can find more from all our great authors at TulePublishing.com, or from your favorite online retailer.

TULE
PUBLISHING